THE ENEMY AT GUNPOINT

Cassius raised his carbine to the loophole and put a bullet close past Lost Bird's ear. The blackpowder smell was plain in the room as he reloaded. Outside, the gray war pony quivered, but did not move its feet. Lost Bird was smiling, and the smile expressed more contempt than he could have shown in any other way.

"You shoot well," his hands said. "You do not shoot to hit. You hit me, nobody in your house will see the sun again."

Rachel startled Cash by speaking almost in his ear. "This is no good," she said.

"You get back where I put you!" he ordered her.

"There isn't going to be any fight," she said. "Let me by. I understood what he said, this time."

"Never mind them damned Indian lies! You're going to—"

"He's telling the truth. I've known all about it for a long time. I'm going to end all this trouble now . . ."

*Books by Alan LeMay
from Berkley*

THE SEARCHERS
THE UNFORGIVEN

THE UNFORGIVEN

ALAN LE MAY

BERKLEY BOOKS, NEW YORK

THE UNFORGIVEN was originally published by Harper & Brothers in 1957. A shorter and somewhat different version of the book appeared serially in *The Saturday Evening Post* under the title *Kiowa Moon*.

This is a work of fiction. Names, characters, places, and incidents are either the product of the author's imagination or are used fictitiously, and any resemblance to actual persons, living or dead, business establishments, events, or locales is entirely coincidental.

THE UNFORGIVEN

A Berkley Book / published by arrangement with HarperCollins

PRINTING HISTORY

Previously published by Harper and Brothers, Ace Books, and Jove Books
Berkley Edition / August 2000

The Penguin Putnam Inc. World Wide Web site address is
http://www.penguinputnam.com

ISBN: 0-425-07680-6

BERKLEY®
Berkley Books are published by The Berkley Publishing Group,
a division of Penguin Putnam Inc.,
375 Hudson Street, New York, New York 10014.
BERKLEY and the "B" design are trademarks
belonging to Penguin Putnam Inc.

10 9 8 7 6 5

1

Dancing Bird River was the Zachary family's name for a little run of live water ten miles below the Red, in the unsettled country west of the Wichita. Their soddy was cut into a slope beside it, in the last miles before the deep-grass petered out into the flinty apron of the cap rock. Some sketchy pole corrals marked this place as a cattle stand, but the house itself hardly showed. Its forward walls were built of the same mud and grass-roots into which it was dug, and so was its roof, which had a good stand of feed. It squatted low and lonely, backed like a badger into the hill; and its nearest neighbor was eighteen miles away.

Inside this hole in the ground, late in the afternoon of March 15, 1874, a dark-haired girl of seventeen was getting ready to put supper on. Her name was Rachel Zachary.

Her brothers had saddled before daylight, and had been gone ever since; but through most of this

day, Rachel and her mother had found their
absence a relief. The soddy was not a cramped one,
as soddies went. The slit of a bedroom Rachel
shared with her mother wasn't much, but the main
room was big for a dugout, even with bunks for the
three boys filling one end. And they worked doggedly at keeping things picked up. "Put away one
thing, put away all," was the first rule of life, in-
doors. Yet with five people in one room and a fraction, the paraphernalia of even the simplest living
hung from the beams, dripped from the walls, and
kept the place forever cluttered. They were seldom
weather-bound; the boys rode longest when the
weather was worst. But on days when they did stay
in, the place soon seemed packed with people.

High above the prairie a mat of black rainless
clouds moved steadily across the world in a seemingly inexhaustible supply, dimming the afternoon
to a twilight that would merge imperceptibly with
the early dark. Under this overcast a wind from the
north blew tirelessly, as it had for many days.
Sometimes it rose briefly to the fury of a full
norther, sending hundred-foot sand-devils spinning
across the Red into Texas; but mostly it just blew,
hard and monotonously, hour after hour, day in
and day out, until silence became unrememberable.

That wind might have come a thousand miles,
Rachel knew, without finding many people in its
path to be bothered by it. Up in Indian Territory,
along the tributaries of the Washita, it must be rip-
ping at some hundreds of buffalo-hide lodges,
sheltering such of the Wild Tribes as were insolent
enough to be wintering on Agency rations. The
mile-long villages of those hostiles could have

mounted enough warriors to engulf a brigade, yet
made no more impression upon the vast emptiness
of the Territory than a dribbled pinch or two of
sand. Surely the wind-moan in the cottonwoods
along the Dancing Bird River must have been the
lonesomest sound on earth.

About midafternoon Mama had gone to their
bedroom for a nap. The partition was no strung-up
horse blanket, such as was common to soddies, but
a decently solid turf wall, plastered with home-
burnt lime. Once the heavy door had closed, Rachel
was alone with the sound of the wind. She didn't
mind that; at least, not for a while. Rachel Zachary
was a shy, thin girl, lightly boned and not very big,
but with considerable wire built into her by the
kind of places in which she had been raised. The
Zacharys had shifted ground a good deal, though
not all of them understood why, always toward un-
tamed land. Now, though, they had stuck it out in
this one remote soddy for going on five years—more
nearly a third, than a quarter, of Rachel's entire
life. While she could not help knowing that this was
a desolate and sometimes menacing place in which
to live, she seldom thought about it any more.

This year had begun with high hopes. Just lately,
in January, Texas had got hold of its own govern-
ment at last, for the first time since the War. Now
the Rangers would come back, and the Border Bat-
talions, and settlers would get some help in their
everlasting defense against the Wild Tribes. At the
same time, the beef market at Wichita was winding
up to boom again, after a series of collapses that
had left the Zacharys about as cattle-poor as they
could stand. They were going to be rich, like as not

—soon, this year, this very summer.

Only, first they must get through this deadly, dragging time of waiting, while winter held on, and on, as if spring were never coming back to the world again. Ben, Rachel's oldest brother, had ridden down the Trinity a month ago to look for trail hands. He should get back any day now, with a corrida of at least twenty men—thirty, if he could find them—and immediately all this dull marking of time would be over. There would be a great swarming of men and horses, and hard-pressing action every day, as their first huge herd of the year was made up for the drive to Wichita.

Ben was twenty-four, old enough to seem at the full power of maturity from the standpoint of seventeen. He had been head of the family since he was twenty, when they had lost their father in the roily waters of a cattle crossing, far to the north. He was their rock of strength, upon whom they leaned in every situation of doubt. Perhaps they all felt at loose ends when Ben was gone. Certainly he could take care of himself anywhere on the frontier if anybody could—even in a wolf-howl of a town of three or four hundred people, like Fort Worth. Yet sometimes Rachel's throat hurt as her thought skirted the possibility that they might never see him again, for this could happen out here, as Papa had already proved. Was he overdue? Well—not really; not quite yet.

She knocked the ash off the wood coals in the fireplace, and set on the three-legged skillet they called a spider. Then she looked at the clock on the mantel beam. It was one of the few truly nice things they had, with a little ship rocking away on painted waves where the pendulum might be expected.

It said exactly eleven minutes of four. She remembered that hour all the rest of her life.

She had been fooled by the unnaturally early dusk; it was still too early to start cooking anything. She set the spider off the coals, and went to one of their two real windows. These, even more than the clock, were their special pride, for they had eighteen panes of real glass apiece. They looked south across the Dancing Bird, so Rachel had to lean her temple against a cold pane to look eastward, past the corrals and downstream. She was hoping, for about the thousandth time, to sight a distant disturbance that would be Ben, at the head of his grand corrida.

Maybe he's remembered to fetch me some pretty anything-he-could-get. To make just one nice dress. . . . She knew perfectly well he had remembered; he always remembered, though often he might be prevented. The shakier question was what it would look like. Men didn't know anything about yard goods. With the best intentions in the world, he might bring her something perfectly awful. In which case she would make it up and wear it anyway—for years, likely—rather than see him chagrined, after he had tried.

He wasn't coming of course. Men never did come while their women watched for them. Only when least expected. But they always watched, nevertheless, so now Rachel went to their north lookout, to see if Cassius and Andy were riding in. The lookout was no more than a tiny-paned tunnel through the sod wall. It was set high, and though Cash could stand flat-footed to fire through it, and Ben might even have to stoop a little, Rachel had to stand on a box to see out. This brought her eyes only a few inches above the ground at the back. Yet this worm's-eye view commanded a surprising reach of prairie, for the land fell away behind the soddy, to rise again in swells and gentle ridges rolling northward to the end of sight.

Most of the time the prairie was worth looking at, for it changed constantly, like the sea, to which so many have compared it. People thought of the deep-grass as brown, but usually it looked almost anything else—purple, or gold, or red, or any kind of blue; for a little while each year, as spring came on, it even looked green. Often, when cloud shadows crossed the long swells, the whole prairie stirred, and seemed to mold and flow, as if it breathed. But nothing like that was to be seen out there now. The land lay winter-defeated, lightless and without color. Out of those dead spaces her brothers would presently come jogging. But she could not see them yet.

Behind Rachel the shadows were growing in the corners, crawling toward the banked embers on the hearth. They brought a faint, penetrating chill, felt more in the heart than in the fingers of the skin, as if the earth itself were dying, instead of just this one bleak day between the winter and spring. And now for once, Rachel became strangely aware of the awful emptiness of this far lost prairie where they lived; and a loneliness took hold of her, with a hollow sinking of the heart. Afterward she came to believe that she had recognized this at once for a premonition of something unknown and dreadful already beginning to happen to them as this daylight failed. But it wasn't true, for no clear thought of any kind came to her, then.

Just as she turned away from the lookout, something out there changed, and she looked again without knowing what she had seen. The first ridge was scarcely a furlong off, and they kept its crest burned off, to deprive horse-thieving enemies of cover commanding the house. On this burn had appeared a dark, narrow object, about three feet high. It looked a little like a scorched rock; only, it had never been there before. She tried to see it better by looking beside it, instead of straight at it; she looked away and glanced back; she moved her head in circles, as an owl does, when it is trying to give shape to something unknown. "What *is* that?" she whispered; and her whisper was lost in the sound of the wind.

Now the object moved, and the mystery cleared, but without reassurance. She had been looking at the upper half of a man, whose horse was hidden by the swell of ground. The oddly behaving visitor now pushed onto the crest of the burn, and stopped again. Even at an eighth of a mile, Rachel could judge that there stood about the sorriest horse she had ever seen in her life; and somehow she knew that the rider was old too, and in all ways as poorly as his horse. She supposed he would ride on in when he had looked them over enough to suit him, and usually she would have welcomed any such diversion. But this time she felt an unaccountable dread, almost a horror, of his coming nearer.

He came no nearer, then. She watched him as long as he was there, yet somehow she never saw him leave. He was there, and then he was gone. Rachel whipped on a coat, meaning to saddle a pony and ride that ridge. She saw it as her bounden duty to keep an eye on the fellow, and see what he was up to, for his actions had no reason unless he meant them harm. At the door she took the Sharp & Hankins carbine from its pegs, and clashed open its sliding barrel, to load. Then she stopped, knowing that she was not going out there, could not go out there. A nameless fear held her powerless to leave the house.

She heard her mother moving about in their bedroom. Soundlessly she eased the sliding barrel back into its seat, and returned the Sharp & Hankins to its pegs. She was building up the fire by the time Matthilda Zachary appeared, misty-eyed and yawny from her nap. "Did I hear a sound?" she inquired vaguely.

Rachel hesitated. Often Matthilda was so absent-minded she missed half you said, but she was capable of sharp flashes of observation, too, all unexpected. She came up with one now. "Thought I heard you breech the Sharp & Hankins," she said.

They spoke with the trailing double vowels of the cotton lowlands, from which most of the early Texans had come. Matthilda was strict with her children about those lapses she regarded as "po' white"; but her own soft speech made the carbine a "Shah-up 'n' Hay-'nkins."

Rachel was silent a moment more, then blurted it out. "There's something spooky going on out there! Back of the north ridge." She saw she had her mother's startled attention. "Some awful old long-hair—he's been watching us. Sitting the dreadfulest old horse, out on the burn . . ." She put a lot more to it, about how she came to look, and all, but actually she hadn't seen much more.

"Poor old man," Mama said.

"What?" She had not conveyed one speck, evidently, of her lonely dread.

"Some old hunter, doubtless; been alone so long he was likely too shy to come in. No matter how much he wanted. What a shame! We'd have fed him, so gladly, if only he'd known."

"Yes, and filled the house with smells," Rachel said sharply. "And fleas, too! I bet he's been with every fat old squaw that never heard of soap between here and—"

"Rachel! I won't have you speaking so unkindly!"

Rachel said, "Well, I think he's harmful to us," and was disturbed to hear a tremor in her own voice.

"Touch of cabin fever," her mother said, gently deprecating. Cabin fever was their name for the sensitive, weepy mood that sometimes came on prairie women in the weeks while spring held off. It came from being shut in, hearing too few voices repeating the same dull things for too long. The tiniest things became magnified into horrid slights and dangers, until you were downright unlivable. And the last thing you wanted to hear was that your troubles were imaginary—especially if you knew it to be true.

Mama said with unwelcome sympathy, "I think this waiting time, between the false spring and the green-up, is just the very meanest time of the whole year." She dipped a pan of cold water from the barrel at the door, freshened her face at the wash shelf, and emptied the pan into the slop pail that served as plumbing. She polished the pan to a tinny shine with a clean flour sack before hanging it up. At the fireplace she pulled the teakettle forward on the hob, so that the boys would have warm water when they came in.

Rachel bided her time in a sulk, confident of getting more of a hooraw out of her brothers. They jogged in pretty late, and took a while shoveling nubbin corn to a dozen winter horses that had come in to be fed. The women never knew when to have supper hot, having no way of telling how long the boys would fool around on chores like that. Matthilda set out candles, and as she lighted them with a fatwood splinter, her hair caught their yellow glow in its silver mist. Matthilda's hair had been white since she was thirty, nearly twenty years ago. Nobody remembered when her hair was any other color, except after she washed it, when it was blue. But they remembered when she had been light and bouncy of step, with quick ungnarled hands, and they still saw her that way, for the changes in these things had come slowly, unseen.

As the yellow candlelight came up, the air outside seemed to turn a darker and more icy gray. Rachel closed the heavy shutters, as they must always do when they made a light inside. The north lookout was now a lightless eye, staring in at them. Rachel stepped onto the chest to pull shut its slide, and a shiver crossed her shoulders. *Somebody stepped over my grave*, she thought. It was what they said when they shivered without feeling cold. She had half expected to find a weird ancient face looking in from close outside. "What *are* they doing out there?" she complained, her patience dwindling.

But when her brothers finally came in, their reaction to her story was just as big a letdown as her mother's had been. She built it up all she could, this time, but Cassius was washing and spluttering, and Andy was noisily trying to straighten a spur, all the way through.

"I don't know what's got into this soap," Cassius said when she slowed up. "Bites like a black-foot weasel."

"Same soap," his mother told him. "You've chapped your hands again. Those buck gloves fend nothing but rope burns. You should have worn your mittens, like I said."

"Cash! Did you by any chance," Rachel demanded, "hear one word I said?"

"Oh, sure. Sounds a little like some old joker stands in need of horse flesh. Andy, remind yourself to go put up the bars. So's we'll know where at to start tracking from, come morning."

Rachel could have killed him. Cassius Zachary, twenty-one, was slim, black-haired, and was starting a mustache, not long enough to twist, yet, but sharply trimmed. He did nearly everything well, and carried himself as if he knew it. Ben often said Cassius had most of the brains in the family, and sometimes this seemed to be true. Like the easy way he picked up languages. Lots of people spoke Spanish, of a sort, and some even a dribble of Comanche; but Cassius could handle the weird Kiowa tongue, which had seventy-four vowels, besides a lot of clicks and nasals, and had to be sung. Of course, Ben spoke it, too, but only because he had labored and sweat over it. Not Cassius! He had heard it, hadn't he? So he knew it. Naturally. Nothing to it. Matthilda said he had learned to read when he was three. And hadn't cracked a book since, Ben sometimes added. Cassius liked raising hell and cattle. Didn't want to know anything else.

And he could come up just a little bit too happy-go-lucky for any use, Rachel was thinking now.

But Andy, by his want of sense, went back on her worst of all. He was not yet sixteen, but already tall, and moved well, so that strangers must have thought him older. As small children he and Rachel had stood together against a world of adults, consoling each other when wronged and left out of things. Rachel had always liked to think she had raised Andy herself, almost single-handed, so that he was virtually her own little child. Only, there wasn't much left of that illusion any more. He was outgrowing her, getting away from her; he could ride horses she could not ride, and go places she could not go, disappearing into the vast unknown world of men. All this made him the more exasperating when he came up with something stupid, and he was an expert at it. So now he looked as owlish as he ever had at eight years old.

"Don't you know what that was you saw? That—" he made it weighty—"was the Ghost of the Bandit!"

This sober idiocy left Rachel speechless, so Cassius took it up. "Ghost? In all this wind? He'd blow away."

"What about the Skeleton in Spanish Armor, down on Devil's River? *He* don't blow away."

Cassius pretended uncertainty. "Well—no; but —you take all that ironware he's got up in—"

"How about that whole platoon of spooks, down on Phantom Hill? Seen time and again, drilling in line!"

"I know, but is it a good *straight* line? Weather regardless?"

"It's perfect," said Andy stoutly.

Most of the feel of danger had left since the men came in. But they had spoiled her story, and Rachel was hurt. One of the little sadnesses that women endured out here in the lonelies was that of never having anything to tell their menfolk when they came home. If the first potato had sprouted in the root cellar, or a jumping mouse had eaten out of Rachel's hand, that was news to be treasured, told to each separately, and discussed at length. Mostly there was nothing at all. Quite a few pronghorns came in sight of the house, of course, and blacktail deer; often they saw a coyote, sometimes a lobo. But the men saw such things all the time. You couldn't interest them with anything short of a bear. And tonight, when for once Rachel had been full of a story to tell them, they wouldn't listen.

She drew into herself, and shut up. Next evening, as twilight closed off another dark, windy day, she felt haunted for a little while, and stole a few glances at the north ridge, to see if the sinister figure would reappear. Nothing happened, though, for two days more.

Then, at the end of the third day, the stranger came again.

2

Matthilda saw him first. This was hardly to be expected, for her eyes were far from the best in the house. One of the things that made Matthilda look younger than she was, lively and interested always, was her bright wide-eyed gaze, which may well have been the result of trying hard to see. On this night, though, she had not far to look. She had taken her sewing basket to a south window, and as her hands worked she kept glancing at the prairie across Dancing Bird River, in hope of seeing Ben coming in. She was very often there. It seemed to Rachel that Ben had hardly got out of sight before Mama had started watching for him.

Rachel was in the root cellar, a sort of pit they had dug as an afterthought into the hill behind. It went down four feet below the level of the floor, and could be got into, awkwardly, through a hole at the base of the wall, behind a wooden slide. Fumbling down there in the dark, Rachel had filled her apron with potatoes, when she heard her mother gasp. Immediately wood clattered on wood as a chair went over; and Rachel bumped her head as she came scrambling out. Matthilda stood at the window, so motionless that she looked rigid, staring at something outside. Rachel cried out, "Mama!" and the potatoes bumped across the floor as she went to her mother.

Just outside, no more than two long steps from the window, sat a strange-looking rider; and Rachel knew at once that this was the man she had seen on the ridge. The startling thing was the concentration with which he leaned from the saddle to peer in. Rachel saw a colorless straggle of beard, some stringy long hair flying loose from under a pulpy wool hat, and an Indian-trade kind of rifle too long for a saddle boot, carried across the withers. And the horse—how could so old a horse be living, let alone worked? Age had turned it a flea-bit white, showing patches of black hide, and scabs of mange. The lip dangled slack below long outthrust teeth, and the unseeing eyes had the staring look of pain peculiar to animals of enormous age. Not a muscle stirred in horse or man, yet the wind made a flicker of movement all over them—a small flying of lank hair and wispy mane, a shimmer of tatters.

The sky was full of mud again, and what little light it had left was behind the horseman, so that he sat in a darkness of his own. A man without a face, except for that wind-wavered suggestion of a beard. And yet, even in that first moment of shock—was there something familiar about him? This frightened instant had a feeling of being relived, as if the same thing had happened someplace else, long ago.

"Pull back," Rachel whispered. "Mama—come away!"

Matthilda said uncertainly, "Can he—can he see us?"

Perhaps there was some doubt of it, what with the darkness of the room, and a possible sky reflection on the panes between, but Rachel felt him to be looking straight into her face. "Of course he can! *Please* don't stand there—" She drew her mother out of line.

"I didn't hear a thing," Matthilda said, bewildered. "I just looked up and—"

Her daughter whisked to the door, and the Sharp & Hankins came off its tree nails into her hands. The sliding barrel clashed twice, clambering a cartridge. Matthilda cried out, "Wait—don't—"

"Ben said to—" Rachel jumped the heavy bar from its slot, and forgot what she was saying as the door creaked wide.

"Rachel! Don't go out there!"

But Rachel was only standing on the stoop, looking frightened, and a little silly, as she stared up-creek and down. No one was in sight as Matthilda came to her side.

"He—he's around the corner of the house," Matthilda whispered.

"Let me go! I'll put a ball through his hat!"

"No! You come in here—please, Rachel, please—"

That breathy, frightened note had not come so strongly into her mother's voice since Rachel could remember. She hesitated, listening for a sound of hoofs, but the great organ-toned wail of the wind through the cottonwoods scoured away all sounds.

Strands of hair whipped across her face, stinging her eyes. Suddenly Rachel wanted to be inside, behind the heavy door, within the thick walls. She was looking meek as she obeyed.

Matthilda's hands were unsteady as she barred the door; she crossed to warm them by the fireplace, so that her back was to the room. This was not like her. The stranger hadn't actually done anything much. Maybe he had been trying to see if anybody was home, never dreaming that women lived here. At first glimpse of them he had fled like a scalded cat. Yet Matthilda, always first to make allowances, had no word of reassurance. She seemed numbed.

Rachel said, "We know that man, from someplace. I've seen him before, a long while back."

"Fiddle," said Matthilda absently.

But Rachel was beginning to remember, not the man, but a happening that was the same. Long ago —six or seven years?—when they lived on the San Saba. . . . She began setting the table in shaky silence.

This time the boys came soon. Rachel saw Andy, first, jogging homeward around the upper bend of the Dancing Bird; and in a few moments more Cassius appeared, looking so sure of himself, so easy in the saddle, that Rachel was comforted in the uncertainty of this dusk. Still, neither of them, nor the two together, could quite take the place of Ben, who could make everything seem all right just by coming into sight.

She held her tongue when they came in, waiting to see what her mother would tell them; for she had a wicked little plan. A name that had been playing tag with her, teasing her by dancing just out of her reach, had now come clear into her mind. She judged it would serve to get Cash's attention this time. Certainly there had been enough fuss and to-do—yes, and mystery made of it, too—that time on the San Saba, long ago.

"Any word of Ben yet? Any sign at all?" Matthilda always asked that first, nowadays; although, unless she was thinking of smoke signals, it was hard to see how she expected any kind of word to outtravel Ben himself.

"Nope." Cassius scooped a handful of home-made soft soap and began to wash. "You all have a good day around here?" He always asked that, too.

"Well . . ." Matthilda wavered, and would not meet Rachel's eyes. "Just a middling ordinary day, I reckon."

Quiet again, under the sound of wind, while Cassius bent low to souzle his face and hair. Rachel waited a moment more, watching her mother. Then —"Abe Kelsey was here," she said.

The effect was explosive. Cassius straightened so sharply his heels lifted off the floor. Rachel was dumbfounded; she had almost scared him through the roof. Well, not scared him, maybe—startled him, more like. His eyes went to his mother, not to Rachel, and held with a hard questioning. *Good lord, I've pulled a trigger. What trigger?*

She had been stretching it, of course; she had no memory of what anybody named Kelsey looked like, way back yonder. She had meant to admit, in a minute, that she hadn't really recognized the stranger. She guessed she had better snatch that mysteriously powerful name back, and in a hurry.

Confession was on the tip of her tongue. Then suddenly it was too late for that.

"I was going to tell you," Matthilda said to Cassius, and her voice was coaxing him not to be mad.

Rachel's heart contracted. Her mother had recognized the stranger and had not let on. When you live so close to people, and they hold things back from you, it makes half-seen things stir in shadows that come all around you. Part of the cabin fever. . . . Cash still stood there, water from his face running down his limp old buckskin shirt, and puddling on the floor from his dropped hands.

"She doesn't mean he came in," Matthilda said. She was faltering now, and near to tears. "He—just sat out there and—looked—"

"How long ago?"

"Well—I guess—it might have been—"

"Twenty minutes," Rachel said clearly.

Cash shifted as if he would rush outside, but changed his mind without moving a step. "But the light was failing. You couldn't have told if— Wait. How far out was he?"

"About seven feet," Rachel said. "He leaned down close, to look in."

"Seven—" He stared at her blankly a moment and his next question fairly crackled. "How come *she* knew him?" he demanded of his mother. "Did you tell her who—"

Matthilda shook her head, and her eyes were ominously shiny. "Why, the child can't have seen Abe since—why, she can't have been more than ten years old. And not even then, unless—and anyway, he's so changed, Cash, just dreadfully. It's uncanny she remembers him now."

More uncanny than you think. This man was faceless, for all I saw. Aloud Rachel said, "A man of that name had an ambuscade with Papa, back in the earlies."

"Papa had falling-outs with a lot of people." Cash reached for a towel, wishing he were shed of the whole thing.

"But Kelsey kept nosing around."

"The child's right, Cassius," Matthilda murmured.

"There was something more to it," Rachel said. "Something queer, that I was never let to know."

"All you need to know is I don't want him around! Let him smell gunpowder—you all hear me?"

It was as if Ben himself had come into the room. No, more as if Papa had come into the room; Ben was quieter. Andy was sitting there gaping, with no more idea of what was happening than Rachel had. Mama went to the table, so that she was behind Andy and Rachel; but Rachel knew at once that Mama put a finger to her lips. "Don't talk so much in front of the children," Rachel put it into words for them.

They made no answer to that. "Bring your carbine," Cassius told his brother, making his tone ordinary. "We'll put the gate poles up."

As they let themselves out, the wind whisked at everything in the house, and set the pans to swinging, but perhaps it was less violent than before. The women moved immediately, both at once, to get supper on. The wheels of daily living began to turn again, as they must always turn, no matter what.

"He's going back where he came from, now,"
Matthilda said, and Rachel knew she meant Abe
Kelsey. "Hear how the wind's dying? Going down
more and more, as he gets farther and farther
away."

It was the kind of sign some of the Indians believed. The Zacharys took no stock in such heathen-
isms, but out here you could sometimes get mixed
up, and confuse the things you really believed with
things that just sort of came with the country. But
it was true that the wind was abating. This should
have made the night a better one for sleep, but it did
not. Their bedding was turning clammy again for
want of sun, so that they were chilled and sweated,
seemingly both at once. Rachel knew she should
have baked their blankets before the fire, but had
put it off, hoping for a chance to get the outdoor
smell of sunshine into them.

Perhaps it was the very quiet that woke her in the
first hour after midnight, so lightly she slept that
night. Once she was full awake, she heard her
mother crying, two yards away, in the other bed.
Matthilda wept so softly, her face pressed so hard
into her pillow, Rachel never would have heard her
at all if the wind had held.

3

Cassius and Andy had to wait for daylight to pick up Abe Kelsey's trail. They followed it easily enough, until they had gone about four miles. Then it disappeared.

They cast some long circles, and found it again around noon. This time the trail led off in a new and unlikely direction; it took them nearer the house than they had been all morning, before they lost it completely. Cassius blew up, and sat cussing so long he turned red in the face.

The trouble with Cash was that he knew exactly who he was after, and why. He thought of Abe Kelsey as a varmint that had to be killed before a worse thing happened, and he was in a sweat to get it over with. But he didn't know how much Andy knew. Nothing, he hoped.

Actually, Abe Kelsey was a most unfortunate man; about as unfortunate as a man can get, perhaps. He was even famous for it, in his own part of the world, which was limited to the prairies south of the Arkansas. Andy and Rachel may have been the only natives of the Texas frontier over ten years old who did not know who he was.

For his story had a riddle in it, and this kept it alive. He had once had a wife and a young son. But he located at Burnt Tree, a tiny settlement of three or four families thirty miles out of Round Rock; and the Kiowas destroyed it in 1863. Kelsey must have married late, for he had been middle-aged even then, and his little boy was only seven when Abe lost him, along with his mother, in the Burnt Tree Massacre.

Supposedly. Two years later somebody brought Abe a rumor that his son was alive, a captive in the lodge of a Kiowa named Pacing Wolf. Abe went up there—and swore forever that he found his son. The boy had even answered to his name. And now a queerness came up. That the Kiowas claimed the boy to be neither white nor a captive, but of mixed blood and their own, was surprising to nobody. But men who had known the Kelsey boy came forward to declare that they had seen the boy dead and had helped to bury him. Thus was born an enigma never completely answered.

But the lower counties were well salted with men who had themselves lost wives or children, or had otherwise been brought too close to the persistent massacres. These were very ready to believe Abe's story without any special scrutiny at all; they angered, and they were men who acted on their angers. Hell-bent couriers raced out in five directions, carrying Abe's appeal for help in recovering his little son. And a posse of more than thirty riders swarmed into their saddles in answer to the call.

William Zachary, then of Round Rock, was one of those who believed Abe because he wanted to believe him. Old Zack, as William was called before he was forty, had ridden with Abe Kelsey in a number of earlier pursuits; he knew Abe as only a so-so Indian-fighter, given to unexpected foolishness and sudden blunders. Yet Zack did not see how even Abe could mistake his own son, only two years gone.

With Abe to guide him, Zack rode on ahead to scout Pacing Wolf's village, days before the posse was complete. He hoped to make a deal for the boy without a fight that would put the captive child himself in deadly danger; or failing that, he wanted to form a strategy of attack that would promise success. He named a rendezvous on Cache Creek where Abe and he would meet the posse.

Abe and Old Zack beat the more unwieldy posse across the Red by more than a week; found Pacing Wolf; and rode openly into his camp. At this point, Zack had already gone to great effort and great risk —and had framed himself into the false position of his life.

For, the instant Zack laid eyes on the boy he knew they had wasted their time. The Pacing Wolf boy was white, or nearly so, but there all resemblance ended, so far as Zack could see. Young Kelsey would have been only nine, in 1865, and all Abe had hold of was a great lout at least thirteen years old. He had actually been on the war trail already, and had the scalp of a little Negro child, to prove it.

Zack talked to the boy in two languages, neither

of which Abe Kelsey understood. The boy was fluent in Kiowa, and knew a little Spanish, but about the only English word Zack could trap him into recognizing was "squaw." He said he had always lived in the lodge of Pacing Wolf, his father, and knew nothing at all about Kelsey except that he was a bad nuisance and got him laughed at. He offered Zack a Mexican concho to shoot Kelsey; couldn't do it himself, for a Kiowa believed that his own medicine would turn on him if he killed a crazy person, or even seriously harmed one.

As for answering to his name—the young savage answered to Set, for Set-Tayhahnna-tay, which means Texan bear. And Kelsey's boy happened to be named Seth.

Time was going to prove that all this common sense could but barely hold its ground, in public opinion, against the farther's total conviction; years later people would still be arguing over it. For a door of doubt had been left open, forever.

Not in Zack's mind. He was convinced that Abe was absolutely wrong, beyond any shadow of doubt, and he told him so, in no uncertain terms. Abe was thrown into an uncontrollable rage, in which he tried to kill Zack, and Zack had to take his carbine away from him. Unfortunately, Zack lost his own patience in this flurry, and smashed the lock of the carbine on a rock. Kelsey carried the broken breechlock with him a long time, and it gave his own version of the story substance for unimaginative listeners.

But a far more unlucky thing happened before Zack got back to Texas. Instead of turning back across the Red, Zack pointed his pony toward Fort

Cobb. Neither the Union nor the Confederacy had
been able to spare troops for a real campaign in the
Indian country, though each side was accused of
efforts to turn the Indians against the other. The
Federals had, however, intermittently garrisoned
Fort Cobb, up in Indian Territory. Old Zack carried a list of brands worn by some hundreds of
horses known to be in the hands of Indians under
Federal protection. Zack's bold demand upon the
Fort Cobb commandant was for a release of the
horses—or a strapping indemnity. He had a case,
and later it was going to rage in the courts for a
quarter of a century. Zack almost, but not quite, got
something on account.

What he did not know was that the Fort Cobb
cavalry was out on one of its recurrent patrols along
the Red. Abe's belated posse, charging out of Texas to rescue little Seth, ran smack into a squadron of
yellowlegs on Cache Creek. The handful of Texans
were told to get the hell back where they came from,
and fast—before they were set upon for taking military action, and out of uniform at that. Whatever
opportunity for rescue there had been was destroyed in five minutes, and never recurred again.

Abe Kelsey forever believed, and persuaded
whom he could, that Old Zack had betrayed the
rescue party to the damyankees; thereby purchas-
ing the friendship of the Kiowas, and perpetual immunity to their raids, at the price of Abe's son. A
stigma of Indian-loving, involving a betrayal totally
unforgivable under any code on earth, was thus
prooflessly affixed to one of the greatest Indian-
fighters, perhaps, that Texas ever knew.

Delusion and frustration seemed to unhinge

Kelsey's mind, after that. He became hipped on at least winning the confidence of the supposed son who denied him. Endless failure only narrowed and hardened his obsession, until he was willing to become an Indian himself, if that would do it. He tagged the Kiowas around, living on what scraps they threw him. He ran whisky to them when he could get whisky, guns when he could get guns. He even scouted out easy kills for them among his own people, which would have made him deadly dangerous if the Indians had trusted a word he said.

And still the Kiowas would have none of him. Fearing to kill or maim a crazy man, they abused him in every other way they could think of, in hopes of driving him away. They robbed him of everything he got hold of, they dumped him in rivers, they played games in which they threw him about. And the boy he thought was his son would do nothing but spit on him.

For all this, Abe blamed William Zachary.

After Kelsey became a squaw man, the Zacharys were able to face down his libel, to some extent. They must have faced it down, or they wouldn't be here. For there was no such thing as a lone cattleman, and never could be, on open range. No practical fence was known. All winter the Zacharys rode themselves saddle blind, trying to hold their cattle. Yet every spring found half of their cows long gone, and their range cluttered with pilgrims, sometimes of three hundred brands. They had to calf-brand for them all, drive the beef with their own, and get the market money back to the owners; meanwhile depending on others to work their own far-strayed cows.

Even in this hateful state of interdependence, Kelsey had been unable to stop them. But presently Abe found another weapon to use against the Zacharys—a far more potent one than his unprovable charge of betrayal. It was a weapon so strange to them that they knew no defense against it; yet so deadly that Kelsey could punish and drive them with it. Even if they killed him—which Old Zack would have done if Abe had not eluded him— it might someday destroy them.

Before Old Zack died, under his drowning cattle in that far, lost river crossing, Abe Kelsey had all but smoked the Zacharys out of Texas.

So now Cassius was furious, baffled, and talking to himself. "Close by, someplace. Less'n six miles from the house, by God. Must be watching us now—"

"How's that?"

"Shut up until you're spoken to!" Cash yelled at Andy.

4

Now Ben got back at last, to the great secret relief of Cassius. Even the weather seemed to have changed for his homecoming. The cloud mat was gone, the sun blazing bright; and the wind gave place to a gentle breeze, still dry, and smelling more of last year's wild hay than of new grass, but of a pleasant warmth. Cash and Andy, having trailed Kelsey and lost him, were cow-hunting to the south that day, toward the Little Beaver, trying to bunch the scattered and winter-driven cattle for a ready gather. As they rode they looked often to the southeast, hoping for a dust that would mean Ben was finally coming in from Fort Worth, and points beyond. They could see a long way in the clean air, but nothing showed.

They were looking the wrong way. In the middle of the morning they were puzzled by a considerable dust, big enough for a company of cavalry, but far to the southwest. Nothing lay in that direction short

of Fort Griffin—more than ninety miles away, for a
horse, which is always having to go around something. Between lay an unholy loneliness. Buffalo
hunters, men bolder than angels and dirtier than
wolves, crossed this wild land in slaughter seasons.
Sometimes they came upon the charred skeleton of
a cabin, and camped upon its graves. Other times
they ran into Kiowa-Comanche war parties, and
found out how came the graves there. During the
War, and the nine years since, the undefended frontier had been pushed eastward a hundred miles.

They went on with their work. Along about noon
the dust was replaced by a signal smoke. They
watched it go up in puffs and long sausages, bitten
off sharply at earth level, blurring out into long
scraves of nothing as they rose; and they recognized
one of the family signals. It meant, "I'm coming in."

Andy let out a long yell— "wa-a-a-a-ah-hoo!"—
of pure celebration. "Whoppee!" he added, finding
he had enthusiasm left over.

Cassius took a more nonchalant attitude, now
that Ben was actually in sight, for he resented his
own relief. "Well, I'll chew up a whistle pig," was
his comment. "What in all hell is he doing down
there?"

"Maybe he taken a short cut," Andy suggested.
Away from the house they dropped very easily into
the looser speech of the cowhands among whom
they worked, having learned very early in life that
this was wise.

They rode southwest toward the dust, and closed
on the corrida in a couple of hours. They saw from
a long way off that Ben had fetched home some thirty riders and a wagon—about the most successful

hiring of hands they had accomplished yet. And he had around fifty head of loose saddle stock; for their range leaked horses so badly, all year round, that they had to bring in replacements every year, on land that should have produced a market surplus. So far, so good, Cassius admitted, subject to a closer look. He had wanted to go after the corrida himself.

Ben himself loped ahead to meet them at near half a mile, and the brothers exchanged a brief, hard handshake. Ben was big, shock-headed; as a boy he had been round-faced and chunky, and even now that he was gaunted, he was so heavily boned that people thought of him as burly, which he was not. Where Cassius had inherited old Zack's flash, Ben had his father's force and authority. Four years as head of the family had aged him to look more than thirty, instead of his rightful twenty-four, which was perhaps why he seemed steadier than his father had been, or his brother would ever be.

"Well, another damned rickety, wamber-jawed wagon, I see," was Cash's opening comment. "But that's all right, I can fix it, in a few hundred hours."

"Had to have it for the cook," Ben explained mildly. "Crippled, of course—or why's he a cook? This here's a spring wagon; Mama will be crazy about it. How *is* Mama?"

"She'll be fine, soon's you show her how to drive two wagons."

"I figure she can run between them," Ben said, to ditch an argument that did not interest him. He blamed himself for the way he and his brother graveled each other, almost on sight. Maybe Ben had inherited responsibility for his brothers too suddenly, and too soon. He got along all right with Andy, because he still thought of Andy as a little boy, in whom any reasonable competence came as a surprise. But Cassius was another matter. He expected great things of Cash—and he wasn't about to get them. The upshot would be that they would lose Cassius pretty soon, in just about the first year he thought the family could stand on its feet without him.

"I guess they must have moved Fort Worth," Cash said now. "I always thought of it as more to the eastward, like."

Ben explained reasonably that he had picked up a few hands there, but not enough. Seemed the Chisholm Trail dreened off most of the Tarrant County riders. So he had turned southwest, racking down the ruts of old Fort Belknap, all the way to Fort Griffin.

"Where a man can find all the damned hide hunters he wants," Cash said. "Them stinkies must have laughed theirselfs sick at the mention of work. No cowhands, of course."

"The buffaloes make it bad, all right," Ben admitted. Only a few stragglers troubled the Dancing Bird nowadays, but farther west there were still buffaloes aplenty. Pretty hard to boon a man with a slow-death job a-horse-back, when he could get rich just banging a gun. Only thing, you had to have your own wagon outfit. Hide hunters with wagons weren't looking for gunbangers; what they wanted was skinners. All those riders, who had sifted down there like sand into the toe of a sock, would sooner starve than skin buffaloes. So Ben had been able to hire some, such as they were.

Both brothers had things they wanted to talk about, but not in front of Andy, or with the overemphasis of haste. So, "Come have a look," Ben said.

They rode back, now, along the straggle of newly hired cowhands, who numbered twenty-eight, plus a cook who drove a six-horse team in the drag. In the performance of these men could lie the difference between calamity and a great year. From the Dancing Bird to Wichita was a drive of only two hundred and sixty or seventy miles—no drive at all, compared to some Old Zack had made to Abilene from below the Neuces River; and they could expect wohaw—a tribute paid in gifts of beef—to satisfy the roving bands of Indians, who had no stomach for a fight with an armed crew anyway. Nevertheless, several thousand head of wolf-wild stock must not be moved, but in some degree coddled, through uneasy country every mile of the way. The herd could get into big trouble any time, any place, if its trail hands were not up to snuff.

Seen from this standpoint, the new hands Ben had to show his brother looked none too encouraging. As usual, the greater number were youngsters; born misfits, mostly, hangdog and unsure of themselves, but with wretched hats cocked jauntily, as if they hoped they were dangerous. One thing was pretty plain about them all. These were wanted men, or thought they were, or they would not have been here. The Dancing Bird was too far from town and too close to the Kiowas to be easy to hire for, no matter where you looked for men. At Fort Griffin you took what you could get. Yet Ben believed he saw a certain toughness, or the makings of it, in these downwind drifters; and he was hoping his brother would see it too.

Cash looked them over with a show of indifference. He had bossed a trail herd when he was nineteen, and believed he had proved himself a cowman. But Zeb Rawlins, with whom they pooled their drives, had been disappointed in the returns, and had never okayed Cash to drive again. Ben might blame himself, but actually most of the ill-nature with which Cash had greeted Ben's return grew out of Cash's resentment over having been unfairly shelved.

"Looks like you did all right," he finally brought himself to say.

So much for that. Ben now sent Andy back to the remuda to cut out any five of the new horses he wanted, for his own string. And the two older brothers drifted off to the flank, where they could talk alone.

Cassius waited until they were beyond earshot of the corrida, before he fired his cannon. "Abe Kelsey was here."

Ben's startled glance acknowledged that he had heard, but he didn't say anything right away. "Close to the house?" he asked at last.

"Rode up to a window. Leaned down to look in."

Another pause; then two questions more. "What kind of a horse was he on?"

"A mighty sorry horse, the way they tell it. I didn't see him. Mama and Rachel saw him."

Ben nodded, gravely. If Kelsey rode a bad horse, it meant the Kiowas still took away his horses as fast as he could steal them; so he had gained no influence with them, or favor. Well, that was something.

And his other question: "Does Rachel—?"

Cassius shook his head. "She hasn't found out anything. Only—this floored me, Ben—she did call off his name. Whether Mama let something slip, or she guessed it from—well, that ain't what signifies."

"No," Ben said slowly. "That ain't what signifies. You want to know something?"

He pulled his horse to a walk, and Cassius waited. Looking at his brother sidelong, Cassius saw he looked a whole lot tireder than a man should, coming off so easy a trip—virtually a vacation.

"Cash," Ben said, "I had to kill a man."

He was looking straight ahead, so that Cassius was able to cover up his first startled, even excited reaction. When Cash spoke his tone was quiet. "The same thing?"

"It's always the same thing. But this time I had no warning. The guns let off, and a stranger-boy I hired that day was down in the dirt. Seems he pulled first, but he was baited into it. The bastard who done it accused him of going to work for . . . a red-nigger lover."

"But when did you—"

"Oh. Me. I stepped out in the middle, and the killer swung round on me. I heard his hammer cock, so I fired."

They were silent awhile. Cash finally smiled a little. "Well, that makes us even." He held out his hand, and Ben gripped it. "I run into pretty near the same thing last year," Cash said. "I kind of figured you knew about it."

Ben nodded. "Wasn't going to say anything, till you wanted to."

"Thanks, Ben." For a moment, there, they were

probably closer than they had ever been in their lives; and they weren't even thinking about it. "We've got to catch this Kelsey and hang him," Cassius said. "We should have tracked him down long ago. I'm thinking of the Rawlinses. No scalehorn on earth ever come stubborner than old Zeb. And nobody hates Indians worse. If Kelsey ever stirs him up we'll have a finish fight on our hands. Else he'll gore us off the range."

"Damn the range," Ben said.

"What?"

Ben held his voice low, but a shake came into it, beyond his control. "Cash, I know, I know in my heart, I'll go after them, and I'll kill them, every man . . . the day they turn on her."

A shade of emphasis fell on the last word, "her," and that was where it belonged. It was Rachel whom Kelsey had been able to turn into a hostage, and a way to get at the Zacharys. In a dozen pioneer crises, the Zacharys had been held defenseless by the special vulnerability of this girl. And their great fear, keeping them forever on their guard through these years, was that she herself would find it out. Their perpetual vigilance in itself had made her far more precious to them than another child could ever have been.

Rachel, called Rachel Zachary, had been raised in the belief that she was their own. But she was not a Zachary, nor of any kin. Nobody knew who she was, or could ever know. It was not even known of what blood she might have come.

Abe Kelsey claimed he knew. He, and he alone, had been present when Old Zack found a naked baby on the prairie, seventeen years ago; and this

gave him the color of authority, for some. After
Kelsey turned on Old Zack, these listened when
Abe pointed to what he claimed was the Zacharys'
strange immunity to raids.

"Kiowa won't touch 'em. Never have, and never
will! Bought themselves scot-free when they sold
out my boy. Even took in a red-nigger whelp on
swap, to bind the deal. Go see for yourself! A squaw
young'n as ever was—growing up in the Zachary
name!"

No worse nonsense was possible. If the Kiowas
had believed for a moment that the Zacharys were
holding a Kiowa child, however fractional of
blood, they would have attacked without let-up. Yet
it was the kind of theory that easily took root in this
blood-soaked ground. In the past twenty years
Kiowa and Comanche raiding parties had killed
more than eight hundred Texas settlers. Among
them had been a great number of women killed by
incessant rape; and a lot of stolen children who died
most pitifully in captivity. The victims were not
only scalped but often gruesomely dismembered.

Ben thought that Texans should at least have
learned by this time that the Horse Indians used
fast travel as a weapon, and great space as a shield.
Old Zack himself had helped teach the Kiowas that
a blood-angry posse might soon be charging in
among their own lodges if they left too short a trail.
Kiowas raided from the top of Kansas to Santa Fe;
they could cross Texas at eighty miles a night to
raid deep in Mexico, and be back above the Red
while the same moon held. Not how far away, but
how watchful, was the measure of safety on this
frontier.

Yet people in the worst-hurt counties still built houses with bullet-leaky walls and tinder roofs, without lookouts, rifle loops, or battle shutters. They let their children wander unwatched, and left their women alone for days while they fogged off on senseless errands. They couldn't learn and wouldn't be told, and no amount of bloody murder ever changed that.

Perhaps a man whose family had been chopped up could not be expected to blame his own negligence. Easier on his peace of mind if he assumed he had done the best possible job, and found other explanations for the better results of others. There were people who asked too recklessly and too often why war parties always passed up the Zacharys, exposed in handy reach, to jump families two hundred miles beyond.

An unheard-of heresy crossed Ben's mind. *A man could learn to hate Texas. He could learn to hate it all.*

Ben himself never feared the Kiowas much. What he feared was a moment of carelessness, at the wrong place or the wrong time, by one of his own people.

They watched the moon. Kiowas on raid might attack by night or by day, but traveled only by moonlight. When the moon was full, you could figure war parites were sifting all over Texas, unseen; while in the dark of the moon you wouldn't cut fresh sign of a single band. The Zacharys allowed twelve days a month for the full moon, and lived differently, then.

They watched the grass. Kiowas wouldn't try a long foray, or any at all, until their war ponies were in shape. So the grass could tell you when the danger time had come.

Most important thing to know of all was that Horse Indians never fought well against walls. They raided for loot, which meant horses, and glory, which meant scalps, and they liked to get them cheap. If your house was proof against bullets and fire, its doors and shutters few and heavy, the Kiowas were unlikely to come against you at all. Only—

Ben now saw something ahead that might change the whole quality of danger on the Dancing Bird, past hope of survival. Suddenly he felt sick in the pit of his stomach, and sick in his heart. A decision he had put off for a long time, and that his father had put off before him, would have to be stood up to, now.

"Bring 'em on," he ordered Cassius; and he rode ahead.

5

Clear of the corrida, Ben jogged slowly, his eyes habitually sweeping and quartering. With the Rawlinses, the Zacharys claimed by right of use a strip some twenty miles wide by thirty or forty long, coming to six or seven hundred sections. The sum total of accomplishment of Old Zack's life lay in their precarious hold upon this land. "Damn the range," Ben had said to Cassius; and now he was wondering if he could ever bring himself to mean it.

The Dancing Bird range was carrying upward of twelve thousand head, about half of which the two families hoped were their own; not counting as many again that carried their brands, but were scattered over half of Texas. They had cows, all right. Everybody had cows, and virtually nothing else. A handful of strays had escaped the early Spaniards, three centuries ago; and these had multiplied into the countless wild cattle that had tantalized and frustrated Texans since before the Alamo. Hundreds of thousands had been killed for their hides, without making a dent. Yet Texas beef remained valueless, until after the war, for want of a market, or any way to reach one.

Then, as the Civil War ended, a railroad poked into Missouri, as far as Sedalia. Ben remembered the excitement that swept Texas. Below the Neuces, where wild cattle ran thickest, a cow might be worth two or three dollars, but you couldn't get it, because nobody had it. The same cow should be worth ten times that, and in cash, at the end of the track. Hundreds of cow-hunting outfits swarmed into the deep brush.

From the Neuces to Sedalia was a drive of more than twelve hundred miles, but William Zachary was only one of many who thought it could be made. With scarcely a dollar, and no place to borrow any, he scoured the brush country, contracting cattle from cow hunters on credit, on shares, or any way he could. He drove north three thousand head, with nine tough brush riders who brought their own grub, plus Ben, then sixteen. Ahead of them and behind them a hundred herds strung out for five hundred miles. Ben remembered his own boyish exultation, greater than he would ever feel again, as 260,000 head of cattle were thrown into the great march.

And he remembered the stunning, crushing disappointment of that year. The Texans drove a thousand miles, to be stopped two hundred short of their goal. Longhorns carried the deadly tick-transmitted Texas fever. Kansas farmers, fearing epidemic among their own livestock, threw up a quarantine barrier, stubbornly manned. The great herds were lost; and so were some of the drovers, who tried to fight their way through, and forever stayed in Kansas.

That was the first year. There had been seven since. That way north became the Chisholm Trail, as the rails pushed westward across Kansas to Abilene, then to Ellsworth, to Newton, and now to Wichita. Two and a half million cattle had made the long march to the railheads, and still they came on. Still the hearts of men and horses broke upon that cruel trail; and still the promise of fortune shone at its end, fabulous as the gold beyond the rainbow—and just as elusive, to most.

Of the seven years since Sedalia, three had been chancy, spotty years, in which they paid off debts in money, to borrow again in cows. Three years had been so bad that they had turned their weary herds and driven them back to Texas—which was how the Dancing Bird got stocked. Of "normal" years, in which successful drives found good markets, they had seen exactly—

One.

Their spring drive in 1870 had paid off every cent they owed. But it was also the last drive of Zack's life, for that was the year he died under his drowning cattle, in the flash-flooded Witch River crossing.

They hadn't made a nickel since. One reason was the treachery of the trail. Stampede, balk, scatter and give-out must be dealt with all the time. Thirst and starvation spelled off high water and bogged prairies; they had wars between rivals, banditry, stock diseases, failures of men and breakdowns of horses. There were freak disasters, as in '69, when grasshoppers stripped half the prairie. The trail boss was a trouble-shooter, at all times so beset that the Indian danger, ever-present and often deadly, was almost the least of his troubles.

But the market itself was more shifty than the trail. The arrival of too many herds close together, or a shortage of cars, or a wobbly day on the stock exchange—anything—could leave tens of thousands of head standing unsold. For a good market, you first needed a country-wide corn surplus, for an unfed longhorn was worse eating than a wolf. And next you needed a shortage of farm cattle, for the huge longhorn, unhappily, was the worst beef animal you could buy. Those vast bawling, earth-rumbling herds set fire to the imagination, until you thought you were seeing the advance of an empire, over the prairie grass. But the desolate truth was that trail cattle were of small importance to the meat supply; in its best years, the Chisholm Trail delivered less than ten per cent of the national kill. Only a special situation could make the low-grade wild beef marketable at all.

In the years since their first costly drive to Sedalia, the Zacharys had been neither lucky nor unlucky in their cattle dealings. They had simply worked along among the inherent paradoxes of the cattle trade. It was a way of life in which you might own ten thousand head of cattle, without a pound of sugar in the house. You might carry your gold around on a pack mule, while you knew you weren't worth a cent. You might strip your range to bunch four thousand head, and find that you had gathered only six hundred of your own. You could start out with two thousand head, and in four years drive cattle worth half a million dollars; and in the end come out with two thousand head of cattle still, except that now, somehow, you owed for them all. You might even, in some long-dreamed-of year, hide a powder keg of gold eagles under the floor of a mud hut—and keep on making your own soap and candles, for lack of time to ride a hundred and fifty miles to the nearest store. . . .

Yet Ben believed his father had left them the means to wealth and power. Here lay their great, deep-grass range, heavily stocked—even overstocked, since the turnaround of the year before. A year of booming markets was due, had to be due, for last year's light buying might result in a national shortage. And the supply would be less, for many Texas cattlemen were discouraged, and more were in no position to drive. All winter long, Ben had made journey after journey, his pack mule loaded with tally books, this time. He had traded his own distant strays for cattle already on his range; when he had nothing to trade, he bought outright—on Zachary credit—hundreds upon hundreds of cows actually using the Dancing Bird grass. Their debts were sky-high again. Ben himself only had a loose general idea of how much they owed.

But this year they could put up a herd with more big feeder beeves in it, and more of them their own, than they had ever driven before. They would make back everything they owed five times over—if only they could make this year go right.

If the Zacharys took this year to move on, to some far-off new land—Nebraska, Dakota, Montana— much more than a great year would be lost. It was one thing for Old Zack to let go of things he had built up himself, and start again. It was another thing altogether for Ben to throw away a stake into which had gone eight years of his father's life—and his life itself, at the end.

I can't do it, Ben thought. *I can't run. Not now. Not yet. We've got to stand, now, here on this river Papa found. No matter what comes. No matter what.*

6

Sometimes Ben felt awkward, and a little bit embarrassed, as he came in sight of the house after being away for a while, for no more reason than that they were always so danged glad to see him. But he forgot that in the first moment he was there, for everything seemed natural, easy, and familiar. He never supposed he knew how to be homesick nor realized how much he missed the people whom he left behind, until he saw them again.

Tears were running down Matthilda's cheeks, and Rachel's eyes had a wet shine, as Ben stepped from the saddle to the stoop. They hung around his neck, asking stupid questions, and making all the fuss they knew how. "Did you bring—" Rachel started to ask, then dropped it. He had never yet failed to do the best he could, and now that he was here it didn't even matter.

In the house, where everything was shined up fit to eat and sleep the Governor, the best they had was ready to go onto the table, as soon as the women could leave Ben alone long enough to get it on. It was Ben's duty to say grace, now that he was home. They had always said grace once a day, and ordinarily Ben's quick mumble didn't put much into it. They had used the same few words all their lives, until nobody really listened any more, or felt any meaning. But tonight, perhaps because he had had a rest from it, Ben said the little prayer so that they heard it again.

"Dear merciful Father, we thank Thee for these vittles, and for all Thy blessings this day. Now guide us, and guard us, and shield us from evil, we pray in Jesus' name. . . . Amen." The others made an inarticulate sound on the "Amen."

At one time Rachel had secretly thought the first part should go, "We thank Ben, mostly, for beating his saddle to death catching up with these vittles—not helped much by all this frolicky weather we're being booned with lately, either." And that short list of chores, repeated daily on the evident theory that the Almighty could not retain, had seemed to Rachel to be failing of attention, to judge by general results. But conformity had shaped an attitude of piety by sheer habit, and she no longer remembered her childish heresies.

Tonight they were all together again, all there were left of them, safe, and snug, and fed; and Rachel was truly thankful. Ben saw how happy she was, seemingly in all ways trustful of her world. He felt a hard twinge of pity, of anger, seeing her so innocently unaware of the black hostility that was hanging over her, ugly enough to darken the lives of them all.

But if any except Ben had a worry it didn't show.
Ben's return with the corrida ended the long tyran-
ny of winter for everybody. He brought the spring,
and the rebirth of their world. Rachel and Matthilda had seen no women except each other for
many long months on end. Now they would see the
Rawlinses, at least, practically all the time, for the
two families must work together closely, from here
on. Or so they thought then; because it had always
been that way before.

After supper Ben brought in the slim parcels he
had fetched home for Rachel and Matthilda. He explained that he was sorry about not bringing more.
Had to carry everything in his saddlebags with his
gear, till be bought the wagon at Fort Griffin. They
found he had brought a piece of blue-checked
gingham, too short, and a piece of red-checked, extra long—had he thought they could use one to
piece the other out? But there was also nine yards of
a flower-sprigged muslin that they wanted to hug
him for; only he was gone from there, down by the
corrals with the rest, by then.

By ten o'clock, when the boys came in, Matthilda
had sent Rachel to bed; and Andy, turning in at
once, was soon asleep. After that, as the owls began
to fly, Matthilda seemed older than she had before,
and Ben let himself go tired. Only Cassius was still
crisp as the three of them took a look at the trouble
they shared.

7

"Cash and I talked to the hands," Ben told their mother. "Didn't use Kelsey's name, of course. Just said a horse thief. Told 'em how he looks. And we put up a hundred dollars."

"A hundred—?"

"Those 'ramuses can't count over a hundred dollars. More would only scare 'em."

Matthilda looked strangely vague, so that Ben wondered if she had followed him. These vaguenesses were appearing oftener, as her age advanced. But now she said, "What if they catch him?"

Ben and Cash exchanged a glance, and Ben said slowly, "Mama, we never told them to catch him."

"What?"

"The hundred," Cassius said plainly, "is for his scalp."

Mama gave a little shuddering gasp. "But Abe couldn't fight them. He wouldn't even try. Why, they'd have to shoot him with his hands up!"

"Yes," Cassius said.

The tears that came so easily nowadays sprang to Matthilda's eyes. She said, "Poor old man," in a sort of plaintive whimper, and sat staring into space. The boys waited in silence for the moment of emotion to pass.

"If somehow, in spite of us, he sneaks up near the house again," Ben said, "I want you to fort up, same as if he had the Kiowa nation behind him. And he's got to be fired on. If nobody else is here to do it, Rachel has to fire on him. And, Mama—for God's sake will you believe me?—you mustn't stop her!"

Matthilda said nothing, but seemed to accept it.

"Now," Ben said to her gravely, "I'm going to ask you to think of something else. I don't know if Kelsey has been around the Rawlinses, or any neighbor. I'll warn Zeb, he's a squaw man and a thief. But Kelsey has friends in Texas, even yet; and the old, black lie he started against us is still alive, just as much as ever it was. If Kelsey gets to the Rawlinses, they may listen to him, Mama—just as likely as not."

"That," Matthilda said, surprisingly matter-of-fact, "is something that will happen, or it won't."

"Maybe it's bound to happen, someday," Ben said. "Maybe, if the Rawlinses hadn't been looked on as no better than damyankees, they'd have been told long ago. Mama, have you thought about what we'd best do, when it does come?"

"Well, we'll have to stop seeing them, I suppose."

"There'll be trouble. No way to work the range with those people, once they turn against us. Every county in Texas has had its gun feuds. We can very easy have one of our own, right here."

"I know," Matthilda said.

"There's one thing more," Ben said; but now he was interrupted.

Rachel had appeared in the bedroom doorway, bare-footed and in her muslin nightie, her hair in long braids. She asked in a plaintive, little-girl fashion, if she couldn't come out and sit up with the rest of them, for a little while. She kept hearing their voices without being able to make out the words. This was a teasing thing, and kept her from getting to sleep.

Coaxingly, Matthilda asked her to keep trying, anyway. "The Rawlinses will be over tomorrow, like as not. We don't want to look just awful." Rachel's eyes went to Ben with a quick appeal, but he did not intercede. The door closed softly behind her.

While she had stood there Ben had noticed again, unhappily, how pretty she had become, still wide-eyed and childlike, yet so plainly a woman, even in the shapeless nightdress. A new, fresh little flower of a woman, as he saw her now, such as any Kiowa buck with eyes in his head would surely want to own. How often would unseen eyes be watching her this year? The Kiowas scouted this place all the time, for it lay on the way they took in search of farther, easier kills. This girl whom he had so long thought of as his sister had suddenly turned into murder bait.

For surely old Kelsey was now preaching to the Kiowas the same story he had started against the Zacharys in Texas, long ago—though to a different

purpose. Strange that so cruel a people should set
such great store by their own children, their own
kin, as the Kiowas did. The deeper the gulch, the
higher the hill, it seemed sometimes. So long as that
sick-minded old man was trying to cadge favor with
the Kiowas, what better way could he find than to
lead them to a long-captive Kiowa child? Not that
they would ever believe one word the old loony said.
But if he kept on dinging the idea into their heads,
one of them was sure to see the advantages in it,
pretty soon. A Kiowa who wanted to think something generally found a way to prove it to himself.

Like, some young buck might get a Kiowa warlock to find out from the spirits if, by any chance,
the crazy old man had hold of something true. He
could hire one of the Owl Prophets, like Sky Walker, or Striking Horse, for a sample, to consult an
owl. With a couple of gift horses in the offing for the
prophet, it was wonderful how the owl would come
up with whichever answer was wanted, about nine
times out of ten. And if a single young war leader
concluded that his people had a claim on the girl he
could very easily find great lashings of fight-loving
young bucks eager to take him at his word, and follow him all out in a holy crusade. Then you'd see
Kiowas come against walls, and with all they had.

"There's another thing," he began patiently,
again. "This is going to be an awful bad Indian
year. Maybe the worst Texas has ever seen. You
realize more than a dozen people have been killed
since the turn of the year, right in the neighborhood
of Fort Sill? They even stole a herd of mules out of
the fort's stone corral. And there's a hundred other
warning signs, as well."

Matthilda shrugged. Not that she underrated the Indian danger; on the contrary, she feared the Kiowas unreasoningly. This year, as Ben described it, sounded about like any other year, to her. "I've never known the time," she said, "but what an Indian could lie right out there on that ridge, and shoot down any one of us he picked."

Actually, a Kiowa out on the ridge was bound to be a scout, alone, or with only two or three others. He wasn't going to start trouble in decent shooting light unless he caught somebody far from support. Or, if he was from a nearby war party, he wasn't going to give that show away, either, by poking into the best-forted hornet's nest on the frontier. Not without even a chance at a scalp. Matthilda would never know things like that. To her the Wild Tribes seemed weird, unearthly, past hope of comprehension; and their cruelties so repelled her that she was forever denied a closer look. Ben was stumped. Nothing he could say seemed to help his case. His mother already held the Kiowas in the greatest fear she was capable of knowing, yet was unswayed by it.

He now attacked the key point of decision with a reluctance amounting to dread, yet head on, having found no other way to come at it. "Mama," he asked, "would you be willing—just for this one year —to take Rachel off to some safe place, like maybe Fort Richardson, or maybe Fort Worth—"

Matthilda was looking at him as if she couldn't believe her ears.

"Or Austin?" he tried again. "Even Corpus Christi—"

"Have you gone mad?" his mother demanded.

He knew what he was up against, then. He felt a moment of chill, almost of panic; he had been hog-tied before now by this gentle, lovingly inflexible will. He was hunting for a persuasion that would move Matthilda; without that, he was helpless to care for them or defend them. He could not very well take his mother and Rachel to Fort Richardson in irons, with a demand that they be held secure. It came to him that the fight of his life was not going to be made in the saddle, or in the smoke of black powder, but here, now, in this room. And it must be made with no weapons he knew how to use. Words never did come to him the way a gun or a reata came effortlessly into his hands.

"We've pushed the work hard," he said, groping. "Cash and me both. We've had a right to hope we'd be so far in the clear, before trouble broke, it wouldn't matter. One good year—maybe this year —and you can school Rachel in Switzerland, or— or—wherever—"

He saw how sadly his mother was looking at him. For a moment he glimpsed a pity as deep as a sorrow, as deep as her love, so that he was nonplused, and stopped. Matthilda no longer believed this hopeful story of a fortune just ahead; she had heard it too many times, since Old Zack's first disastrous drive to Sedalia.

Matthilda Zachary would have hated and feared the prairie if no Indian had ever ridden it. The galling month-long winds; the dust that sifted forever from the walls and roof of the hole in the ground where they lived; the spreading stains of mud that leaked through with every rain; the few poor things they had to do with, so that endless toil showed no return; the cruelly harsh, home-boiled soap, which made cracked, hurting hands the price of just keeping clean—all this Matthilda could have forgiven. But she could not forgive what seemed to her the prairie's vast malignance, as boundless as its emptiness, and as mighty as its storms.

A grass fire, a blizzard, or a parching drouth was always dotting the earth with carcasses, so that the deep-grass everywhere hid uncounted bones. For all its birdsongs, its flowers, and its wind-turned grass, the prairie kept changing into a horrid maw, that could swallow the labors of whole lifetimes in one savage night. It had taken her husband, and had even withheld his lifeless body, to be thrown away. The bright will-o'-the-wisp he had followed, and which now led on his sons, was part of a monstrous and cruel lie. *I know that, now,* she told herself. *But men have the hearts of little boys. They love to make up big golden dreams, to treasure as if they were true. . . .*

"We'll talk about it when the good year comes," she answered Ben.

"Mama, I tell you—will you believe me just this once? You've got to get her out of here now, before the first Kiowa Moon—or it's going to be too late!"

"What little money we have wouldn't carry us a step out of Texas. And I'll never take her to a Texas town again—never. I'll not see her heart broken, and her life ruined, before my very eyes. Have you forgotten Round Rock? And the San Saba? The whisperings, the snubs, the turned backs—while the poor little thing turns bewildered, and so cruelly hurt— How long can that go on before somebody says it to her face?"

"Says what to her face?" Cash asked sharply.

"Do I have to say it? I will then! Red nigger. *Red nigger!*"

It was strange to hear Matthilda speak the rough words, forbidden in her house. She might pronounce "Negro" as "Niggra," but to her nothing on earth could have been a nigger. The disused words had effective force, even shock, as they heard her say them.

"Tell me," Matthilda said, "you could bear to hear your own little sister called that?" Sometimes they could not tell whether Mama forgot that Rachel was not her own, or whether she was just playing her chosen role.

"I'll hear no man say it twice," Cash promised.

"It won't be said by a man, or to you. It's Rachel will hear it said." Matthilda had left an infant daughter under the swept sand of a Round Rock churchyard. From the very first, Rachel had fulfilled for Matthilda a deep maternal need. Perhaps it was the same need that makes a mare break loose, and travel a hundred miles to haunt a cactus patch, where once she dropped a stillborn foal. Her face twisted now, and she sounded as though she were crying, while her eyes remained strangely dry. "Have you any faintest idea of what that would do to her?"

They supposed they knew how she'd feel; but maybe they didn't. Perhaps men who live mainly in the saddle can never entirely put themselves in the place of a young girl when the world turns its back upon her, and draws off.

"She's so dear, so precious," Matthilda said. "How can you even think of letting that happen to her?"

"I'd choose it before I'd risk her death," Ben said stubbornly.

"It's the same thing."

"What?"

"Do you believe she'd stay on a minute, once she thought she was drawing harm? She wouldn't care where she went, or if she lived or died. We'd never see her again." She was pleading with them to understand, and at the same time despairing that they ever could. "I don't believe you know her at all!"

"I sure don't see how it serves any useful purpose to hold her here, trapped, in the one most dangerous place she can be!"

"I can protect her here," Matthilda said.

There it was, the softly indomitable purpose that came before everything else in Matthilda's world. Because of it she had made Old Zack bring her here, which he never would have done of his own accord, knowing how she felt about the prairie. And because of it she stayed, in spite of every appeal Ben could make. "I can protect her here." It was the end of argument, standing stronger than hope or fear. Stronger than common sense, too, of which it was the very opposite, Ben thought. He supposed that what he faced here was a female way of thinking. To a male, plain physical danger was the first consideration; it had better be, if he was responsible for a family on the prairie frontier. Matthilda's conclusions would always be in some part incomprehensible to him.

"What when the Kiowas come?" he asked her.

"Well, then, we'll fight, I suppose."

She knew no more about fighting than she knew about Indians, and would be no help whatever if they were forced to a defense of the soddy. Probably she could not have said a thing like that in so maddeningly casual a way if she had known what she was talking about. Yet she had touched the weakest point in his whole position. This place could be defended, for the brothers, and Old Zack before them, had made sure of that. Even over-whelmingly outnumbered, they stood a pretty fair chance of giving attacking Kiowas a licking.

"Nothing more I can say," Ben mumbled, baffled and defeated.

But there was something he could say to Cassius, when their mother had gone to bed. "You saw the hands I hired," he said.

"They look all right to me. I told you that."

"Could you take about twenty of 'em, and get four thousand head to Wichita?"

Cassius flared up, roweled on the same old gall. "What the hell you want to ask a thing like that for? You know it damn hootin' well!"

"All right," Ben said. "It's your herd, Cash."

"It's what?"

"I'm staying back."

8

Five of the Rawlinses arrived next day, to visit overnight while Zeb Rawlins and Ben straightened out their affairs.

"Let's not mention Abe Kelsey to them," Matthilda asked of Rachel. She made it oddly confidential, and urgent.

"Why?"

"It just isn't needful. I can't see it's needful at all!" Tears came easily to Matthilda's eyes, but Rachel was surprised, and a little shaken, to see them appear now. "Promise me. Please promise!"

It was the last thing she said to Rachel before their visitors came.

Zeb Rawlins and his wife, Hagar, appeared first, with a team and rig. All hands but Rachel and Matthilda were out horse hunting; they used ten horses to the man, so driving in a hundred and fifty head more was the first task of the spring work. The Rawlinses' two grown boys were out with the hands, and Georgia Rawlins, nineteen, had tagged along, as Rachel would have done had she been allowed. Zeb and Hagar Rawlins made a peculiar couple, unlike in most ways, yet held uncommonly close together by the circumstance that each had a handicapping "infirmity," of which they never spoke, and to which neither yielded an unnecessary inch. "Two old crocks," one of them might say with curious tenderness, when realizing that the other was concealing pain; but never a word more.

The nature of Zeb's infirmity had been unclear. Zeb was tall sitting down, and short standing up; his thick arms and shoulders had the great strength that sometimes goes with this build. But he moved with a slow, ponderous step, and always traveled by team, unable to mount a horse or sit a saddle. The Zacharys, inventing an explanation, had once believed that Zeb carried a bullet in his heart. Later the boys had learned what Zeb had was a "rupture"—a hernia of the type for which out-country folk knew no remedy but the truss.

Impeded in movement, but a heavy eater still, Zeb had become vast of heft and paunch; but he handled a team with great skill, once he made it to the seat. He now wheeled his rig close to the house, to let his wife dismount directly upon the stoop; then doffed his hat with a broad gallantry, bellowed at Matthilda that he hoped she was well, M'am, and was off like a runaway to look for the horse hunt.

Hagar Rawlins was taller than her husband, gaunt, grim-jawed, with hollowed cheeks and deep-set eyes. Rachel was afraid of her, for she had often caught Hagar eyeing her strangely, as if with antip-

athy, or perhaps with some nameless suspicion. As
soon as Hagar was afoot, her own physical handi-
cap was plainly visible, though puzzling as to ori-
gin. She was not the sort of person you asked about
such things. Something was wrong with her ankles,
as if the tendons had been cut; she painfully shuffled and flapped, dragging or slinging her helpless
feet in misshapen moccasins.

Matthilda and Hagar embraced, as was custom-
ary, though it had always seemed to Rachel that
Matthilda brought all the affection there might be
in it. Hagar was from eastern Tennessee, "so fur
back in the hills," she liked to put it, "the sun don't
never shine." She could ridicule her own back-
ground, but she was "easy throwed" by Matthilda,
who was likely to confide that her father had been
schooled for the ministry, partly, and had read
Latin and Greek. Around Matthilda, Hagar would
have sieges of speaking carefully, in mincing forms
she imagined elegant. Then she would backslide,
and catch herself again; so that her language kept
kind of running out and in, like a sliphorn.

But today Hagar brought news, and they could
see at once that it had changed her past all imagining. The Rawlinses had an older daughter called
Effie, who had been gone from the Dancing Bird
country for a year and a half. She had taken down
with lung fever, and gone into a decline; as a last
resort she had been sent to Fort Worth for a pro-
longed doctoring. No matter how many children
you have, the one in danger becomes precious out of
all reason; and no light of faith had sustained
Hagar. "They never come back," was what she said
the day she watched Effie out of sight.

Yet Effie had rallied; Hagar now had word that her daughter's recovery was complete, and she was coming home. To Hagar it was a miracle and a resurrection. There was warmth, now, even serenity, in the deep-hollowed eyes that had so often chilled Rachel; and a great weight seemed lifted from them all. Perhaps none of them had realized the degree to which this dour, strong-willed, and embittered woman had dominated their prairie.

And more. While convalescent in Fort Worth, Effie had made good her time by catching herself a young man, of pretty good family at that, by all reports. She was bringing him home with her; they were to be married—out here, in her father's house. The Zachary women spent little time regretting the monotony of their lives; perhaps they did not even know how barren of reward their lives actually were. Yet they treasured every least diversion, and made the most of it. Now, suddenly they had a wedding to look forward to.

Rachel had never known Effie very well. She remembered her, perhaps unkindly, as watery-eyed and washed-out, with a bluish, translucent look. Thinking of Effie as a romantic figure was none too easy, but Rachel took this hurdle in her stride. Immediately, she began to imagine what the wedding would be like. Since she had never seen one, her mental picture of it flowered most wonderfully, unrestrained by facts. She couldn't seem to help seeing the whole doings spaciously mansioned, with great numbers of handsome people coming to it. All were beautifully dressed, especially the women, whose many-hued gowns were reflected in a floor as brightly polished as wet ice. None of this would ever

be. The few families who might possibly get there
had never seen the kind of clothes Rachel was imagining, and never would in their lives. And the wedding would have to contain itself in the log house of
the Rawlinses, which was hardly bigger than the
Zachary soddy. As for polished floors—the
Zacharys at least had a wooden floor, long since
scrubbed white as bone, and it had never reflected
anything yet. The Rawlins floor was of dirt. . . .

In her present mood Hagar talked readily and
unabashed, in the language of her own hills. The
hampers she had brought, as was usual, carried a
huge baking of crackling bread, and much more.
When Matthilda made the conventional protest—
"Why, Hagar, you shouldn't have!"—Hagar said,
" 'Tain't nawthin', Mattie." Probably nobody else
had ever addressed Matthilda as "Mattie" in her
life.

Along toward sundown they heard the first day's
horse-gather coming in. The deep-dug back wall
often brought the sound of hoofs into the house,
through the earth, from a long way off. Today they
listened for half an hour to a faint humming in the
ground, increasing slowly to a tremor, then to the
drumming of hundreds of hoofs, before at last they
heard the whooping of the hands. The riders were
hazing and frolicking, showing off because Georgia
Rawlins was with them; they poured the herd in at
the gallop, running like a storm. The uproar sent a
dust cloud sky high as they choused the winter-wild
stock into the long night corrals across the Dancing
Bird.

Georgia Rawlins came on in. She was a big girl a
couple of years older than Rachel, tall as her moth-

er, and strongly made; handsome, rather than pretty, but bright-eyed and full of bounce, from hours in the prairie wind. She came in briskly, with a loud but shy, "Oh, hi, everybody!" Her great shapeless riding skirt was held up in front of her, avoiding both stumbles and embraces, for it embarrassed her to be hugged by women. She bolted for the bedroom, to change into other clothes she had carried in a roll behind her saddle.

This was the girl who would normally have been Rachel's best friend; there was no choice of others. But both families tacitly understood that Georgia was Cash's girl. Supposedly they would marry at some undetermined time, when Cash got around to building a place to live. This threat stirred up a certain amount of possessiveness in Rachel, so that she very easily found faults aplenty in Georgia, and not much else. Probably no girl would have seemed worthy to Rachel, where her brothers were concerned. She took to noticing that Georgia moved like a tomboy, always ready to climb a corral, or the like, in ways that showed her legs; and could cuss like a man, though she wouldn't try it in front of Hagar. *More like a man in girl's clothes,* Rachel told herself, but without much conviction. If there was anything unfeminine about Georgia, the boys didn't seem to know it.

Georgia reappeared in full-skirted blue cotton. The dress looked familiar, for it was the only decent one she had, but Rachel had to admit, with a twinge, that she looked all right. Georgia had a lot of mouse-blond hair, which she had tied back with a blue ribbon. *Wrong color blue,* Rachel hoped, without looking too closely. But she envied Georgia's strap slippers, new since they had seen her. *Finally got shoes on you, I see. Had to rope and throw you, of course. And stockings, too—will wonders never cease. Now, if next you hear of underwear . . .*

What Georgia thought of Rachel was not known. Most of the time she seemed unaware of her.

Soon, though, the men began coming in, and no awkwardness of any kind could long survive the excitement of a house full of people. The two Rawlins boys, though lacking in flash, at least were young men who were not Rachel's brothers. Charlie was the youngest Rawlins, and the one nearest Rachel's age. He had sad, slow-moving eyes in a shy, quiet face—an empty face, Rachel thought it. The Rawlins heavy-set strength had missed Charlie. Only unusual thing about him, and it was kind of ridiculous, was his great tangle of dusty-looking hair, which stood straight up. He kept plastering it down with water, but it no sooner stopped dripping than it began to spring up again, a tuft at a time— Ping!—like wire busting loose in a freeze. Rachel knew that Charlie's eyes followed her moonishly, whenever he thought she wasn't noticing. She found this pleasantly exciting, even though she didn't care anything about him.

Charlie's brother Jude, of an age somewhere between Ben and Cassius, was a likely sample of what his father must have been, before salt pork and inactivity crept up on him—bull-necked, hammered down in the legs, and heavy of bone and muscle. Andy stood in awe of him, admiring his strength.

"Why, he's got leaders in his wrists thick as the haft of a brand iron," Andy said once. "Thicker even."

"And Ben can throw him over his head," Rachel tacked onto it.

Jude stayed close to his father and Ben Zachary, listening doggedly, in hopes of learning something.

Cassius was the one who outshone everybody, when he finally came in. Ben, in his old, worn clothes, still looked like the boss; even while he was talking with a courteous deference to Zeb Rawlins, Ben still looked like the man in charge. But Cash was all dressed up, astonishing Rachel, who had not noticed what he was wearing at breakfast, in the sleepiness before dawn. Black leather shirt, wrapped high in the throat, like a stock; black trousers, after he took his brush leggings off. Black, silver-conchoed leather cuffs and belt. Rachel thought he looked wonderful. Ben's eyes, though, may have been belittling when they rested on his brother, as if he thought Cassius a fool.

After supper Ben and Zeb Rawlins got their heads together over the bookkeeping that was to Ben the meanest chore in all the cattle business.

Rachel saw that Zeb Rawlins kept slowly shaking his head, while Ben might be having a hard time hiding his opinion that Zeb had the outlook of a one-horse sod-buster. Zeb would reap half the benefit of Ben's winter trades, but he had not okayed any buying. Hard feeling always developed when two outfits started even, on the same range, and one came out way ahead of the other; so Ben wanted to give Zeb half the profits on purchased stock, while guaranteeing him against loss. But Zeb thought Ben highhanded, and a plunger as well. He was stubbornly sitting back in the breeching.

They didn't get far, and it was just as well.

Georgia, harder to squelch than a prairie fire, got
Cash to his feet, then Charlie and Jude; and of
course Rachel. They pushed things back and
started up a singing game—a kind of a scamper,
first, in which one stood in the middle, and a boy
chased a girl around him until he caught her. Then
others like that, with clapping and stamping for
music, the Rawlinses as tickled as kids with the
noisy wooden floor. Couldn't have been more childish, actually. "Stole old Blue! And I know who!
Here I come, and I see you!" Pretty silly, but plenty
loud. Ben and Zeb had to give up.

"If only Effie was here," Hagar kept saying. She
was very much here in their minds, a part of the
great day acoming, that had been such a long, long
time on the way. With Effie, they had in this one
room all who were to have a part in the bust-up of
the Dancing Bird range. Or rather, all save one,
who was in nobody's mind; unless, perhaps, the
shadow of a wretched and doomed old man sometimes crossed Ben's thought or Matthilda's, like a
ghost of the living, unasked and unwanted.

The room became hot; when the girls blew their
hair out of their eyes, little damp tendrils were left
stuck to their foreheads. "Now swing the other!
That's the wrong one! Go right back where you
started from. . . ." One rompy, let-yourself-go night
like this had to last them all for a long time. Rachel
wanted to hold onto it, as if it were the last night in
the world.

It was the last, for these people as a group. They
were never again all together under the same roof.

9

It began to rain; not in the good old soaker they really needed, but in bursts that doused the prairie hard and briefly, with spells of sunshine and rainbows between showers. Ben walked out bareheaded in the first rain that fell. He spread his arms to it, and turned his face up to be rained on, getting whopped all over with drops as big as dollars. The Dancing Bird rose, and the grass started. Winter-gaunted cows and horses gorged themselves into bloats and colics, but all would be well with them now, for the time being.

In the house the women eyed muddy stains spreading upon the whitewashed roof boards, and swore the sod roof must be shingled over this year for sure. But the house would get no attention now. All day long Jude's hammer rang at the forge, as he repaired the wagons and shrunk new iron to the wheels. Every few minutes came a yell, the angry squeal of a horse, and a splatter of hoofs, as somebody fought to get the hump out of a range-wild pony.

Every year they had the same argument about whether Rachel was to be allowed out around the hands. When she was little Matthilda had feared she would get her head kicked off, and later that she would hear too much rowdy language. Now that she was a young lady, the objection was obvious. About every third girl in Texas ran off with some young cowhand, who might amount to something later, but showed no signs of it at the time. Rachel always lost the battle, yet won the war. Gradually she would begin sifting out, on useful errands that somehow became more frequent by the hours; till even her mother got used to it, and accepted that nothing was actually happening to her.

This year Ben felt that the whole thing had better be handled a different way. He didn't say anything, but come afternoon the day after the Rawlinses' visit, he rode to the house, and hollered for an extra slicker. When Rachel brought it to the stoop, he sung out, "Rachel's with me, Mama!" And he had her up behind his saddle, and through the Dancing Bird, before objection could be raised.

Only thing, he explained to Rachel, he wanted to see something before he turned her loose on her wild lone, so she would have to stay put where he told her. "Right—square—here," he said, letting her off on the fence of the round busting corral.

She sat on the top rail, hugging her luck, for here was put on the best show they had. Half a dozen of the best rough-string riders got a few dollars extra for working the round corral. The corrida Ben had hired was full of youngsters who had ridden before

they could walk, and most of the time since. They
would fight anything that wanted to fight, so long
as they weren't crippled up. But the round-corral
busters were expected to turn a mustang into a saddle horse without any wasted roughing, and this
took a kind of horse-savvy that had to be born in a
man.

Into the round corral, half a dozen at a time, were
hazed the horses that had never before felt rope—
called "colts," whatever their ages might be. All
were geldings, age-hardened at full growth; the
Zacharys rode no mares, no fillies, and no colts under four. Like the longhorns, the Texas mustangs
came of Spanish stock, abandoned upon a strange
continent long ago. After running wild for three
centuries, beset by wolves, drouths, and bitter win-
ters, they had a runty look, but an almost incredible
toughness and endurance.

With the range-wild colts came the meanest bad-
actors from the rough strings, the ratchet-heads
that never knew when they were licked, but had to
be fought out all over again every spring. These
knew what they were up against, and were not
afraid of it; they fought wickedly and cunningly,
bucking as they had never bucked when they were
fear-crazed colts. You didn't have to be thrown to
get hurt riding horses like that. Rough-string riders
were smashed up and through before they were
thirty.

Not every year, but once in every few hundred
horses, a killer might turn up. Usually there was
nothing about him to warn you. Any colt was likely
to strike, or lash out, or try for you with a snap of
the teeth fit to take off your arm, as you worked

around him. Or he might groan, deep in his chest like an angering bull, as you snubbed him short for saddling. None of this meant anything. A killer almost never charged a man on foot, as a stallion might do; he might even stand quiet, as if earlier handling had cured his fear of men. But when his rider was thrown he turned like a lion, and trampled with whirling, stiff-legged jumps, sometimes savaging with his teeth.

The rare killers hardly explained why nearly all the young riders wore pistols; and neither did the unlikely chance of a dragging account for it. If a thrown rider's boot caught in a stirrup, almost any horse would kick him to death in a hurry. But this happened so seldom that few had ever seen it, and it could be made impossible by using tapaderas, such as the brush-country riders always wore on their stirrups. In any case, neither a man slammed hard on the ground nor one stirrup-dragged by a runaway was likely to draw and fire soon enough to do himself any good. Even the bystanders, invariably taken by surprise, generally failed to take effective action in time.

But the only boy you saw unarmed was one who hadn't been able to get hold of a gun. They wore them belted snug and high if they were going to ride, with a slitted thong on the hammer to keep the gun in the holster; or slung them low, tied down to the thigh, if they expected to be afoot. They wore guns to break horses or to brand calves, or when they weren't working at all. Most of them took their guns to bed. A seven-pound gun could develop an almighty heavy drag, in fourteen or sixteen hours of riding, but only a thunderstorm could cause it to be laid away. For gun wearing was a fashion; maybe it was a fashion set by men in trouble with the law—but a fashion just the same.

So, when a rough-string boy who called himself Johnny Portugal came sidling along the fence to where Rachel was perched, he was armed with a huge hog-leg of a percussion revolver, like most of the rest. He leaned an elbow on the top rail close to Rachel, and crossed his feet in a pose of ease. His mouth seemed uncommonly full of large teeth, and the grin he flashed as he looked up at her showed them all.

"You been living around here long?" Johnny asked pleasantly; and that was as far as he got.

Perfect, for Ben's purpose, because nothing even remotely off-color in Johnny's remark confused the issue. Ben had not set out to teach these saddle tramps their manners; he didn't give a hoot whether they had any or not. What he wanted was to warn them against messing around Rachel at all.

Ben spun Johnny Portugal by the shoulder with his left hand, and with his right hand swung what could be called a slap. His hand was open, and the blow rang like a slap. But the heel of the hand carried Ben's full weight from the heels. Johnny's feet seemed to fly up, his hat sailed off, and his head cracked a five-inch pole as he hit the fence. He ended sitting in the mud against the bottom pole, and in this position grabbed for his gun. His thumb failed to flick the thong from the hammer on the first try, and he had to start the draw again. Ben stood waiting with an appearance of patience while Johnny Portugal fumbled. The gun came out at last; and Ben instantly kicked it over the fence.

Cassius had come over the fence, and was standing beside his brother, looking happy and interested, as Johnny Portugal looked up. Rachel remembered afterward that Cash had been fooling around nearby, accomplishing nothing, all the time she had been sitting there. One brother on each side of the fence, watching the bait Ben had put out.

"He gets it from our old man," Cassius told the seated man. "Old Zack broke a Comanche's neck with a slap like that, right in the middle of a Kiowa camp. Indians always called him Stone Hand." Well—that was the way it was told in Texas, though the story had been fixed up a little, by later narrators. Actually, the Comanche had only been knocked out—which the Kiowas had taken as a good joke on the Comanche.

"I got time coming," Johnny mumbled, rubbing his head, and then his jaw.

"We pay off in Wichita," Cash said.

"I ain't fired?"

"What for? You're the party done all the sufferin', so far."

"You're lucky it wasn't my brother," Ben told Johnny.

"Tell me he hits any harder," Johnny said, "and I walk back to town!"

"He doesn't hit at all," Ben said; and they walked away.

Matthilda could have found no cause for complaint, after that, in the averted eyes, the ducked hatbrims, or the wary circlings of cowhands who had to pass Rachel. It was as if she had learned to rattle.

10

While it lasted, the lively horse-handling made every day a fiesta, but it was over in less than a week. The colts would have to learn their work as it went along. The cook wagon and the bed wagon began to roll. From here on the corrida would get home only every third or fourth night, coming in long after dark and pulling out before the first light. A couple of hands were left at the home layout, cleaning out the well, or mending saddles, or burning lime; there were always plenty of odd jobs to keep them busy while they served as a garrison. And one of the brothers always came in overnight when the corrida was out. This seemed all the precaution that was needed, for the moon was at deep wane; and even when it waxed again, the Kiowas would remain pinned for one moon more, while their ponies regained weight.

Almost every day Rachel rode out to the wagons with whichever brother had slept home. The range hands were rounding up, cutting out the beeves that would make up the first drive, and chousing them into bunches that would finally be thrown into one great herd. The Zachary boys worked cattle in the hell-for-leather way Old Zack had learned in the brush country, where you rode full stretch or lost your cow. Often Zeb Rawlins watched the parting of the cattle from his buggy, and Rachel knew he was sometimes angered by what seemed to him a brutal roughing of the stock. But she wasn't going to worry about old Zeb's opinions or anything else, while these treasured days of the green-up lasted, to her the most precious of the year.

Part of it was the good smells, of cows and horses, and leather, and beans boiling, and salt pork frying, sometimes the spice of trampled sage; while everywhere, and above all, the fragrance of young grass responding to the rains made a magic like nothing else ever known. It rose upon a new warmth, gentle, moist, and living, from the unlocked vitality of the earth itself—the smell of hope, of promise, of a world reborn. Under the ground and upon it and in the air, every winter-deadened thing awoke, turned young and eager; and human hearts rose singing in answer.

And partly it was the sounds. From the increasing herds came a continuous bawling that is like no other music on earth, to cow-folks' ears. Underneath it ran a perpetual soft, deep tone that was the voice of the sod itself under the beating of innumerable hoofs.

Before long she was sleeping out with the wagons half the time. Matthilda had never been so easygoing with her before. The truth was that Matthilda had been unable to shake off the forebodings she had been made to feel by Kelsey's appearance on the Dancing Bird. Often when she looked at Rachel she seemed to see a shadow hanging over her, menacing the child's place in the world, and her will to live—perhaps threatening her life itself; and she was moved to a loving pity, in which she wanted nothing in the world so much as for Rachel to enjoy a free and happy time, in her innocence, while yet she could.

Out in the overnight camps, Rachel was the only one ever allowed to sleep in a wagon, sheltered by its bowed canvas. Even Ben and Cash, even the cook, slept on the ground, and would if it were under water. At night the herd was quieter, though never entirely still. When a critter lay down it made a big, contented-sounding "whoof," as it settled, knees first, into the trampled grass. If there were thunderstorms they would shuffle themselves all night, tense and ready to run, and all hands might have to stay in the saddle. Even on quiet nights the cattle might get restless, for no apparent reason, snuffy and always listening. What did they listen for, spooks? Wolves? They could get themselves strung up until the crash of a falling cigarette ash was enough to explode them, and they would jump and go, all at once. One night when they broke they like to ran down the wagon, rocking it as they blundered past, until it almost turned turtle.

Singing to the cows seemed to quiet them, and help to keep them from going snuffy, nobody knew just why. Maybe it covered up small sounds that the cattle might think were suspicious, and gave them something meaningless to listen to. Or maybe it kept them assured that the two or three men who rode spur-jingling and saddle-creaking round them all night weren't up to anything. So all night long some of the hands would be singing out there, while they slowly circled the bedded herd.

The long rides between the wagons and the house, yellow-slickered in the bursts of rain, were almost the best. It was only when she was alone in the vastness of the night that the prairie ever made Rachel afraid. They were getting a lot of rainbows; once she counted eleven in a day. Between showers, all over the prairie, the meadow larks were singing. When she was learning to talk, way back in the first year she could remember, she had known the meadow larks were saying "Happy—new year—to you!" And they were saying it yet.

But the day came when Rachel realized, with a hard shock of disappointment, that the spring work was almost over. She could not understand how so big a herd as they were going to drive could have been made up so soon. But now the long-winged chutes went up, for a quick road-branding of the herd; and that was always the last thing they did. As the hands began bunching the cattle for the push through the squeezers, Rachel knew the lovely green-up time was done.

11

Jude had forged eight stamp-irons for each of the
two squeezes they built, so that plenty of irons were
always cherry red, no matter how fast the critters
came through. Using plenty of branders and plenty
of fires, they branded a cow on both sides at once;
while ear-markers cut a dangling strip of skin,
called a jingle, on each ear, at the same time. The
cows went through there on the run.

For a road brand Cash was using a kind of
Galloping X, only he said it was a bird, and that it
was dancing. Plenty big, and burned high on the
ribs, it could be seen as far as you could see the cow;
and the jingles served to identify an animal that so
much as raised its head in the middle of a herd. Zeb
Rawlins had some grumbling to do about the size of
the road brand, which he declared cut down the
value of the hide; and he disliked the ear jingles,
which seemed to him a senseless disfigurement. Ben
undertook the job of assuaging Zeb, and fending

him off, determined that the tough job ahead of his brother should be made no harder; and the herd was branded as Cash wanted it.

Then suddenly all grumbling stopped. Georgia Rawlins, who had been riding virtually alongside Cash every day, came out no more; Jude and Charlie took to scouring distant corners of the range on their own, far away from the wagons. Only old Zeb still sat lumpishly in his buggy, watching over his interest with what looked like a jaundiced eye.

"Reckon they got the word," Cash said.

"Yes," Ben answered.

Together they rode to Zeb's buggy.

"Zeb," Ben said, "you got something you want to say to me?"

"Well, no; not now," Zeb scratched his jowls, looking them over with the stoniest eyes they had ever seen in a human head. "Not right now . . ."

They knew they had got answer enough. Kelsey had been to the Rawlinses—or else had stirred up somebody else, who had carried his lie to them.

Cassius was for dragging the whole thing into the open, and at once. Settle the matter once and for all, so far as it concerned the Rawlinses and this range, in a single explosion, as violent as needful. He never did have any use for a waiting game.

"Red niggers," he said through his teeth, furious enough to go to the guns. "We're all of us red niggers to them, right now! You going to stand hitched for that?"

"What about Georgia?"

"Georgia will stand by me or she won't," Cash said in his anger. "And right now I don't care a hell's hoot which it is!"

Ben judged it was time to get his own back up. "Now listen here! You bust up this drive, and you'll never boss another—you hear me? Because I'll bust your Goddamned back! You get that herd to Wichita, before you talk feud-fight around me!"

Cassius wasn't worried about his back, or what his brother might do, but the thought of having his drive broken up before it even started threw a scare into him. He shut up.

12

Rachel drove her mother out in the democrat wagon to see the herd start off. Matthilda always announced, on the eve of every drive, that she didn't believe she'd go out this time. The chill of the darkness before dawn made her knees hurt, and when you'd seen one you'd seen them all. But hot coffee and the excitement of the move-out always changed her mind when morning came.

They began to hear the moaning of the cattle a long way off, and the sound of the herd, coming to them across the long prairie miles, carried a sense of its great mass, as vast in proportions as its importance to their lives. For an hour the herd remained hidden from them by the roll of the land, while its earth rumble increased imperceptibly, and its voice developed until they could hear the bawling of individual cows. Then they came out upon a ridge that Rachel had chosen the day before, and below them moved the herd.

The first drive of the year always seemed new, as
if it were the first drive of the world. The longhorns
themselves were spectacular—almighty tall, gaunt,
long-striding beasts, armed with horns spreading
six, eight, and even ten feet; and Cash was driving
more than four thousand head. They had moved
some bigger herds than this, and driven them a
whole lot farther than this one had to go. But you
couldn't look at this broad, slow-moving belt of
horned stock, seemingly stretched out as far as the
eye could reach, without feeling that here was the
most portentous pilgrimage ever undertaken by
man.

Far out ahead the point rider rode at a walk, followed waveringly by the lead cattle, a long way
back, held loosely to the line by the forward swing
riders. No single critter had yet emerged as leader.
Rachel picked a slab-sided claybank steer, of great
height and spread of horns, as the one she'd bet on
to be plodding in front when the herd raised
Wichita, someday, beyond the curve of the earth.

Behind the leaders the herd was a rebellious
muddle for a mile and a half, but a winding backbone, where the cattle were thicker, was already beginning to show. In a couple of weeks the cattle
would put themselves into traveling order of their
own accord. But even in this first disorder, their
very numbers gave the long straggle the effect of
moving at a measured pace, and with a great, slow
majesty. They went past for a long time.

A steer broke for the brush, so far off that it appeared no more than a humping, tail-high speck;
but as a pony streaked after it, closing in long
jumps, Rachel knew the rider was Andy. He got the

steer by the tail, and busted it end over end; where-after it trotted back where it belonged, satisfied. A hard disappointment was ahead for Andy, and Rachel wondered if he knew it yet. Ben and Cash had told Andy a thousand times that he couldn't be spared from home, but Andy wanted so badly to go up the trail that he wouldn't believe they meant it. Only yesterday he had cleaned and mended all his gear, and packed his bedroll ready to go. But Ben would turn back tomorrow, with the six hands Cash was leaving him, as soon as the herd was across the Red. And when he did, Andy would be with them.

Up from the drag came the chuck wagon under its narrow-hooped canvas, bounding most marvel-ously behind six apparently unbroken horses. It looked like a runaway, but the brake wasn't on. This manner of driving seemed to be one of the ways range cooks expressed their defiance of the fate that had made them cooks. After the chuck wagon followed the bed wagon, not visibly driven at all. Some unfortunate green hand with the job of nighthawk, who herded the saddle stock by night and drove the bed wagon by day, rustling wood for the cook in between, was probably already asleep among the bedrolls, letting his team follow that of the cook as it chose.

Behind the last cattle the cavy of saddle stock, something around a hundred and seventy head, came wandering and loafing along, let to move about as the ponies pleased. And finally Cash came loping from the farthest tail, on his way up to the point. He came up the ridge to the democrat wag-on, and leaned from the saddle to kiss his mother and his sister, then galloped forward. The point was already out of sight beyond a distant rise.

Matthilda reached for Rachel's hand, and they held onto each other hard, as the last of the great herd passed beyond them, and out of their world.

13

After the herd was gone, the work went on; and for a while it seemed pretty lonely around the little soddy.

The Rawlinses came visiting no more; but the present coolness was easily explained, entirely aside from any part that Abe Kelsey might have played. Effie had been delayed, and Jude had stayed home to wait for her. None of the Rawlinses, except Georgia, thought Cassius could handle any part of the drive without Jude along, and Hagar had actually wanted the drive held up, until after the wedding. Even Zeb saw that this was ridiculous; the market would not wait for Effie, or anybody else. But Zeb himself could not forgive Ben's failure to consult him before making Cassius trail boss, for Zeb had hoped to put Jude in charge. Rachel could understand why the two families had better stay away from each other, for awhile.

And Ben was gone all the time. Cash had left Ben

with six men and Andy, as well as both Rawlins
boys—theoretically; though Jude was supposed to
ride and overtake the drive after his sister's wedding. There was no Indian danger yet. The moon
had been full as the herd rolled, but now it was on
the wane; the Kiowas would let their ponies
strengthen on the spring feed until the moon waxed
again. Ben left two men at the house—though even
this seemed hardly needful—and worked a single
wagon far out. He was trying to catch up with the
calf-branding in the far corners of the range, so that
he could work closer home when the danger time
came.

Meanwhile, Rachel was having a harder and
harder time getting away from the house. The inside work had piled up some, during the green-up;
but aside from that, Matthilda seemed to feel lone-
lier, and less secure, as Cassius got farther away.
No sense to it, of course. But Rachel was finding out
that the less sense there is to a thing like that, the
harder it is to talk away. This quirk of the mind
went back to the year they lost Papa up there, in the
crossing of the Witch River, Rachel supposed.
What few times Rachel did get out to the brand-
ings, Georgia was always there; that was what
made her mad.

Andy rode home every day or so, but Ben got
home only once during that wane, and he might
much better have stayed away. He came in very
late, and drank his coffee without sitting down.
"You all right, here? I'm fine. Work's going fair, I
guess. No, they haven't heard from Effie, far's I
know. You folks need anything?" He filled his
pockets with cold vittles, and was actually at the

door, when he turned back to cut Rachel's girth for her, once and for all. "Oh, by the way—Sis—you'll have to quit all this ramboodling around the country. You've got to stay home."

"Now wait a minute!"

"For a lot of reasons," Ben explained. He had found Indian sign almost every day he had been out. No big war parties, looking for fight—ponies not ready, yet, to shake off a pursuit. Mainly horse thieves, playing hide-and-sneak. But the whole Indian situation looked bad. Fort Sill troops had been fired into—not just once, but three times that he knew about. Ben predicted a full-out uprising, come summer. "Just wait till their ponies are ready. Then you'll see!"

"Well, they're not ready yet! Never heard such a far-fetched excuse in my life," Rachel argued. "What are you up to out there you don't want me to know about?"

"Who, me?"

"What about Georgia? I notice she rides on the wild loose every day of the world! Everyplace you do!"

"Who's Georgia? Oh, Georgia. I'm not running Georgia. It's you I'm responsible for," Ben answered her, making out it was all a matter of sweet concern for his sister's welfare.

Rachel was left low in her mind, and haunted by suspicions. Georgia pretended to be helping with the tallies, but Rachel thought it was mighty funny that she was always to be found tallying for Ben. Never felt called on to help her own brothers, who got on fine without any put-in from Georgia, seemingly. Not much to go on. Rachel couldn't really convince herself that anything was wrong. All she knew for sure was that a spring of seeming promise was turning into something pretty tiresome, with fly season not even begun.

But now Abe Kelsey was in the Dancing Bird country again.

14

Kelsey did not come to the house this time, though he might have been on his way there. Neither Rachel nor Matthilda saw him. If Rachel's understanding of her younger brother had been less acute, she would not have known about the ugly thing that happened then, in those days before the Kiowa moon.

One afternoon Andy rode in two hours before he could rightly be expected, in a dusky rain; and Rachel ran down to the corral, a carbine under her slicker, to unsaddle for him, in case he was of a mind to catch up with a few chores. One look at Andy's face brought her up short. He had a greenish pallor, for one thing, like something under water.

"Andy! You're fetching down with something!"

"No—oh, no—I'm fine—" He tried to keep his face turned away from her as he stepped down.

"Then you're hurt. Either a colt stacked you,

or—" Another possibility struck her. "Is Ben all right?"

He nodded, and pushed his rein into her hands; and he ran around behind the trough shelter. She could hear him being sick back there, as soon as he was out of sight. She tied the pony, and got a gourd of water from the well by the Dancing Bird.

Andy gulped at it. "Tell me one thing. Was he here? Did you see him?"

Confused, she almost said, "Who, Ben?" Then she understood. "No," she answered him. "I haven't seen him. But I think you have. Today."

"I didn't say . . ." He let it die out, and made a vague move toward his pony.

She said, "You weren't going to tell me that, were you? And there's more you haven't told me. *Which of you killed him?*"

"Nobody," Andy said, and looked as if he wanted to be sick again. He drank the rest of the water. "We had a chance at him. But somehow—something went wrong."

She got the rest out of him, then. Andy had been with Ben, a long way out from the wagon, when Kelsey showed himself. He came toward them, first, as if he wanted to talk—maybe had been watching for a time when they were apart from the others. But when they pointed their horses at him he lost his nerve, and ran for it. Andy thought he must be trying to lead them into an ambush; he pulled up, yelling at Ben. But Ben went on, so Andy drew carbine and followed. Kelsey rode a pretty fair horse this time, but with no grain to it, of course. Ben closed on him fast, and pulled his pistol. Kelsey took one look back, and the next thing he did was unbelievable. He pitched away his rifle—and went tearing on with his hands up, kicking his horse full stretch. Ben seemed flabbergasted; plainly he didn't know what to do. He could have gone ahead and shot Kelsey, but he didn't seem to think of that. He hesitated a few seconds, then stuck away the pistol and shook out his reata. And the rest was a nightmare.

Kelsey was jerked off his horse, but the loop had got an arm and a shoulder, as well as the neck, and he hit the ground alive. Ben didn't seem to know what to do about that, either. He just spurred on. . . .

"When finally he stopped, and I come up, there wasn't nothing on that reata but . . ."

Rachel let him skip that part of it.

"Ben threw away his reata, rather than step down and loose it," Andy ended.

"You don't call that killing him?"

He shook his head. "We went back to the wagon, for tools to dig a grave. And it started to rain. Took us two hours, before we got back where we left him. And when we did . . . he was gone from there."

"Didn't you cut for sign?"

"It was raining hard by then. We couldn't find out anything." They never did find out how Kelsey left there. "I never knew Ben to foozle so. I suppose I should have shot Kelsey, somewhere in there. I guess," Andy finished uncertainly.

"Why should you?"

Andy stood opening and closing his mouth. "Ben told us we had to," he said finally.

They stood out there talking a long time, though Matthilda twice came to the door of the house and banged on the triangle. Andy didn't know anything more. But talking had got some of the kinks out of him, and he returned to his normal color. They didn't have to explain anything to Matthilda, which was just as well. The truth was that they didn't know then just what had happened—whether Kelsey was alive, or dead, or what.

That night Rachel wept a little, silently, into her pillow, thinking sentimentally about her brothers. She was sorry for Andy; in this mood she thought of him as still the little innocent-eyed boy of whom he sometimes reminded them. And she was sorriest for Ben, the one who had always been so steady, so gentle, and so kind, yet had somehow been driven to saddle not only himself but his brothers with a commitment to murder. Perhaps he still did not know whether he had killed the old man or not. But if he had, he had done it in the clumsiest way it could be done, and she could believe he might be haunted all his life by that.

She hoped for a while that Kelsey was indeed dead, so that the whole nightmare was over with. Then she thought how awful it was if the corpse was stiffening somewhere out there under the brush tonight; and she was horrified at herself, and filled with a sense of guilt.

Why does he haunt us so? He has a reason. He had it before, and all along. Or Ben would not have called his death. What evil thing was it we did—or Papa did—long ago, that makes this happen now?

She believed she would be able to make Ben tell her, now.

It did not work out that way. Before she ever spoke to Ben again, another thing happened. This time it happened to Rachel herself, and to nobody other, except as everyone in the family was affected by a disaster to one. And the world as Rachel knew it turned from beneath her, past all possible recovery.

15

During the night the rain stopped; the skies were clear, the day after Kelsey was dragged. Rachel plotted to get a horse saddled and out of there. She meant to find Ben at once. She knew about where his crew was at work.

Only a year or so back, it had been hard to get Matthilda to go and lie down, or to take any daytime rest at all. But her afternoon had hardly begun when the bedroom door closed upon her. Rachel was out of the house in the same minute. She walked past the corrals, and along the Dancing Bird, pretending to size up the driftwood brought them by the spring rise, in case Matthilda happened to be watching her out of sight.

In another minute, as soon as she had given her mother a chance to doze, she would have turned back to rope a pony.

She never got it done, for Ben appeared unexpectedly, and Georgia was with him, stirrup to stirrup. They came surging up out of an arroyo some distance downstream and Georgia was laughing, having a great time. Then Rachel saw her do an odd thing. Georgia's laughter stopped abruptly; she checked, and whirled her horse in what looked very much like an attempt to get out of sight. Too late, of course. Georgia recovered herself at once, and stopped where she was. Her horse shied, she explained afterward. It was not important. What mattered was the way Rachel took it. For her resentment of this girl suddenly popped sparks like a sap log.

You weren't coming to the house at all. You tried to get back, without I saw you. Rode here to be with him—but didn't want us to know! I knew it was you made Ben hang my saddle up.

Georgia exchanged a word or two with Ben. Then both waved at Rachel, and came on at a walk. Rachel saw she wasn't going to have any chance to talk to her brother at all, not even here in their own house, what with this interloper butting in.

Sure. Come right on in. May as well, now. Make yourself right at home, just as cool as a hung hog. I've had about enough of you! It never occurred to her that Ben could be blamed.

She was getting ready to fix Ben something to eat, and wondering if she could bring herself to set a plate for Georgia, when Georgia dismounted at the stoop, letting Ben take her pony to the corral.

"Ben lost his reata," Georgia said as she walked in. "That's a man for you. Doesn't even know where or how, seemingly. Had to come in to get a rope."

Rachel must have known that it was jealousy had

hold of her, a very different jealousy than she had ever felt when Georgia was fooling around with Cassius. For just a moment she wondered whether she had better start a war she could not finish, or risk an open bust-up with any member of that other family with whom they were already having difficulty enough.

"Been seeing a good deal of Ben lately, haven't you?"

"I help keep the tallies. It frees a man for the work. Anyway, we have to keep a cross-tally. For Pa."

"Who's cross-tallying for Cash? Oh, I forgot. Cash is way far up the Wichita Trail. Out of sight, out of mind. I guess that's plenty easy, for some."

Georgia answered shortly, but reasonably. She had not come looking for this fight, and felt no need of it. "Get this through your head. I'm not bespoke. Not to Cash or anybody else. When I am, I'll tell you."

She moved away, toward the wash bench; and Rachel, turning to the table, picked up the long Bowie knife with which they carved, and cut a paper-thin slice from the pot roast. The run of the honed blade through the meat felt good to her in her present mood. She knew she had said enough. She had a chance to drop it now—the last chance she would have in her life; but she couldn't let it alone.

With her back to Georgia she said, "Ben isn't fixing to settle down. He likes to ride free on the trails."

Georgia stood looking at her sideways. She hadn't angered yet. Her riding had taken the winter

softness off of her, and now she was thoughtfully
rubbing the palm of one hand on a hip bone.
"Neither am I fixing to settle down," she said. "Not
for a while, anyway."

"Then why do you keep tolling them on—each
behind the other's back? We have a name for that,
where I come from!"

Georgia's eyes seemed to go higher in her head,
signaling that if Rachel wanted fight she could have
it. "Oh, hell, Rachel! Why don't you quit acting
like a brat?"

"I won't have you coming between Cash and Ben
—you hear me?"

"I hear you very well," Georgia said slowly.
"You sound like a spying little sneak, to me."

Rachel's head came up. "I am Rachel Zachary,"
she said. "Everywhere in—"

"You're what?" Georgia got in.

"Everywhere in Texas, they know who the
Zacharys are. And do you know how many people
there are in Texas can give a Zachary slack? Not
one!"

"That's right," Georgia answered. "It's a big
pity you ain't one."

Rachel stared, no more than puzzled then.

"You're no Zachary," Georgia made it plain for
her. "You're no tittle of relation to a Zachary."

"You out of your mind?"

"Why, I knowed it first time I seen you. Look at
yourself! Where's the Zachary bone? You got bones
like a snuff stick. Look at your hide! The sun ain't
hardly touched you, and already you're the color of
a red hog in a mudhole. You couldn't pass for a
Zachary in a thousand years!"

With shock, with bewilderment, Rachel saw that
Georgia believed what she was saying. She stam-
mered out, "How do you think I got here—if—"

"You're nothing but a catch-colt, a foundling—
picked up bare-nekkid in the road, at that! You
don't know who you be, or what—and you never
will! And everybody knows it."

Rachel's lips turned white, and curved in a little
smile, while her eyes went wide and fixed. The knife
in her hand poised in front of her, edge upward, and
she moved toward Georgia, light and quick on the
balls of her feet.

From the bedroom door Matthilda screamed—
"Rachel!"

She stopped short, and the knife clattered from
her hand. Before her eyes the room careened and
darkened, so that she almost fell.

Georgia had retreated from her, stumbling over
her awkward riding skirt. She was not a girl who
scared easily, but this time there was horror in her
eyes; for she knew she had never been nearer death
in her life. Before Rachel's vision had cleared she
was gone.

Matthilda held Rachel in her arms, conforting
her, crooning to her. "There, now, there . . . dear
girl . . . dear, dear little girl. . . . Everything's all
right."

"What did she mean? Mama—what could she
mean?" Rachel was shaking weakly, but her mind
was working again.

"Don't think about it. Put it all out of your mind
—please, Rachel—please!"

"She believes it. I'd have known if she was making it up. Mama—is it true?"

Long ago, Matthilda had known this moment might come. In her mind she had rehearsed what she would say, forming two opposite answers, hoping to know when the time came which one to use. One was a straight-out denial, relying upon vehemence and a pretended astonishment. "Why! Shockin'! Fiddlesticks!" The other was meant to be a natural and easy acceptance as of something unimportant. "Why, yes, dear. Of course. Didn't I ever tell you? Never thought about it, I guess. . . ." An uneasy feeling had remained that neither answer could save the tranquillity she desired for Rachel above all things. Some third way seemed to be hovering just beyond her reach; she never found it.

But the years had come between, dimming the danger and the need. She had almost been able to forget that Rachel was not her own, because she so wanted to forget. Now as she reached for the answers she had devised she could not remember what they had been.

She faltered, "Why—why, Rachel—why, I—" And in that moment of groping it became too late.

"So it's true, then," Rachel said.

16

For almost a week Rachel tried to find herself, while
it seemed to her that not a single familiar compass
point remained. Her whole identity had been struck
away. These familiar people among whom she lived
were in reality strangers; they fed and sheltered her
by tolerance and charity, not in accordance with
her rights, for she had no rights. Sometimes she recalled moments of rebellion, and times she had as-
serted herself, and she was shamed. There was self-
pity in it, and a chill of fear, as if she had been sleep-
walking all her life upon the edge of an abyss. *It must
be people like me who become fancy girls*, she thought,
without ever having seen one in her life. Mama had
sometimes spoken with horror of the dreadful wom-
en who preyed upon the cowboys, in the wild towns
at the end of the trails, thanking God that her sons
would never go near women like that. But a girl
who belonged nowhere and to no one couldn't be
expected to care where she was or what she did,
Rachel thought now. She wanted to get away, and

lose herself where nobody knew her, and who she was couldn't matter. Yet she did not know how to turn her back on these people who had done everything for her that had ever been done in her life.

She tried to find out how the Zacharys had come by her in the first place. Matthilda was tempted to invent an elaborate story, giving Rachel an inspiring family history and a romantic orphaning. She would have done it, too, had she not known perfectly well that she would be tripped up by it, soon or late. She compromised by telling part of the truth. Rachel's natural parents were unknown, she admitted, and this was true. But here she began changing the facts a little bit. Lots of wagons were on their way to California, she said, and Rachel had accidentally got left behind by one of them. At a rest-over camp, called Possum Stop. It wasn't there any more. Nobody knew which wagon, or why the family never came back to look for their baby. Maybe they'd been fooled on where they lost her— looked a long time in some wrong place. Or . . . it was possible something happened to them. . . . It came out a whole lot more lie than truth, before she wiggled out of it, perhaps because so little truth was known.

Matthilda tried to comfort Rachel every way she could think of, for she was as miserable as the girl. She tried reasoning. "Every family has its bad people, and its useless people, and its good people, and its great ones. You are you. You can be what you want to be. What else matters?" She tried religion, in her own conception of it, which was vague, but of high integrity: "God is love. We are his children. We are bound together and sheltered by our love for

each other, and His love for us. For love is what
God is." Rachel wasn't listening.

She had often told Rachel that men hated to see
women cry, and that she must teach herself never to
weep before anyone. But when everything else
failed, Matthilda herself fell back on tears. Now she
let her lip quiver, and her eyes brimmed. "I wanted
a baby girl so much. I was so happy making your
little clothes. All of us loved you so, and wanted you
so—didn't you want us?"

Rachel did love Matthilda very dearly; which
was not hard, for no gentler spirit could be imagined. Matthilda could be shocked, or hurt, but no
one ever saw her angered; and she lived for her children to an all but fatuous degree.

But now Rachel was cloyed and repelled. She
hated herself for it, and she pitied Matthilda, but
that was the way she felt. Wanting to be left alone,
she pretended she was satisfied, and that everything
was all right.

She asked, "How much do the boys know?"

"Andy doesn't know. He wasn't born, then. And
Cassius—well—I don't believe he ever thinks about
such things. Ben knows, of course; he was seven,
then. But we promised each other it would be our
secret. We wanted you to be just our own." Then,
pleadingly, while those ready tears threatened
again: "We don't need to say anthing to them. Or to
anybody. Ever." She wanted everything put back
just as it had been before. But Rachel did not feel
that this could ever be.

All my life I'll wonder who I am.

She stayed out of the house all she could. She
doubted if either Ben or Andy noticed that anything

had happened to her, but she stayed away from them, too, what few times they came in. She was watching the tadpoles in a still slough of the Dancing Bird, without seeing them at all, when a strange new idea came to her.

Why, then, Ben isn't my brother. He isn't even my cousin. He isn't any relation at all. . . .

Of course the same thing was true of Cash and Andy, but with them it seemed to make small difference; her affection for them could stay the same, whether they were brothers or just childhood friends. But with Ben it was somehow a peculiarly disturbing, even frightening thought, hard to get near to, after thinking of him as a brother for so long. She circled it skittishly, as a puppy scouts a fascinating new thing that may bite.

Ben had always been much in her thoughts, a good deal more than the others had ever been. She had never realized before how often she wondered where he was and what he was doing, whenever he was out of sight, which was most of the time. But now she reached into the past, and most of the things she remembered best were mixed up with Ben. They were the only ones in the family who kept playing jokes on each other. Like the time Ben sneaked the little green frog into the water pitcher. Rachel had not let on, but after she refilled his water glass the frog was in that. Ben pretended not to see it—seemed about to drink it down, when Mama squealed. Then they both had laughed so hard, over nothing worth it, seemingly, for the others just stared at them, seeing nothing funny.

Farther back. There were the talking animals—the dwarf owl, only as big as your thumb; the spotted coyote, the mud hen, and the red mare. For a couple of years, when Rachel was seven-eight years old, Ben had kept bringing home accounts of conversation with such-like critters. They told him all kinds of stories, mostly without much sense to them, and never with any moral, unless it was useless. ("Never stick your head in a clam," the mud hen had advised him.) Whatever became of them all? They just kind of died out. Perhaps Ben knew when she outgrew them.

Still farther back, when she was four, five, and six. Moments of mixed terror and delight while Ben was introducing her to horses. She had first been on a horse in his arms, but later had stood barefoot behind his saddle, arms around his neck, while he chased a dodging brush rabbit, and almost roped it. Later, through over-confidence in an old roping horse, he had got her a fall that knocked her senseless; but she hadn't blamed him. Those were the same years when she had been most afraid of the dark, and sometimes when she had been sent to bed alone he had come and sung to her while she went to sleep. His songs were the same woebegone, bloody, yet somehow soothing ballads the cowhands sang to the cattle: "Pore young dying cowboy, Never more he'll roam, Shot right through the chest five times, He ain't never coming home. . . ." Could it be that Ben had been only eleven years old when she was four? She couldn't remember when he hadn't seemed as big and safe as a fort.

Even before that. When she was three, and had nightmares, she remembered running in her nightie, over floors icy to her bare feet, to jump into Ben's bunk; for he was the one who never sent her away.

In a few days she was thinking: *All I want is to wait on him, and take care of him. Even if he married somebody else, I'd be happy if I could just work for him all my life.* But later she knew it wasn't so. *No—I couldn't stand for anybody else to have him. I'd rather die.*

She began to light up again; and Matthilda was so relieved to see it that she never dared to ask her what had come over her.

Rachel sent a note out to Georgia, next time Andy stopped home. "I take pen in hand to say I'm right sorry," she wrote. "I had no call to act up so. You taken me by surprise, first off. But I see now you told me something I bad needed to know, and I'm right thankful."

Georgia's prompt answer was scrawled on a leaf from a tally book, and appeared to have been written in the saddle. *During a fit of pitching,* Rachel criticized, but was glad to get it. "Freind Rachel," it began, and went on to express relief. She hadn't told anybody what their Donnybrook was about, and hoped Rachel hadn't. All Ben knew was that she "got run the Hell out with a bucher Nife." Laughed fit to die every time he throwed it up to her. What she needed was her mouth sewed up, Georgia finished.

Whatever it was the Rawlins family had gone so sour about seemed either to have been withheld from Georgia, or had not affected her. So they fixed it up, as they thought, and just about in time. For now the moon was coming full again; and this time the Kiowa war ponies would be tough and full of run.

17

During grass season they were under the Kiowa Moon only a few days more than half the time; but the fort-up periods were such a nuisance that they seemed to come directly on top of each other, and to last forever.

While the moon was full you must never leave the house unarmed, and even in broad daylight you must never go alone beyond gunshot of support. You must fort up every night, battle shutters barred and weapons ready, as if certain of attack while you slept. After dark you could strike no light, and even the ashes on the hearth must be drenched, lest a coal should wake and show a gleam. You must remember where the plaster-covered loopholes were in the walls, and be ready to knock them open with a blow. When a Kiowa scout came feeling out your defenses, you had better whistle a shot or two over his head without hitting him, as a persuasion to look farther. The water barrel must be kept filled from the well by the creek, the homemade ammunition kept in supply, the gunlocks taken down over and over. There was a lot more. The very success of all these precautions made them the more difficult to maintain; for it was pretty hard to keep up to scratch when nothing ever actually happened.

Ben had been saving the work near home for the Kiowa Moon. Of the six hired hands held back from the drive, he had meant to give half to Zeb, for the Rawlins defense, but Zeb, perhaps in a spasm of thrift, had accepted only two. Ben could only hope that the Rawlinses were getting a little something done, now and then, over at their end of the range; for though the Rawlinses were maintaining a taciturn truce, they could not now join forces in a single range crew every day. Of his remaining four men, Ben picked the best shots, a couple of boys named Tip and Joey, for a permanent home guard; while with Andy and the other two he got on with the calf branding, bringing all hands in every night.

Rachel and Matthilda, who were cooking for them all, made breakfast in the dark, over a little Indian-sized fire that they masked as best they could. But Ben waited for daylight before he saddled now, and spent a while cutting for sign—sometimes a couple of hours, before leading off for the work. Even so, the boys came in dog-tired at the edge of night. They ate enormously and in silence, and were asleep with their clothes on before the women could wash up and get out of the room. Yet loneliness was banished from the Dancing Bird while so many people were around, even if they were sound asleep.

Rachel watched her chance to catch Ben alone.

For a couple of days it seemed as though there was
no way this could be done. He had turned short of
speech, and was showing strain, as if he did not like
what his houndlike casting told him was happening
around there, during these moonlit nights. Sometimes she thought he had guessed what she was up
to, and was wary of being pinned. But on the third
day of the Kiowa Moon he broke a stirrup leather,
and had to stop in the saddle shed to rig another.
And there she cornered him.

"Funny how seldom you ever seen one. An Indian, I mean." he said, and rambled on as if trying to
avoid questions by doing all the talking himself.
"Once or twice I've seen a little speck, a long piece
off, on a ridge, where nobody ought to be, and
that's about all. But there's lots going through here,
just the same. I've cut three trails in two days. One
of eight-ten horses, ridden in travel file, without any
loose stock; and another—"

"Ben," Rachel cut in, "is Abe Kelsey dead? Do
we know yet if he's dead or not?"

He did not look at her, but his hands stopped
their work. When he answered his words were tone-
less, without any ring, or jump. "He's alive," Ben
said.

She did not make him go into how he knew. He
was lacing leather again and would soon be out of
there. "I have to know one thing," she came
straight at it. "What was the great hurt we did Abe
Kelsey?"

"Us? Hurt Kelsey?"

"He hates us, Ben! Why? Because Papa
wouldn't help him get back his son?"

"The Kiowas don't have Kelsey's son—never did

have him. Kelsey's boy is in his grave at Burnt Tree."

"Sure looks like a father would know his own son."

"Would, huh? That one damn-fool notion has kept the whole thing a-simmer! I talked to this Seth two years ago. In Kiowa, naturally. He already had two squaws, and three-four kids. All this at sixteen? That buck is twenty-two if he's a minute!"

"Ben, you mean to tell me that old man would fetch down a raid on us just because Papa wouldn't—"

"A raid? Him? They wouldn't move an inch for him."

"I heard he's virtually one of 'em!"

"They'd have killed him long ago if he wasn't crazy. They bat him around, and misuse him, and take his stuff away from him—you saw the horse they left him with. But let him scout for them? Hell! They'd never believe a word out of him."

"Then why are we so set on killing him?"

He hadn't seen it coming. He had dug his own trap, and galloped straight into it. He opened his mouth, and closed it, and for a moment wouldn't look at her.

I've got him, now. I'm within one inch of the truth, right this minute. Ten seconds more, and all this mystery will be over. . . .

But Ben balked; he could think of no dodge, but he balked anyway. He met her eyes, not with candor, but with plain obstinacy. "Horse thief," he said shortly, and shut his mouth like a trap. He knotted the stirrup-leather lacing, finished or not, and took his saddle by the fork, to go out.

She was beaten, and she knew it. Nagging him would serve no purpose. She asked him, "Does Seth ever come here, Ben?"

He stopped. "Maybe. I don't know. We find tracks where Indian ponies come and go; sometimes moccasin tracks, close in. He could have been here a lot of times. Why?"

"Want to see what he looks like."

He said with a startling intensity, "I pray God you'll never see his face! Because if you ever do, there'll be war paint on it."

He left her; and she was disheartened as she thought how near she had come to a glimpse behind a dark veil. They were coming no closer together. He would go on treating her as a sister, even thinking of her as one, probably, until Rachel herself made known to him that she was undeceived. But he was preoccupied and edgy all the time now, so that the time never seemed right.

Ben had been wrong about one thing. Seth came the next day, without war paint, and in plain light.

18

Texans always called him Seth. Even when they tried to say Set-Tayhahnna-tay they couldn't get the singsong gobble to it that a Kiowa would understand. He had been no more than a fable when Abe Kelsey first called him Seth, a riddle, in an old man's tale. But since then he had become a reality to be dreaded, in his own right. There were other white and near-white warriors, such as Red Hair, Kiowa Dutch, and Kiowa Frank, and perhaps many more less widely known. All of these had been captured, enslaved, and finally Indianized, when very young; only one or two of them remembered their native speech. The Kiowas had no chiefs, either hereditary or elected, nor any other constituted authority with powers of discipline. A war chief was any man who could scheme up a raid and persuade others to follow him. The white war chiefs had made their names in open competition, by the boldness, ingenuity, and ruthlessness with which

they made war on their own race. Most believed the
white warriors more savage than the Kiowas of
blood, but this was because of the resentment
aroused by their anomaly of race. They could equal
the cruelty of their adopted people; they could not
hope to exceed it.

On the day Seth came, Ben left the others haul-
ing water to the house, while he rode circle alone to
read what news of the night had been written upon
the prairie soil. He was back in twenty minutes, and
had the up-horses moved to the corral nearest the
house, where they were covered by its guns. Then
he brought Andy and the hands into the house and
forted up. The battle shutters had been opened to
let in the first sun, but now they were barred again.
They pried the plugs out of one shutter loophole at
each of the two windows facing the Dancing Bird,
and opened two loopholes in the door.

Two cowhands were put up at the window loops.
The one called Tip was gangly and hatchet-faced,
and in this situation was tense enough to ring like
the blade of a knife. His eyes darted about the
room, and came to rest on the fireplace. "Ain't that
chimney pretty big?"

"It's got iron hooks built into it, big as scythe
blades," Ben told him. "The buck that jumps down
it will stay there."

Mama was puttering in a cupboard, pretending
that nothing was happening; but she was careful to
make no noise, except for a soft, almost tuneless
humming, that was rapidly working on Rachel's
nerves. She tried to think of some way to tell Mama
to stop, but none came to her. She opened the ammunition chest under the rifle rack, got out a hand-

ful of rim-fires, and took them to the cowhand called Joey. He was a tow-headed, Dutchy-looking boy, with white eyelashes, and China blue eyes which he was too shy ever to raise to Rachel. He thanked her without looking at her.

Suddenly everybody was motionless and silent, a man at each loophole, with no places left over from which to see out. Mama stopped her humming and held perfectly still, her hands idle in the cupboard. Ben said, "Ground your carbines, you fellows. I'll kill the man who shoots before I tell him." Perhaps they didn't know him well enough to be sure whether he would do it or not. He seemed so relaxed and easy, even pleased with the whole situation, Rachel was not sure she knew him herself.

He spoke now in a queer, soft tone. "Sis . . . Speak of the devil. You want to see what Seth looks like? . . . Let her look, Andy."

What she saw was astonishing. Three Indians sat their ponies on the near bank of the Dancing Bird, in full view of the house at less than fifty yards. They were recognizable at once as Kiowas; their strong, flat-stomached build, prepotent in the Kiowa blood no matter how diluted, could not be mistaken for that of any other Indian. They carried carbines in their hands, but wore no paint, no head-dresses. They rode light Indian-made saddles with elkhorn trees or none, and the tails of their ponies were blowing free, instead of clubbed for battle. In all ways, these three were equipped for travel, not for fighting.

"There's fifteen or twenty more of 'em around someplace," Ben believed. Kiowa warriors would take any risk to put you off your guard. "He's a whopper, isn't he? Big as Satanta."

She knew then, for the first time, which Seth was.
You couldn't tell he was a white man, at the distance. Kiowas came in as many sizes as white men
did, but when they were big, they were big all over,
heavy-limbed, but never paunched like a Sioux or
Comanche.

"Carbine, Andy," Ben said, still casual, still as if
pleased, but concentrated, now. He reached back
without turning from the loophole, and Andy put
his own Spencer in Ben's hand. After working with
Andy all his life, Ben did not need to ask if a ball
was chambered. "I'm going to waste one," he said,
raising his voice to reach Tip and Joey. "Now don't
be poking your muzzle out! I'll tell you when."

Ben took aim unhurriedly, but fired without delay. Rachel saw the Kiowa ponies stutter their feet,
yet they were held in place so closely that their
riders only swayed lithely at the hips; their heads
and shoulders were not displaced an inch. The
three remained relaxed, and Rachel saw that they
were grinning. They glanced at each other, before
their eyes returned to the house. Seth raised his
right hand in the peace sign.

Rachel was awe-struck. "Medicine," she whispered. "They think they've got bullet-proof medicine!"

"Not them," Ben said. "I know all three. The one
to the left of Seth—there's a tough one! That's—
that's—" he tried a Kiowa word—it sounded like
G'yee-tau-tay—under his breath. "Wolf Saddle, I
guess you'd call him." Kiowa names were shifty to
translate; this one might mean "Rides a Wolf," or
"Wolf on his Back," for all Ben knew. "And the

other—" he hesitated again. Traveling Hawk? Wandering Eagle? "That's Lost Bird," he settled for. "Meaner than Seth himself, if that's possible. Those buggers know what they're doing." He handed the carbine back to Andy. "They even know what I'm doing," he added.

The used shell went bouncing and twinkling across the floor as Andy ejected it. A thin, sharp smell of black powder came to Rachel's nose, bringing a nervous sense of urgency, and an impatience with Ben, who could dally over shades of meaning, as if nothing deadly and immediate was hanging over them. Yet he was right. The behavior of these Indians did not explain itself; they had no exact parallel for it in their experience. A thing like this had to be waited out. The worst thing you could do was to let yourself be choused into any kind of move at all before you knew just what was up.

Outside, Rachel saw Seth speak shortly to the others, then start his horse straight toward the house, at a walk. His right hand was still up, in the sign of peace. Wolf Saddle and Lost Bird followed on either side of him, unevenly, despising any discipline of formation.

"Uh-huh," Ben said. "Well, I'm going out there."

Mama cried out, "Ben! Please! I won't let you—"

Ben was wearing a Colt's Dragoon revolver, in a holster black with years of saddle-soapings. Both had belonged to his father. He had the weapon close-belted on his left, butt forward, for a cross-draw in the saddle; but now he loosened and turned the belt, so that the gun hung lower, and on his right. He said, conversationally, "I'll have to ask you to be quiet, Mama. I'd hate to have to shut you in your room."

"Why!" Mama gasped. Ben had never spoken to her like that before; but Papa would have said it, and meant it. Matthilda did not speak again.

Ben took a look at his percussion caps. "Bar the door after me," he told Andy. "You fellows—Tip and Joey—better poke your front sights out, soon as I'm on the stoop. I won't shoot unless one of 'em swings gun on me—and don't you cut loose until I do. All right, lay holt of this bar, here, Andy."

He went out on the stoop, hatless, and stood lightly, his hands hanging empty. The three Kiowas stopped in front of him, their ponies spread a little, less than two horse-lengths away. Andy took the loophole Ben had left, and each had his own, now, except Mama, whom Rachel forgot for the next few minutes. When next noticed, Matthilda was at the table, her Bible before her but unopened, her hands folded upon it; she sat staring at nothing, and took no part in what followed.

Seth took a deliberate look at each of the carbine snouts, where they now poked through the shutter loop-holes, well to the right and left of the door. He smiled a little, faintly contemptuous, mildly entertained. Andy had not brought up his weapon, but Seth let them see that he noticed the loopholes in the door, behind Ben, too. Rachel studied him with the fixity of apprehension. His hair hung in two braids in front of his shoulders, and looked to be a rusty red, in spite of its shine of grease, which must have darkened it. A mixed-blood Kiowa might have had hair that color.

But the low-bred face, punkin-rounded, and what they called owl-nosed, showed an uneven splotching, as if it wanted to freckle. And the narrow-set eyes were wrong. They were muddy blue, bloodshot by wind and sun. The lashes were invisible, giving the eyes a baldish, lizardy look. His shirt and leggings were of fringed buckskin, almost new, and his moccasins were heavily decorated. It had cost a lot of Texan horses—some of them doubtless Dancing Bird horses—to buy the squaws who made him stuff like that. But the breech clout that converted the leggings to trousers was of the dark blue cloth to be found only in officers' tunics; and this might or might not have been given to him.

She was thinking of a story told of this white Indian. A dozen others were told, and a hundred might be someday, without adding anything more. Two years ago, far down near the Rio Grande, a small farmer had come home to find the remains of his wife—or parts of them, for they were not all in one place. Their four-year-old daughter was missing. Pursuit was organized, and recovered what was left of the baby girl a hundred miles away. The stripped and mutilated small body, a pitiful rag, had been left impaled upon a broken post oak. Since then the two scalps had been seen upon Seth's medicine shield, the wavy light chestnut of the mother's hair beside a curly soft tuft of fine-spun pale gold. Surely Ben must be wasting his time, trying to talk to Seth; for how could anybody reach a kind of people who found honor and glory in a deed like that?

Seth's eyes settled upon Ben, and held steadily, waiting for Ben to speak first. The marauder looked self-satisfied, insolent and sure of himself; yet Ben outwaited him. Finally Seth grunted, and began to talk in signs, letting his carbine hang in the crook of his arm. The conventionalized signs his hands made ran off smoothly, and very fast; yet the message was simple, and Rachel could understand it well enough. "We come as friends. We came to talk to our friend," Seth's hands said; then added, "Sometimes friends are given gifts."

Those in the house understood no more, for now Ben did an exasperating thing. He refused the sign language known to everybody on the prairie, and made the Indians speak in their own tongue. To show off? To impress them? Presently Rachel knew he had done it so those within would not know what he said.

The Kiowa sentences came in slurred bursts, full of clicks, drawn-out nasals, raised and lowered tones. Rachel saw Seth's companions intensify their concentration as they tried to follow Ben's Kiowa; it had a right to be pretty bad. At first Rachel tried to guess what was being said in that outlandish tongue. She thought Ben might have told them that in his understanding it was those who came to talk who brought gifts. Seth smirked, and took from round his neck a slender gold chain, with something like a quid of tobacco on it. He tossed this at Ben's feet, but Ben caught it with the toe of his boot, and flipped it into his hand. He barely glanced at it before putting the chain around his neck. Seth seemed blanked by that. He paused a few moments, looking Ben hard in the eye, which seemed strange in a man like that.

Now Seth went into a long, unhurried speech, and Rachel took a look at the other two. Wolf Saddle was the chunkiest of the three, with a broad and yellowish face, as if he might have Comanche blood. His brief interjections seemed to be jokes, for whenever he spoke the other two laughed.

The other Kiowa, called Lost Bird, was in some ways most remarkable of the three. His skin had the dark yet ruddy sun-char of the full-blood Kiowa; but his hair, greased though it was, looked to be auburn. His face was smooth, lineless, placidly at rest. When Rachel had looked at him for a moment, she realized a strange thing. This face was beautiful, and in an odd way, as a girl's face should be beautiful. She was fascinated, and at the same time repelled.

As if he felt her gaze, Lost Bird turned his head and looked her straight in the eye; she felt as if the whole door was suddenly open in front of her, and not just the loophole. His eyes were green, now— no, a dark yellow. They darkened as he tried to see into the shadows behind the loophole, until they seemed almost black, and surface-lighted. Yet as he turned his eyes to Seth again they appeared the gray of pale slate. She had a frightened sense of having known eyes like that before, though she was certain she had never seen Lost Bird in her life. A moment of uncertainty weakened her middle, so definite that she felt a touch of nausea.

But he began to speak, and the illusion was gone. He spoke with broad gestures, flowing or emphatic. His voice rose and fell; his chest puffed, and his head lifted with hauteur. Yet he became smaller as he spoke, until his threat was no more than that of a deadly weapon with the legs of a fast horse, controlled by nothing with any depth of mind. He had

talked no more than a minute when he ended upon
what was obviously both a question and a demand.
Ben was standing close enough to the door so that
Rachel saw a drop of sweat trickle down behind his
ear, only a few inches from her eyes.

Instead of answering at once, Ben spoke in English to the people behind him. "Andy. I want a few
cartridges. But stay where you are. Let Rachel
bring them to you."

By his softened tone Rachel knew Ben was smiling, and she wondered if the Indians knew by this
how angered he was. Did you have to know him to
tell that? She became scared again, aware that he
was close to an explosion of temper that could bring
disaster upon himself and them all. She could not
see his right hand, but felt sure it had not moved.
*Never touch your gun without you draw it, never draw it
without you shoot to kill,* Papa had taught.

"I want two fifty-caliber metallic, and one rim-
fire forty-four," Ben said.

Andy unbarred the door to put the three
cartridges in Ben's hand. "Bar it again," Ben said
and Andy obeyed. They saw Ben toss one cartridge
to each Indian. Then he made a brief final
statement in the Kiowa tongue.

The three sat quiet a moment more, their eyes
fixed on Ben, faces as expressionless as mud. None
threw their cartridges away. Seth kept tossing and
catching the gift cartridge without looking at it. He
took another slow look at the carbine snouts sticking out of the shutters, on his left and on his right,
and he looked at the loophole where he knew Andy
must be. Then he spit at Ben's feet, and unhurriedly turned his horse.

The others followed Seth, walking their horses slowly, their backs exposed arrogantly to the carbines in the house. Andy softly lifted the bar, and Ben slid inside. The Kiowas jumped their horses out of sight over the cutbank of the Dancing Bird.

"That may be all, for now," Ben said; but he kept Andy and the hands on watch for a long while more. Nobody on earth was Indian-wise enough to say for sure whether an attack would come, or when.

"We're getting kind of low on metallic," Andy said, and it was a question.

"I told them to use those when they came again," Ben answered him.

Mama let her lip tremble, now that it was over. She whimpered, "I only wish those people would stay away."

Ben said, "There weren't any people here, Mama. Those were Indians."

Rachel moved close to Ben, so that she could make her tone low, yet urgent, demanding. "What did Seth want of us?"

He turned to her slowly, took her face between his two hands, and for some moments looked straight down into her eyes. He had never done that before; and, though she met his gaze steadily, the unaccustomed fixity with which his eyes probed into hers so flustered her that her mind would not work. She had long had a notion that she could tell what he was thinking, if he would meet her eyes, but this did not work for her now. It came to her that she could not read his mind because he was trying to read hers, so that all she could see was the questioning at the front of his mind.

Then a twinkle appeared, and his face softened with the first warmth before a smile. "They were trying to buy you," he told her.

It seemed so far-fetched, so unexpected, that she couldn't tell it from the kind of foolishness with which he often put people off, when he didn't want to answer them. She heard herself reply nonsensically, in kind. "Well, did you sell me?"

"I held out for more horses."

But later she saw that she had no real reason to disbelieve his statement of Seth's purpose. She was chilled, and shaken. There was something dreadful about the impassable gulf between the Kiowa ways of thinking and those of her own people. Sometimes it was hard to believe that this strange bloody-minded red race was human at all. It was as if giant lizards had come here on horses, mouthing and grunting their unearthly language that so few white men had ever understood.

And there was something else. If Seth was determined, or believed himself humiliated before the other war chiefs, the hard strike of his answering raid would be the same as if sense and reason were behind it; and the unbelievable cruelties in the event of victory would be no different.

Mama suddenly exclaimed, "Ben! Take that dreadful thing off!" He had forgotten Seth's gift, but now he took the gold chain from around his neck, and looked at the dried human ear it carried as a trophy. Then he threw it in the fire.

19

Two days passed, and the moon was dead full, but Seth did not return. No new Indian trails appeared upon Dancing Bird land. For the moment the country seemed to have emptied of Kiowas. Ben doubled his precautions, turning more irritable every day over the time lost from the work while they scouted the terrain. But the prairie remained blank and still.

Unexpectedly, on the sixth night of the Kiowa Moon—in the very heart of danger—Effie popped up in the foreground of their lives again. Ben brought the word when he came in at nightfall, the Rawlins split of the crew having been joined up with his own early that morning. It seemed that a rider had reached the Rawlinses pretty late the night before, and hollered them up. His news was that Effie and her promised young man—his name was Harry Whittaker—were only one day behind him. The messenger had left them at Fort Rich-

ardson, when he was sent on ahead with the word.
They meant to come right on.

"Why, she must be home right now!" Matthilda
marveled.

Ben supposed they were. The rider, whom Ben
knew only as Gus, had come from Fort Richardson
in a day, having changed horses at the Rountree
ranch, forty miles out. Call it about seventy-five
miles from Fort Richardson to the Rawlinses, with
a road of sorts for fifty miles of the way—Effie's
spring buggy should make it with fair ease in two
days, stopping overnight with the Rountrees.

These times and distances became of sharp interest, a little later.

The wedding was to be in four days, giving Effie
three days with her family, during which the family
could get acquainted with their new in-law. Matthilda was mildly shocked by what seemed to her an
unseemly haste about these arrangements. She was
not at all sure it was decent.

"So long as *that's* all you see to worry about," Ben
grumbled.

"Jude and Charlie turned right around and high-
tailed for home, soon as they give—gave us the
word," Andy complained. "Let theirselves right out
of a full day's work." Ben had been setting a furious
pace, and Andy had been trying to outdo him.
Trying to get their pay raised, it looked like to more
easygoing men, who saw no call to get in a frenzy.
"Not that Jude and Charlie are any good around
cattle. But they could anyway try, couldn't they?
Effie wasn't even looked for, until way late. They
could just as easy have put in a short ten-hour
day—"

"They had to ride to meet their sister, of course," Mama told him. "It's the least they could do."

"Trust them to do the least," Andy commented.

"Ben!" Mama rebuked them. "He's picking up all this unneighborliness from you!"

Ben denied this. He didn't hold with all this galumphing around the country in raiding season—with the moon right smack on the full, at that. He understood this Whickaty, or Whittaker, or whatever his numpish name was, had some side riders with him—didn't know how many. But the fact that he had sent his rider, this Gus, riding far into the night all alone, proved *he* didn't know what he was doing. "Her brothers should have met her in Fort Worth, if you ask me," Ben gave his opinion. "And then kept her where she was!"

But he hadn't found out who the preacher was to be, though Harry Whittaker surely must be bringing one. Didn't even know who-all was coming. The Rountrees, doubtless—about six of them—but how many more? How were his womenfolk to know what-all to bake, if he didn't even get the main facts? Ben had made a failure of it, they made plain to him.

Ben grumped and complained. He supposed they would make him responsible for getting them over there somehow, if they had to fight every foot of the way. Needn't blame *him* if it cost every scalp in the dang family. He saw himself called on to whup the whole Kiowa nation, like as not, with only five carbines including Rachel's—Mama would have to take the driving lines, soon as they were jumped. She'd better get some practice with the four-horse team, for she'd have to flog full stretch, when they made their run for it. If anybody got through alive they'd be lucky. "But of course all that means nothing to you folks. Not if some jug-haid female is shotgunning herself a man. Damn those people anyway!"

They were paying no attention to him. The Zacharys, by previous arrangement, would go over the day before—which left them only two days to get ready. They were in a panic over all the baking they must do. And when it came to what they should take to wear! Weeks of forewarning apparently had not readied them at all.

Rachel was excited for a little while, or thought she was, because she had expected to be, once. But presently she became aware that the events between had given the long-anticipated occasion too much chance to go stale. Effie's wedding was only something that had happened to most of the people in the world, up to now, and would go on happening forever probably, to generations unborn. Too little had been said about whether the Rawlinses really did want them, after all the coolness there had been. And they were overriding Ben, again, on the subject of precautions, which was exactly how people who should know better lost their hair.

Matthilda, though, had a theory that if you worried enough about something it didn't happen, and this often seemed to work. This time, as they came in sight of the Rawlinses', it seemed to have worked again, up to here, for they had met with no alarms on the way.

In dry seasons the Dancing Bird was no more than a few hundred yards of stagnating slough, where the Rawlinses had built. They called it "The

Branch." The trees that had once fringed the water had gone into the cabin, a considerable barn, and a line of stock shelters, and the brush had been burned off to help the grass; so the whole place could be seen in virtually naked detail, from a long way off. The peeled-log house with its shake roof made the Rawlinses feel better-fixed than the Zacharys, who lived in a hole in the ground. At the same time, the Zacharys felt above the Rawlinses, who had no wooden floor, but lived on dirt, like pigs.

Both families had hauled their few window sashes, hinges, and such like, from the ruins of a hamlet twenty-five miles to the east. Its name had been New Hope, before its abandonment under the Indian threat, during the war; everybody called it No Hope, now. No one ever expected its people to come back. But Zeb Rawlins had a rigid puritanical streak in his honesty. He searched out people who claimed to be property holders in No Hope—including some who had never heard of it before—and paid them off. While doing so he learned that the Zacharys had never taken this trouble; and he had distrusted them, as on the shifty side, ever since. The Zacharys, who took pride in the belief that their word was hard money anywhere in Texas, would have been dumbfounded had they known.

Andy rode to the wheel of the democrat wagon, as they came in view, and offered to pick up some mullein leaves for Rachel. Girls rubbed their cheeks with these leaves, to bring out a glow. It worked better for other girls than it did for Rachel. Her skin was the even, biscuity tint of a Plymouth Rock egg; a flush came slowly to it, and was soon gone. But she was going to accept, when Andy added, "Charlie's home, you know."

"What's that to me?"

He pretended surprise. "Why, I've kind of been looking for you two to run off, 'most any time."

Matthilda made it worse by saying, "Now, don't tease her, Andy."

"What's wrong with Jude?" Rachel demanded. "You all holding him in reserve?"

"It's only," Matthilda fumbled, "Charlie seems more your age. There aren't so very many boys, out here on the—"

Rachel was furious. "I've got no more choice in the matter than a heifer pent up with two bulls!!"

"Rachel!"

"Well—two, he-cows, then. What one won't rise to—"

"Rachel, that's enough! Shockin'!"

Still beyond sound of a hail, they saw Georgia come out of the house. She gave them a sketchy wave, as if uncertain it could be seen, and trotted for the corrals. Rachel knew Georgia would be entirely game to straddle a bareback horse, skirts and all, and come walloping out to meet them. But another figure appeared in the doorway of the cabin, and Georgia stopped.

Rachel restored herself by filling in the inaudible exchange. " 'Georg YAW!' " she imitated Hagar. " 'You git back yar!' 'Naow, Maw—' " she switched tones, as Georgia was seen to answer back —" 'I got a call to the—' 'GEORGyer!' " They saw Georgia turn back. " 'Aw, dern it, Maw, heck,' " Rachel finished for her as she disappeared into the house.

Ben and the hands were riding the ridges far out on either side, and Rachel's show went kind of flat. Andy seemed not to have heard, and Mama just looked pleasantly good-natured and vague. Matthilda was often smiling, often gay, but when you tried to remember when she had laughed out loud, you couldn't think of any time. *Oh, well—Ben would have laughed.* It was the last, nearest thing to a light or trifling moment that they had.

Effie had not come home. Her brothers had expected to meet her only a few hours out, but no one had come in that night. When there was no sign of them next day, Gus and the two cowhands assigned to the Rawlinses had been sent to search the road. But three days had now gone by, and no word had come.

20

A hot sun had come out—and to stay, though they didn't know that yet; it had quickly dried the prairie. But Ben recalled that it had rained pretty much all day and all night, while Gus was riding from Fort Richardson, and most of the next day, too. Effie's party must have laid over where they were. Even if they had started from Richardson, the hub-deep mud might have turned them back. Some of that red clay took time to dry. And if they lamed a horse . . .

Hagar said, "Yes, we thunk of that." Her deep-set eyes had receded into her head, and she looked hollowed everywhere, as if she had not eaten or slept.

"I'm sure they're all right," Matthilda said. "They're bound to get here. I know they will."

"Yes," Hagar said without emphasis. "I expect they're safe somewheres, Mattie."

Zeb had welcomed them quietly and gravely, and

since had sat staring into the fireplace. Once he said, "Being's Ben and Andy are here now, I believe I'll just hitch up and—"

But Hagar said, "I'm going with you, if you do." And that was the end of it.

Nobody could find much to say more. They had expected to find the cabin thronged, but it had become a sad and awkward place to be. Rachel and her brothers took time carrying in all the fancy cooking they had brought. More stuff piled up inside than there was any place for, and every added hamper made plainer how different things were here than they had expected. Hagar sat inert, looking cadaverous, even failing to protest when Matthilda and Rachel got supper on.

As they gathered at the table, it was Hagar who pulled herself together in an effort to dissimulate. "Like one time in Hog Scrape," she said. "We had this here bull goose—" She checked herself, and looked timidly at Matthilda. "He-goose—"

"Gander?" Matthilda suggested.

"This here bull gander," Hagar accepted. The men ate doggedly, as if set on keeping up their strength, as Hagar rambled on. Hog Scrape was what Hagar called the Tennessee hill village where she had been born; actually it had some commonplace name. Willetsville? Like that. Over the years she had piled up enough anecdotes about it to fill a history book. Rachel had always thought her stories funny, and so had Ben. But most people, looking for a point and not finding one, were only bewildered by Hog Scrape. Hagar's own family took the tales in stolid silence. Tonight Ben was preoccupied, and Rachel could not find the funny part, either, under the layers of foreboding.

It seemed the gander had settled in Hog Scrape of its own accord. Didn't belong to nobody. Used to sally up and down the board walk like he owned it; dogs learned to slink out of his way. Got to know everybody, friendly-like, and right neighborly, too —always helping folks out. Like if a drunkard was asleep in the street, the gander would run the hogs off, and make the teams go around him. Only, there was this lay preacher they had in Hog Scrape, kept running the gander out of meeting. Claimed he wasn't housebroken, rightly. Until finally the gander had enough, and took exception. . . .

She trailed off, as if she judged nobody was listening, and Matthilda tried a politeness. "I used to know a . . . What was his name?"

"Harlow," Hagar answered. "Only name he answered to, anyway. Though, naturally, he couldn't tell you; small use asking him."

Matthilda looked puzzled; she had meant the lay preacher. But Hagar's stories generally escaped her, somewhere along the line.

"So Harlow called a feud on this here lay preacher," Hagar picked it up again. "'It seemed the gander made about the worst enemy a man could have. Everytime the lay preacher come in view, Harlow taken after him, hissing, and wing-whopping, and tearing the feller's britches; and him awhooping and acussing, and abusing in anyplace on anybody, for cover. Sometimes five times in an hour . . .'"

She got up to fill a platter, shuffling painfully, but talking on, unwilling to be helped, as always. She said it got so everybody was throwed by such dern carryings-on, and there was talk of a law. Some wanted a law against ganders, and others wanted it against lay preachers—both had their followings. But in the upshot, one evening when a cloud set itself down on Hog Scrape, the lay preacher thrun a shot at the gander, and missed, and taken the constable in the leg. And the constable, he answered fire, out of anguish; and—

She was coming back to the table when she stopped abruptly, and her wandering story stopped. She stood looking downward, as if not seeing the dirt floor, but something deep beneath. Zeb bumped table and bench as he surged up ponderously, to go to her; but before he could leave his place, Hagar let the platter fall. She dragged herself to a seat by the fireplace, and there folded up.

"I can't go on," she said, and hid her face. "I can't play up no more."

Zeb came to her, and put his hands on her shoulders. "Best you lie down a spell," he said gently. "I'll heat up some—"

"No," Hagar said in a dreadful voice. "No—I can't stand it back there—all alone in the black dark—"

The Zacharys had no way to leave there. No place for them all to sleep, either, until the main room was changed around, and shakedowns fixed on the floor. The Zachary hands went out to spread their blankets in the barn, and Ben and Andy slipped away to join them as soon as they could. Georgia had a narrow bed, in a lean-to room like a horse stall, and she offered this to Matthilda, then to Rachel. But there was not room for both, and neither would desert the other. Georgia made more coffee, and withdrew. At another time Rachel would have suspected Georgia of going out a window to fool around the boys, but the notion had no interest for her now.

At last Zeb, who had been dozing in his chair, made a feeble effort to take Hagar off to bed; but retired alone when she refused. *Maybe he doesn't want to be alone with her either,* Rachel thought. And after that the three women just sat, while the night dragged on.

Rachel had been asleep in her chair when she was startled awake by Hagar's voice. There was no clock in this room, but the embers in the fireplace were low, as if the night was old.

"I pray God she's dead." Hagar spoke out strongly, her voice dry and harsh in her throat.

"Hagar," Matthilda protested helplessly.

"I know whereof I speak," Hagar said. "I was in the hands of red savages, long ago. . . ."

And this became the dreadful night in which they learned what had crippled Hagar, and made her strange. They did not know how to stop her, or to close their ears, no matter now much they might wish forever they had never had to hear.

Hagar had been orphaned, by the time she "come of full growth." Two uncles and a brother were starting for California, by wagon across the plains, and she had made them take her along. But they were late at Independence; the last wagon train of the year had pulled out a week before. They could not afford to lay over until spring, so they joined one other belated wagon, and set out to overtake the train.

They never caught up. A woman and her three-year-old boy, from the other wagon, and Hagar herself, were the only survivors when the Indians struck. She had never known what Indians they were; all the Horse Indians looked alike to an inexperienced eye. "In number, they was eleven, after their wounded died."

She judged they knew how the savages had used her then, and the other woman too. For a few days the two women took turns carrying the child as they rode the bareback Indian ponies. But one day the mother could comfort the little boy no more, and he began to cry. Hour in and hour out he cried, until they came to a stream. There an Indian took the child by the feet, and slung him high in the air, into the river. He was hardly more than a baby; didn't know what swimming was, but there under the river he fought for his life. Soon they saw him crawling to the bank, slipping in the wet clay, but making it out of the water.

A young savage fitted an arrow, and shot the little struggling fellow in the face. The child went under—yet, in a few moments appeared again, floundering and strangling. The arrow had fallen away, but the little face was streaming blood. The bow twanged again, and again the river closed over the child's head. Then, unbelievably, the little boy appeared one time more. One eye socket was empty, but he was trying still. It took still another arrow before the child went down to stay, under the muddy water.

The mother slumped to the ground, and could not be beaten to her feet. The savages scalped her before they went on. Hagar worked herself free of the horse upon which she was tied, and tried to get hold of the bowman, to kill him with her hands. After that they always bound her ankles together with rawhide, under the horse's belly, when they rode; and that was how they crippled her forever.

"At first I prayed to die. Wouldn't you think, as time run on, the body would die and let the soul go free? No; it ain't that way. I know now why we're taught beasts have no souls. It takes the soul to tell the body when to die. But the soul goes faint, and lies as though dead. Naught is left but an animal, and the animal schemes to live. . . ." Hagar had at last stolen two of the fastest horses the savages had, and got away. Some soldiers found her, finally, on a wagon trail.

"The body heals as best it can. But it was Zeb Rawlins raised me up among the living again. A whole man, then, and a proud one, and I told him all. Yet it was Zeb gave me back my soul. Or so I thought, until this very now. . . ."

Hagar's voice had gone lifeless, a dragging monotone; yet she felt the need of telling them one thing more. "This one thing I know. The red niggers are no human men. Nor are they beasts, nor any kind of earthly varmint, for all natural critters act like God made them to do. Devil-spirits, demons out of red hell, these be, that somehow, on some evil day, found way to clothe themselves in flesh. I say to you, they must be cleansed from the face of this earth! Wherever one drop of their blood is found, it must be destroyed! For that is man's most sacred trust, before Almighty God."

"Suppose," Matthilda said, with surprising self-possession, "suppose a little child—a helpless baby —came into your hands—"

A dreadful glow came up behind Hagar's cavernous eyes. She extended her hands, gnarled and clawed, and they were shaking. "A *red nigger* whelp? Into these hands?"

Matthilda remained steady, and rode it through. "I have no question to ask," she said.

Hagar crumpled weakly, and her words were faint. "If Effie is in their hands tonight . . . how can I ever again say . . . God's will be done. . . ."

Rachel held deathly still, hardly daring to breathe. She believed Hagar Rawlins to be insane.

Ben was harnessed and hooked before dawn; and he found his womenfolks more than ready to be taken home.

21

Two days more, and the Kiowa Moon had waned.
Matthilda thought Ben should take Andy and his
two hired hands and go help look for the missing
wedding party. But Ben had become wary since
Seth's visit. Moon or no moon, he would not leave
his womenfolk alone.

It was Georgia who rode out to where Ben was
working the calves, with the word that Effie was
dead. An ambush in the ruins of No Hope, only
twenty-five miles from home, had left no survivors.
Those last rains, as the year turned dry, had not
only delayed discovery, but prevented pursuit.

Ordinarily the Zacharys would have been expected to hurry back there. But in this situation
Georgia believed, and told Ben, neighborly custom
did not rightly apply. Shy off, she advised them, at
least until her sister's body was brought home.
She'd be able to tell better, then, how her mother
was going to ride this thing out; and she would se-

cretly fetch word. Might be the Rawlins cabin would be no fit place for visitors of any kind, she put it tactfully, for quite some time to come.

She and Ben agreed upon a rendezvous, where he could look for her at certain times. By picketing her horse on the crest of a particular ridge, she could let him know from about five miles off if she was there; save him some of the ride. She'd come there any day she had something they ought to know.

Now there was a strange delay. Ten days passed before the body of Effie Rawlins was brought home. It turned out that Jude had gone on down the Trinity, all the way to Fort Worth to have a proper casket built. He had even tried to get silver handles, but had not found them in supply. The coffin he at last brought back was strong and heavy as a safe, with the lid sealed down, and no way to open it intended.

But Hagar was determined to make sure for herself that the body Jude had brought home was really Effie's. Though they did all they could to restrain her, she got up in the night, found tools, and forced the coffin lid.

Inside she found only a sealed lead box, about a foot wide, by thirty inches long.

22

Time was getting on to where they could begin hoping for Cash to get home, pretty soon. They never could tell, within a matter of weeks, how long their trail drivers were likely to be gone.

In the end of the soddy's main room, between the bunks that filled the corners, stood a huge cabinet, with a leaf that let down to write on, which they called the "secretary." Papa had made this, the winter his broken leg was healing, and it was the only really good piece in the house. Its main structure was of heavy walnut, but the doors and drawer fronts were of fruitwood, covered with carvings of birds, leaves, flowers—even a few antelopes and buffaloes could be found on it. Within, along with their bushels of stock tallies, and the family Bible, and a great pile-up of odds and ends they never used but didn't know how to throw away, were stowed the logbooks of every drive they had ever made. Three times they had made two drives in the

same year, and once they had made three, so that in
the seven years since '67 they had accumulated
logbooks covering a dozen.

Rachel had dug these out, and had been poring
over them since the drive first rolled. But no part of
that long push seemed ever to have gone twice just
the same. No two drives took exactly the same
route, for one thing. The Wichita Trail had a destination at its other end, but outside of that it was no
more than a name, and not any one particular way.
Weather made a big difference; in wet years the
herd plugged slowly through hock-deep mud, and
every creek became both a hazard and a hard day's
work. The grass made a difference, for if it was poor
the weakening cattle must graze slowly all the way.

Thunderstorms could spook a herd into stampede after stampede, or a herd could go "spoiled"
of its own accord, and run four nights a week. What
with the time it took to gather, after a run, and the
exhausted state of the cattle, the boss might get to
thinking he lived on the trail now, making one drive
his lifelong work. And the worse the conditions, the
more you needed a corrida of fast, game horsemen
who knew how to handle this wildhorn Texican
stock. You never did have enough men like that.

After the first week or two Rachel didn't even
know which river Cash would be crossing next.
Ben's old logs showed that he had not always been
sure himself. She found places where he had noted
the time of certain crossings, but had put the names
in later with a blunter pencil. Not so with Papa's
logs. These were hastily scrawled, and sometimes
illegible, cross-scribbled in every direction with
notes on losses, stuff issued from the wagons, and

every kind of thing. But if he didn't know where he
was, he said so. The boys made a great legendary
figure of Papa as a trail driver. They claimed nobody had ever seen Old Zack lie down while he had
a herd on the trail. Maybe once in a while you
might see him doze a little, sitting on the ground
with his back against a cook-wagon wheel. But even
then he would have a cup of coffee in his hand, so
that if he went full asleep it would spill on his legs,
and get him up from there. Any real sleep he had
was actually in the saddle; he used up about five
horses a day.

Old Zack had left them no record for the drive
from the Dancing Bird to Wichita, for they were
still driving to Abilene, far up in the eastern part of
Kansas, at the time of his death. Ben's second drive,
in 1871, had made Wichita in four weeks and two
days, which was his best time, and would have been
a credit to his father. He also had made the same
drive in nine weeks and three days. Cassius had
made one drive, which the Rawlinses had sat out, in
1872, in five weeks even, which was cracking good
time. You could call six weeks good time, and seven
weeks pretty fair. No telling, though, how long
they'd be held up in Wichita, waiting to sell, and
sometimes they had to load the cars, holding until
cars could be had. Call it a week or two—maybe a
lot more. Then it would take about ten days for the
riders to get back. There was no part of the opera-
tion not hedged all round with ifs and providings.

During this time occurred one of the small-seem-
ing, unreadable things, the seriousness of which
was hidden at the time it happened. They lost a
horse, which was a common-place if anything was,

except that this one went missing in broad daylight, out of the up-horse corral. Well, somebody must have turned it out, though no one would admit it. The animal was a sleepy old pony named Apples, because it had some Appaloosie blood, shown in a pale, speckled wash across its hindquarters. It might never have been missed, except that it happened to belong to Andy, who called it his night horse; he hunted, and complained, and harped on his loss, until everybody was sick of hearing about Apples.

Cassius had now been gone upwards of six weeks, and they were coming into the just-barely-possible area. The land was already yielding dust again where the grass was poor, or the run off had scoured the earth barren. So now they watched for a distant stir-up.

But when they sighted one, early in an unseasonably hot afternoon, it was in an unlikely direction; and it was a Fort Worth posse that came there, before Cash ever got home.

The light, intermittent dust the posse made was seen by Ben from where he worked a long way off, and he judged at once that it could only mean more trouble. He came on in, with Andy and his two hired hands. By lathering the horses, he got home just ahead of the slower-moving posse. Immediately he sent Andy up to the house, with word that Matthilda and Rachel were to stay inside, whatever happened. And shortly after that, nine riders came jogging around the corral to where the Zachary men waited, sitting their sweated horses.

The man in front, gray-thatched and gray-mustached, with a dried-out look, Ben knew for Sol

Carr of Tarrant County. He had been a Ranger,
once, before the War Between the States, and
would be one again, now that Texas could bring the
Rangers back. Ben did not know why his father had
disliked Sol Carr but remembered that this was so.
For the time being Carr was head of a loosely organized bunch of volunteers from the Fort Worth
neighborhood. They chased thieves and war
parties, and some of them rode all the time.

Behind Sol Carr and to one side, respectfully
aloof, rode an Indian in the butternut clothes of a
cowhand, but with no dents or creases in his hat.
He had the squat look of a huge frog, and graying
pigtails hung beside his jowls. Ben believed this to
be a Delaware called Humpjack, who had scouted
for troops and Rangers against the Wild Tribes
since long ago.

Most conspicuous, because they hung back and
would not meet his eye, were Jude and Charlie
Rawlins. But Ben could have named three of the
five others. He had exchanged powers of attorney
with them, for handling drifted cattle. They nodded
slightly, noncommittally and without smiling, as he
looked at them one after another; and this confirmed that the posse was hostile. The chilling thing
was that these were ordinary men, who were Texans and cowmen, but not renegades, nor of any special faction. Sometimes a kind of tide seemed to run
across the empty spaces of Texas, a tide of senti-
ment, of opinion, so that far-separated, lonely settlers were swayed the same way all at once. To
stand against such a thing was to stand against the
State. Sooner or later the guns would start clearing
their throats, and you might find yourself fighting

feud after feud, without any future or any end.

Behind the mounted men, a tenth man drove a light wagon, with a horse tied to the tail gate; and the led horse was Apples.

Andy swung down. "That's my horse you got there! What's that contraption you got on him?" Apples was carrying an Indian saddle of sticks and straps; it looked to be broken.

Somebody shouted, "Let that horse alone, boy!"

"That thing's eating him in two! I got to get it off him!"

But Ben said sharply, "Come back here, Andy!" And his brother obeyed.

Carr dismounted now, without invitation, and Ben stepped down to meet him. They stopped two paces apart, and did not offer to shake hands. Both had left their carbines on their saddles, but Ben wore his holster slung low on his right, and Sol Carr was similarly armed.

"We've been following out the No Hope massacre," Carr said to Ben, "and we've been lucky. Found out quite a bit." He let an edge come into his voice, as if he were talking to a man under arrest, or about to be. "I'm here to learn the rest of it from you."

Ben flared up, but his voice remained quiet. Rachel, watching from the house, heard no word of what followed.

"Those were your last words in that tone," he told Sol Carr, "while you stand on my land."

"You can back that up, too," Carr said, dry as the dust, "just by taking on all these men. How many do you figure you'll have time to get?"

"One," Ben said.

Maybe the old Ranger modified his tone, some, then—or maybe he didn't, actually. Certainly his purpose was not softened.

"We taken a prisoner," Carr said. "A white squaw man, and I believe you know him. Name of Abe Kelsey."

"We've been looking for Kelsey a long time," Ben said.

"That's as may be. What interests us, he was mixed up with them red niggers at the massacre. Laying aside what he says he was doing there, he anyway messed into it enough to get himself shot up. And we got him."

"Alive?"

"Just about. We got the names of the main war chiefs out of him. Seth was there, and so was Wolf Saddle. But he says Lost Bird was the leader. Though he may be protecting Seth, seein's he claims he's Seth's old man."

"If he's alive," Ben demanded, "why haven't you hung him?"

"We may get around to it," Carr answered. "Meantime, he's spieled off a whole string of charges against you. I thought you might want to face him, and answer him. I've got him here, in that wagon."

"Let him lift his head," Ben said. "And I'll put a ball between his eyes in the next tenth of a second!"

"You'd shoot an unarmed man?"

"Yes," Ben said.

"Then I better tell you what he says myself. Bein's I'm in better shape to shoot back. He says, to start, the Kiowas used your place, here, for their point of assembly."

"The three you named were here," Ben acknowledged. "We forted up, and stood 'em off."

"He says Lost Bird learned from you that the people they massacred were on the road, and there was no other way the red niggers could have learned of it."

A stir of surprise ran over the posse as Ben laughed in Carr's face. It was a nasty laugh, with promise of fight in it, yet unexpected. "The Rawlinses are the people we have to work with," Ben said.

"They're also the damyankees that crowded in on your range," Carr reminded him. "Your old man had his eye on this grass for a long time. When he finally come to settle on it, Rawlins was ahead of him, and he had to go splits. It's possible to believe you wanted them out of here."

"Oh, good God almighty," Ben said with contempt.

"There's plenty to say it's the Kiowas you have to work with, not Rawlinses, if you want to last where you are. They say this foundling girl, this foster sister of yours, you people have raised—"

He broke off, stopped by the blaze of pure murder that had lighted Ben's eyes, contradicting his smile. "What about her?" Ben prodded him.

"They say she's the key to your understanding with the Kiowas," Sol Carr went on coolly. He had been startled, but he was not the man to be frightened. "Kelsey says your old man found the girl on the prairie, and rescued her. And she proved out to be a Kiowa quarter-breed baby, lost out of a drag litter—Lost Bird's half sister, out of a white woman captive. They say the Kiowas are friendly because you're raising one of their own."

"Carr," Ben said, "if you don't have enough
Indian-savvy to know that's impossible, it's no use
to talk to you. You ought to know there's nothing
could bring the whole tribe down on us any quicker
than if they thought we was holding a captive
Kiowa child!"

"I would have supposed so," Sol Carr admitted.
"Only there's one thing more. After the massacre,
Abe Kelsey made his way here. His horse had been
hit; died about two miles out. He's showed us the
bones, stripped clean by the wolves. God knows he
was in no shape to catch another. He says you people gave him a horse. You gave him that horse, right
there. You helped him get away on it. And he got
back to some of his red niggers—what time he could
keep up with 'em."

"That horse was stolen," Andy said. "Out of this
corral right here. And within an hour of noon!"

"Nobody around at all?" Carr said with disbelief.

"I had two men here all the time," Ben told him.
He glanced at Tip and Joey, and found them looking blank, and frightened.

"Do you accuse the two men?" Carr asked sharply.

"I do not! I don't think they know anything
about this at all."

"Yet somebody gave Kelsey this horse!"

In the moment of silence that followed, Ben saw
Sol Carr look past him, and start to say something
more, then close his mouth again. Ben had not
known that Matthilda had left the house, until she
spoke from behind him.

"I did," Matthilda said clearly. "I gave him the horse."

23

Matthilda had not explained to Rachel, as she left the house, what it was she meant to do. Rachel made as if to go with her. Perhaps she would not have obeyed an order from Matthilda to stay back; perhaps Matthilda knew it.

"Ben won't like this," Matthilda said. "Please don't make him mad at you, too."

That worked. Rachel stayed at the window, and watched Matthilda walk down there, to butt in on the men, where she wasn't wanted. But mostly her eyes were on Ben. She thought, *I ought to be there. I'm the one should be beside him, now.* Suddenly she went and got the Sharp & Hankins, and chambered a cartridge. If a fight broke, she was sure she could not fail to get some of those who were against Ben. About one with every shot, at this range, firing from a rest. After that she felt better about staying where she was.

Down by the corral, Sol Carr lifted his hat to Matthilda, and spoke courteously, covering his objections to being thrown off his line of attack.

"I remember you, M'am," Carr said. "You are Mrs. Zachary."

"And you are Sol Carr," Matthilda responded, "who tried to do my husband out of six thousand dollars."

Carr may have reddened a little, but his tone did not change. "I understood you to say you gave Kelsey this horse. Did you realize, then, he had come direct from the No Hope massacre?"

"I realize nothing of the kind. The day he came here was more than two weeks after the massacre."

That stopped Carr for a moment or two; but he said, "He had been wounded, though?"

"He had a gunshot wound in the limb," Matthilda said. "A new one. The blood was fresh on the bandage. It wasn't a bad wound, then. I should judge it's bad now—I can smell green-flesh from here. You'd better get him some doctoring, or you won't get him as far as his trial!"

"M'am," Carr said, "this is his trial."

"I'll be interested to hear the verdict," Matthilda said saltily.

"What was your belief, then, as to how he got wounded?"

"I supposed he was caught stealing horses. Our horses, likely."

"You thought he was a horse thief," Carr said wonderingly. "You knew he was a squaw man. You knew he's spread tales against you, to your great harm. Yet you gave him a horse to get away on?"

"Yes," said Matthilda.

"M'am, in God's name—exucse me, M'am—why?"

"Poor old man," Matthilda said. "I was sorry for him."

"After all he's done, you tell me you were sorry—"

"Suppose one of my little children had been taken by red savages," Matthilda said. "Do you think there's anything I wouldn't do, any lengths I wouldn't go to, to bring my child back to me? I have no doubt I would go crazy, as crazy as Abe, before the end of it. Of course I'm sorry for him!"

There were a lot more questions. Like, where were the two men Ben had left at the house, while Matthilda was giving away Apples. Smoked out, Tip and Joey admitted they had been reining a couple of colts, and had jumped a loafer wolf. They had taken after it, to rope it, and run it a far piece. Tip like to got a loop on it, but his colt spooked at the rope, and throwed him. Joey had had a hard time catching Tip's colt for him, so, all in all, they had been out of sight maybe two hours.

But the backbone of the posse's purpose, if it had been to involve the Zacharys, had been broken for the time being, on the sheer incredibility of Matthilda's honesty.

Rachel saw the posse leader step into his saddle, at the end of it. Then Ben mounted, though he made Andy and the cowhands stay at the corral. Matthilda turned away, and plodded slowly up the hill to the house, her face white, but held as rigidly expressionless as she could make it. Behind her all the horses began to shift and move; and it was Ben who led out, not in the direction from which the posse had come, but upstream.

As the wagon moved, Abe Kelsey dragged him-

self up with scaly old hands to hang over the side.
Clear up at the house, Rachel could hear him plainly, wailing and pleading.

"I'm an old man—I'm a pore old man—I ain't
got no friends—I ain't done nothin'—I'm a pore old
man—You got no right—"

She could hear him for a long time, over the
sound of the hoofs, as the cavalcade moved off, and
trailed out of sight beyond the upper bend. Mama
reached the stoop then; she fumbled at the door,
and Rachel opened it for her. Matthilda was crying,
now, quietly, and steadily; she could not, or would
not, answer any of the many things Rachel had to
ask. Without speaking a word, Matthilda went to
her bed and hid her face there, crying still.

It was almost sundown when Ben came back,
and unsaddled slowly. A little after that the posse
passed, going back the way it had come, but on the
far side of the creek. The old man in the wagon no
longer made any sound; and Rachel knew, by this
time, why the posse had gone upstream. There was
a big pin oak, up there, a whopper for its kind and
place, with a limb of suitable height and girth. An
old tale had it that a bandit had once been caught
here, and hanged upon that tree. Some said, and
Andy liked to believe, that this ghost from long ago
still haunted the Dancing Bird. No matter whether
that legend had any truth in it or not.

The Dancing Bird had a ghost to haunt it now.

24

Ben came in reluctantly. He didn't want to talk to anybody. His black moods were uncommon, but when he was in them he could bite, and he was in one now. Rachel knew no way to approach him, or question him. He paced, sometimes beating a fist into his palm, his lips moving in long strings of silent blasphemies. Or else he sat sullen and bitter on the edge of his bunk, burning holes in the floor with his eyes. He didn't hear you the first time you spoke to him, and when he did hear you he snapped. When it was time to feed him he ate doggedly, straight through one thing after another, with no idea of what he was putting in his mouth. Later, Rachel would wish she had served him a cloth potholder, to see if it would go down, but such an impertinence was unthinkable while the black mood was on. She would as soon have bitten a mule on the ankle as trifle with him, then.

Andy only picked at his food, and stuck close to

Ben, refusing to meet Rachel's eyes. A mumbled, "I d'know," was all she could get out of him, and she knew it wasn't his fault. He had been told to shut up, and stay shut up. She was alone, now, beyond the wall of this secretiveness; everyone in the house knew things that she did not. The hands came in to eat, but they kept their eyes down, and their mouths as close shut as Andy's. The Kiowa Moon would soon be riding above them once more, and Ben updated it a number of days. He wouldn't say just what he was expecting to come against them; perhaps he was not entirely sure himself. But it was plain he felt easier with all the carbines within ready call.

Once Rachel asked him outright if it was horse stealing Kelsey had been hung for. He said it was not.

"Mixed up in the No Hope massacre," he said.

Andy saw a chance to put in, for once, without telling anything more than Ben had said. "They charged him with aiding and betting on hostiles."

"Abetting," Ben snapped. "Aiding and abetting, damn it!"

"What?"

"Nothing! Don't talk so much." But he let down enough to tell Rachel a little bit more. "He was with Seth, when they killed Effie. By his own admission."

"They were trying to pull us into it some way—weren't they?" she pressed him. "Weren't they?"

He blazed up. "Who told you that?"

"Why—nobody—"

"Then forget it! And stop making up things!" Sometimes she tried to find out what the

Rawlinses had done against them, or were waiting
for a chance to do, but nobody would give her a clue
to that, either.

"No way to fight them," Ben said once. Sometimes, now, he seemed less grim than discouraged,
which was a new thing. "Jude and Charlie can
shoot, all right, if you give them all the time in the
world. So can old Zeb. But they don't know how to
fight anything that shoots back. If they hurry a shot
it goes wild. Any one of us could put all three of
them down. Only . . . it would be like a man
shooting a bunch of boys."

As bad as that, then. Bad enough to send Ben on
the shoot, to smoke out their neighbors, except that
he wasn't ready for outright murder, yet. She saw
he was sorry he had said so much; and she could
draw out nothing more. Ben paced and fretted,
sometimes pulling weapons off the gun rack in an
irritable pretense of examining them. He was like
that now whenever he was in the house. Daytimes
the men loitered and puttered; no more work on the
range was attempted.

That waiting time lasted barely a week, as the
Kiowa Moon came on, though it seemed a lot longer than that. The seemingly hopeless stack-up of
chores melted away. The house got whitewashed,
and even received a wash of lime and brown sand
on the outside. Only the mud-leaky roof stayed the
same, for lack of shingles. The cowhands took to
playing endless games of high-low-jack on a blanket
under the trees by the creek.

There was a day when Andy thought of something he could do; and it was a different kind of
thing than had ever entered his mind before. He

started out to build a pansy bed.

Matthilda had always had pansies, every year of their lives. Even when time pressed hard, she had managed to grow a few, for seed to be saved over. If they moved during the growing season, a few pansy plants had to go along in bedding boxes, so that the little flowers would not be lost out of their world. Matthilda loved the little faces, which came out more distinctly upon her blooms than they ever did upon any others, and in more different bright colors. Sometimes when Matthilda bent over a bed of them, working the lumps out of the soil with gentle fingers, Rachel could have sworn that all the little flowers turned upwards, and peered into Matthilda's face, as if trying to talk to her. Why not? Matthilda sometimes talked to the flowers.

The pansy bed Andy made beside the stoop was built up more than knee high, with stones from the creek. He carried the first stones in his arms up the slope, but later hitched the work team to the stone boat, and went at it right. After a while, Ben and the cowhands got interested, and pitched in, and before they were through they had a raised bed on either side of the stoop, each six feet across, and so solidly built that they were an easy bet to outlast the house by half a century. The boys hauled dirt from the corral, hoof-churned and manured by five years of horse-critters; and lightened it by mixing in sand. Matthilda hummed gaily, her face shining, as she set out the tiny plants she had already started. Surely the pansies would grow here as they had never grown before, if only they were still here to see them.

Suddenly the waiting days were over. Eight men

of Cash's corrida got back, with the reduced remuda, and both wagons. But Cassius was not with
them.

25

Ben met the stripped-down corrida half way to the Red, and for a few minutes had a great sinking of the heart as he saw from a long way off that Cash was not with his wagons. He found Johnny Portugal straw-bossing, in charge of bringing the wagons and the remuda home. They still did not know Johnny Portugal's right name, and probably never would, but he had turned into as steady and loyal a hand as they had, since the day Ben had slapped him down in the round corral.

Cassius had ridden on ahead of them, Johnny told Ben at once. Said he had a side trip he wanted to make, on the way home—something he wanted to see, though he didn't say what. So, the morning of their fourth day out of Wichita, he had taken a fast horse, and a spare on lead, and was soon out of sight. He had told Johnny Portugal to take his time, so the corrida wouldn't scare hell out of the family by getting home ahead of him. Johnny said he had sure thought he was traveling slow enough; he was eleven days out of Wichita. Which meant they hadn't seen Cash in a week.

Ben took the corrida on in, and by the time he got home he had worked out a lie. Cassius had always wanted to see where Papa was lost, he told them, and Ben had explained to him how to find it. It would take him a far piece out of his way, because the rivers were down now; the corrida didn't have to take the roundabout way the herds took in flood season. But the country Cassius would travel was safe now—no game in it, and so no Indians. Johnny Portugal had really made very fast time; Cassius could hardly be expected for two or three days yet. And so on and so forth. Not a word of it had any relationship to fact.

He had supposed that Mama would assume at once that she had lost her son to the dreadful trails, as his father had been lost four years before. Ben himself thought it entirely likely that Cassius was dead, and that they would never find out what had befallen him. A night-long hysteria would not have surprised him. But Matthilda, who could dissolve so easily over trifles, had a way of stiffening surprisingly when truly serious and deadly threats hung over them. She accepted Ben's conjectures as though they were entirely reasonable; and if fears haunted her all through the dark hours, he was spared them.

Cassius came in the next day. He was gaunted and hollow-eyed; like his father, he was another who could never be caught asleep while he bossed a cattle drive. And he was saddle-weary to the bones from recent hard riding. One of the two horses with which Cash had left the corrida was dead, Ben learned later. The one he still rode was taxed so far past endurance that it might never recover full usefulness. The carbine was missing from his saddle boot, and Ben lent him his own, lest the loss attract attention when they reached the house. But Cash himself was sound, and in high spirits, in spite of his fatigue, and that was the main thing.

As they rode in they agreed to stick with the story Ben had already invented—that Cassius had visited Witch River, as a sort of shrine, because his father had been lost there. Actually, so far as he knew, Cash had been nowhere near it; didn't know it when he saw it, or how to find it.

Nobody but Ben ever learned the story of where Cassius had been, or what had been his errand. Ben himself was not told right away, or all at once. Events at both ends of the Wichita Trail called for a making up of minds, so that the tale of Cash's unaccounted days was easily pushed aside.

But what Cash had done was of graver portent than he thought. He had conceived a bold, brilliant, and wholly farfetched stroke; execution involved great personal danger, while the odds against accomplishing anything useful were enormous— which were perhaps the factors that made the plan irresistible to him, once he had thought of it. He was unabashed to have obtained no immediate result. He might or might not have set some wheels turning, but if nothing ever came of it at all, he would not be surprised. What Cash did not realize, and perhaps never fully understood while he lived, was that the action he took in those eight days he was missing in Indian Territory might prove more

dangerous to them than anything that had ever
happened to the Zacharys before.

Cash had begun by reasoning that Rachel was a
Kiowa or she was not; and the truth must be in
existence somewhere. If it was, the place to find it
was in the lodges of the Kiowas themselves, for they
had always kept better records of their history than
any other Indians on the plains. He imagined that
Striking Horse, a Kiowa warlock Old Zack had
once known, could probably lay hands on the facts
if anybody could. So Cash had gone to find out.

Four days out from Wichita he had left his corrida, and gone in search of the renegade village with
which Striking Horse traveled. The Kiowas were already as good as at war. A furious burst of murders
and scalpings was rushing them toward a showdown that could destroy them. A Texican who rode
alone into a Kiowa village might not ride out again.
"But sometimes," Cash explained himself, "you
have to call for the turning of a card."

Striking Horse was an old man who for a long
time had been what the whites called a medicine
chief. The term did not fit too well into the patterns
by which the Kiowas lived, for the Kiowas had no
official medicine men. A medicine, or spirit power,
might deal with anything, from wet joints to bullet
proofing; almost every Kiowa warrior had a power
of some kind.

What Striking Horse had was a gift of prophecy
supposedly conferred by owls, which the Kiowas
feared as more or less supernatural, and connected
with the world of the dead. He kept with him an owl
skin with a bladder in it, enabling him to produce
an owl on order by secretly inflating one; and the

showpiece among his sacred possessions was a giant thigh bone of a Man-Eating Owl. A man had to be a strong warlock indeed to fool around with owls.

Old Zack had once been Striking Horse's friend, up to a point, and in a way. Striking Horse had been prominent in the Eagle Sign Society, a group of magicians devoted to sleight of hand. It had amused Zack to contribute to Striking Horse's reputation by some simple gifts.

And it was Striking Horse who had given Cash's father the name of Stone Hand, the time Zack knocked a Comanche senseless with a slap. Cash had reason to hope that the father's name would serve to place the son.

Striking Horse had the gray eyes of his Spanish mother, and the dark skin of his father, who was half Crow; he was a Kiowa by virtue of only a quarter of his blood. So Cash knew the Owl Prophet when he found him. He did not find him quickly, or easily, or without certain moments of great risk. But he got there.

Cash opened by giving Striking Horse his carbine, and all the ammunition he had for it, with no strings whatever attached—thereby putting himself just as far outside the law as the old Indian was.

After that, piecing out his battered Kiowa with quick-running sign language, he had told the Owl Prophet about a medicine dream he claimed to have had, in which he was shown a thing that actually happened, long ago. He had seen a Kiowa village running away from a great force of Tayhahnnas. While he watched, a baby was bounded out of a drag litter unnoticed, and so was lost; and this was what the dream had been sent to show him, for here it ended. He had even been made to know in what year this thing had happened. But something was unclear. The baby had seemed to be a Tayhahnna child, held captive by the Kiowas. Cash made out that it was necessary to his medicine to know whether this was true, or whether the lost baby had been a Kiowa child. This was what he had come to find out from the Prophet of the Owls.

Striking Horse brought out his history calendar, and gravely spread it before Cassius. This was a spiral figure, delicately drawn upon a deerskin, and filled up with tiny pictures, each representing a summer or a winter; for the Kiowas counted time by seasons, rather than years. Each spring and fall the calendar keeper added a little drawing that stood for an event. The single event served to bring the season back to him, reminding him of all other events. A number of Kiowas kept these wheels, each one differently. The Owl Prophet's wheel went back so far it had grown bigger than a grindstone.

The old Indian told Cassius to point to the time, on the calendar wheel, when this thing happened in his dream. At first it didn't seem as though this could be done. Counting back didn't get anywhere, for the calendar keepers commonly left out seasons, or whole years. But Cash studied the wheel; and presently saw a winter distinguished by a speckled face. He had heard of a smallpox epidemic among the tribes during the winter before Rachel was found. So now he pointed to the summer following.

After due thought, Striking Horse decided he didn't remember any baby being lost that summer. Must have happened in some other village than his own. He said he would ask some other calendar keeper sometime, when he ran into one. If he found out, he would send word. He put the carbine away, and offered Cash a smoke.

"I guess I was a damn fool," Cash said. "Wasted a carbine, likely. Still . . . the Kiowas don't generally lie. Except to damyankee commissions," he qualified it, "who lie all the time. He might find out. I remembered afterward he never asked where to send word. But I judge they know how to find us, all right."

Yes, I judge they do, Ben thought. *Too dang hootin' well.* He was hiding a bitter anger, for his immediate conviction was that Cash had made out death warrants for them all. The thin nonsense about a dream could not have fooled Striking Horse for a minute. So here was Abe Kelsey at their throats again; doubtless he had tried to tell the Indians a thousand times that the Zacharys were holding a captive Kiowa girl. Now old Kelsey was dead, and still they weren't shed of him at all. He was even safe from them, for they could never again hope to hunt him down and kill him as a solution to anything. He put Ben in mind of John Brown, whose dead body had got into a song, and helped bring on a war the South could not win. *And here we got another damned hell-raising old hooter amoldering in his grave, while his mischief goes marching on. I suppose the old son of a bitch ain't ever going to lie still.*

Small matter whether the Kiowas had believed Kelsey or not, now that Cash had run to Striking Horse and virtually confirmed the whole thing. *Cash didn't realize,* Ben told himself, keeping his mouth shut and his face still until he could get hold of his anger. He had to remember that the dangers with which Cash had been tampering had been far less plain at the time Cash set off up the Wichita Trail. *He didn't know. . . .*

"I don't know why we never thought of this before," Cash said. "Papa could have proved long ago she hasn't a drop of Kiowa blood, right out of those Kiowa history calendars. Easier then than now."

Ben saw, then, what had blinded Cassius to his mistake. Their mother's wishful assumption that Rachel was of pure blood had stood in Cash's mind as an unquestioned truth, without alternative, since before he could remember. Only Ben knew why his father had never gone to the Kiowas for an answer.

William Zachary had believed Rachel was a Kiowa child. Perhaps, for all Ben knew, he had known it for certain.

No use to tell Cash that now. "You did a brave thing," was all Ben said, at last.

But nothing about Striking Horse, or the missing eight days, came up to mar the triumph of Cash's return, that first day.

26

Cash had made his drive in thirty-one days, and it had leaned him to the bone. By all accounts, he had no more than dozed against a wagon wheel once in a while, and the rest of the time had slept in the saddle, or not at all. Once his deals were made, the rest of his time was spent in retrieving his cook and the best seven men that he had from Delano, Wichita's whisky-and-women suburb, across the Arkansas River.

The same collection of saloons and dance halls had been called Nauchville, when it stood outside Ellsworth, and Hide Park at Newton. Each time the railhead advanced, these shaky buildings were pulled down and flat-carred, to be set up again at the new shipping point, with the same cadre of bartenders, faro dealers, and girls—plus the new faces of additions and replacements. It was a cowhand's paradise, such as no man could rightly appreciate until he had behind him the brutal hardships of the trail. But Cash finally combed the men he wanted, heavily hung-over, out of the sawdust floors of Delano. He believed he knew them, now; and he was paying them the highest wages offered on any trail.

He could afford it, for he was riding the high wave of success. After the heartbreaking drives from which the Zacharys had turned their cattle back to trail them home again, after years in which they had dumped whole herds at the price of hides in order to pay off their men, Cassius had sold high at last.

Until Cassius got home, Ben had not touched the huge strongbox carried in the cook wagon. It was built of heavy steel plates, and it took four men to carry it into the house. Instead of padlocks, it had blacksmith-welded iron straps, and they were the better part of an hour getting it open at all.

Inside, sewed up in a great number of small deerskin pouches, Cassius was carrying a little more than $104,000 in gold.

Ben was chilled as it got through to him what Cash had left in the hands of the tough renegades Ben himself had hired in Fort Griffin. Cash claimed he knew his men. Ben didn't believe anybody knew these men, or any men, well enough to justify trusting them with a fortune like that. Well—they had got there with it; that was the final answer to that.

They moved the carved secretary Papa had made —it weighed about a ton—out into the middle of the room, to get at what they called the Glory Hole. This was a trap door, fitted of random-length planks so as not to show, with a keg set into the earth underneath, to keep their money in. It had been empty, or nearly so, most of the time for quite a while. But

tonight they filled it up again; and tried to realize
that they were rich.

After Rawlins had been paid some thirty thousand dollars for his lesser share of the herd, and they
had paid off seventy-five or eighty other brands for
nearly a thousand strays they had driven and sold,
and when they had paid off twenty-two thousand in
debts, they would still have thirty thousand dollars
left—a fortune, clear and unencumbered; plus a
couple of thousand head of breeders and young
stock, not counting calves and yearlings, standing
on the range.

They could send Matthilda and Rachel to safety
far away, to the east coast, or abroad; they could do
anything they wanted to now—if only they could
find out what it was. For now Matthilda balked.
She feared even to cross Texas with Rachel while
Kelsey's hanging still had the whole doomful dis-
pute over her birth still fresh in everybody's mind.
They were certainly safe here, with a corrida, now
with a strength of twelve men plus the Zacharys
themselves, right here on the place. She wanted her
sons with her, at least as far as the Mississippi, and
they certainly could not leave the work now. Wait
till the work was done this fall; it all would be easy,
then.

She made it sound natural and sensible to delay
their departure, for the sake of safety alone. But
Ben felt a deep foreboding. Rachel probably came
first, in his mother's heart; he was fairly sure of
that. Yet he began to doubt that she would ever
leave her sons, of her own will.

After Matthilda went to bed Ben and Cassius still
sat up, talking all through most of Cash's first night

home. Andy slept, unbothered, but Rachel lay
wakeful in her bed, listening to that ominous-seem-
ing, indistinguishable mumbling, on and on. And
though she knew what times they poured themselves fresh coffee, not one word they said came
through the heavy door. Bird songs were starting up
along the Dancing Bird before they quit. Yet they
were up, red-eyed but unfriendly to sleep, in the
early dawn.

First thing they did was to send a rider down the
Dancing Bird with a note to Zeb Rawlins, naming
the halfway point at which he must meet them, late
that day.

27

Zeb Rawlins and his two sons met the three Zachary brothers on a stripped and barren flat ten miles down the Dancing Bird. The wheels of Zeb's buggy crackled as they cut through the baked and curling crust, for here an endless network of earth cracks made cruelly visible the damage this year had done the range. Jude and Charlie carried their carbines in their hands as they rode on either side of their father; and Zeb himself carried a long rifle in his lap as he drove. Saddle horses and buggy team were freshly groomed and tail-plucked, and every inch of rigging had been rubbed to a shine, under the film of the fast-gathering dust. This spit and polish, as much as the weapons in their hands, bespoke a predetermination that this showdown should be official, final, and complete.

Each of the Zachary boys saw at a glance that only the two carbines were repeaters. Jude's weapon was a Triplett & Scott, and Charlie's a Henry;

but Zeb's rifle, with its uncommonly long 30-inch
barrel, was an old cap-and-ball Snyder—the weapon of a man who means to shoot once, and make the
one shot do. The Zacharys left their carbines in
their boots, but they were wearing their revolvers.
Cassius had his father's Dragoon; Ben, his big
Walker Colt, with a 9-inch barrel; and Andy, a
Confederate copy of the Whitney, with which he
had proved to his brothers he could "wipe their
noses for them," if ever he got anybody to hold still
for it. All three wore their guns butt first on the left,
for cross-drawing, when in the saddle.

The two parties pulled up with the noses of their
animals a horse-length apart.

Zeb Rawlins sat motionless, looking so solid and
immovable that the buggy was made to look frail.
Ben noticed how his great weight bore down its
springs. Probably these two had never had any
chance of understanding each other, from the first.
Zeb had been born of corn-country pioneers, up on
the Ohio River; every time he had ever mentioned
such a thing as a "gant-lot," Ben had had to stop
and figure out all over again what he meant. If
either of the two had actually fought in the War,
they would never have tried to work together at all.
Yet Ben no longer wondered how a man unable to
ride could undertake to whip the open range. Zeb
had a motto: "When Bull takes holt, heaven and
'arth can't make him let go!" It was neither a
slogan nor a preachment; it was a description of the
man.

"My brother sold your cows," Ben said shortly.

Zeb's eyes went to Cassius, who spoke briskly.
"Twelve hundred and nineteen head, as loaded at

Wichita. Average for the herd, twenty-six dollars and eight cents a head. Your pro-rate of cost, one thousand and four. Leaves you thirty-one thousand, seven hundred and ninety-one dollars and fifty-two cents.''

Watching Zeb's face, Ben could see no change in his neighbor's dark and heavy mood. Cash had described a great golden flood, all but unbelievable, after the lean years that had gone before. Ben supposed Zeb must already have had news of the market from another source. There was a short silence.

"You'll be paid off in gold coinage," Ben said. "Say when and where."

"I'll send for what's due me," Zeb said.

They waited, until Zeb Rawlins was ready to go on.

"The charges made against you have not been fully proved," Zeb said. "Not yet."

"Watch your God-damned mouth," Ben said; and he saw Zeb's jowls begin to purple and shake.

"My daughter has been murdered," Zeb said, still speaking with slow weight. "Her mistreated remains are under the ground. It's enough for me that any part of the blame could be charged to you at all, by anybody whatsoever. Yet I'll do this one thing more. I'll buy out any rights you think you have here, together with whatever cattle of yours you don't want to drive off. Figure up your price, and send me word what it is. But I want to know soon!"

Ben answered so reasonably that Cash shot him a glance of angry disbelief. "I might buy, or I might sell," he said. "Either way, I mean to cross-brand, first. There's too many cows on this range owned by marks on paper, and not enough owned by the right marks on cows. If you want me to work yours, too, send a rep. It'll cost you the standard fifty cents a head."

"I'll send a rep," Rawlins conceded. "See that you keep your damned iron off the odd-brand cattle until he comes!"

Ben's voice rose in anger for the first time. "I'll brand any damned critter I see fit!"

"All I want," Zeb roared back at him, "is to get you red-nigger lovers to hell off my range!"

"You've got no range," Ben said dropping back into his drawl again. "This is Texican land. It'll take a sight more than a fat-gutted damyankee son of a bitch to put me off it."

In the quiet that followed, Andy shortened his reins, and flipped the ends out of the way of his draw.

"I'm sick of looking at them," Ben told his brothers. He turned his horse; and the moment for gunfire went past.

But something else had happened that might build up to a bigger and longer fight than any six men could have had, on the flats by the Dancing Bird.

Up to here Ben's trouble had been that he loved the Dancing Bird country for itself. Even the Kiowas had been a boon, in a way, holding this grassland in trust for them, until some good year would enable them to buy land scrip, and take it up. Ben had a hundred long-range plans. He had picked a dozen places where he wanted dams, to establish permanent water in far, dry grasslands where now only brief flash floods ran. He had located clay he could haul from a long way off to line the tanks behind the dams, so that the waters would not seep away. He was experimenting with a hedge of wild-rose bramble to stop winter drift, and the everlasting shuffle-up with half the brands in Texas. With fences up he could grade up his stock, bringing in bulls that otherwise wasted themselves on anybody's cows but your own. He meant to bring in fruit trees, and Mexican labor to raise garden truck; he planned to build such a house as would be a showpiece forever.

Now he had his good year; he could think in miles of land, instead of pounds of powder. But if he was going to scrip this land, he had no time to lose. Once the Rangers came back to make this border safe, the country would flood with people, and all this beautiful grass would begin to go under the plow, never to be recovered again. Confederate Texas had sold land scrip by the wagonload, to finance the War. Much of it was still knocking around, and could be cheaply had. But a lot of it had been used to tie up land by map landmarks, as a speculation. Ben saw reason to think that some of the country he now used was already the private property of absentee owners who had never seen it yet. These would have to be bought out at a stiff advance in price.

Because of this he could not expect to buy all of the range he used at once. But he could get title to both sides of the Dancing Bird, though he paid a thousand dollars a section, where once four dollars in scrip would have been enough; he might be able to take up a part of the Little Beaver, and a strip along the Red. With his water secure, he could count on scooping up the rest in other good years, later on.

Or else—the returns from this one good year

could be used to run away once more. It had to be one thing or the other, and right away. History would not stand back and wait much longer.

Once Ben would have been willing to give up the Dancing Bird, drive a stocker herd to some new land, and start again, rather than drag his family into a war he might not be able to win. But it seemed to him now that if he gave ground this time, he would never make any stand again.

He no longer believed that he would ever be able to give up this land.

28

A week passed. Ben and Cash alternated days on the range, one staying in with two or three hands, picked for their interest in gun-fighting. The range crew quickly whipped through the last of the calf branding, and began to sort the cattle and shove them around. They started cross-branding, adding the Dancing Bird brand to cattle otherwise branded, but their own on paper. Whichever one was home spent many hours a day at Papa's carved secretary, sorting and rebooking the hopelessly complicated accounts and tallies.

The Rawlinses did send a rep, at last, and the Zacharys were glad to see that Jake Rountree was the man who had let himself be talked into the job. Jake was nearing fifty, a stooped, gaunt man with wild eyes and a look of perpetual fatigue. The tired look may have been the result of chronic malaria; some days he complained of a general ache. The years of bad markets and irregular weather had all but squeezed him out of the cattle business, so that his own outfit was hardly more than a token and a hope of building again. Żeb Rawlins was paying him a strapping hundred a month—had had to pay it, in order to get him, hard up as he was. Ben promptly put a hundred a month of his own on top.

Jake knew cattle. Neither Cash nor Ben ever had any trouble with him. "Trying to give everything away," was his only objection to the way they were handling the bust-up. The Rawlinses, for the time being, stayed off the range.

But afterward, when the parting of the herds was complete? Doubtless Rawlins could comb up a corrida. He could even scrape up a corrida of Yankee outlaws, if that was what he wanted; he could throw fifty killers onto this range. Maybe both outfits would be cool and careful, at the first. Then bickerings would begin, and presently somebody's temper would break. Once the guns began to smoke, how could they ever be quieted again? They didn't know. They did the work in hand, judging that they would know how to handle what came next, some way, when they saw what it was.

Meantime their debts had to be paid, a big job in itself; for all those thousands were owed in dribbles, to hundreds of cowmen, spread out over most of Texas. It was a job Ben felt he had to do himself; wanted to find out what kind of friends he still had in Texas, for one thing. He would be in the saddle many weeks, and he was eager to get at it. As soon as he got Cash and Jake Rountree well started with the cross-branding he would be on his way.

As Ben bored into the range work, setting a brutal pace for the corrida, Rachel was watching the calendar in a little horse race of her own. Ben's birthday was coming up; she wanted him to be home for it. She had thought of something she could make for him, something that would have no practical use at all, but which she hoped would look pretty to him, and surprising.

The calendar had no chance in a race with Ben. Three days on the range, three nights in a deluge of papers at the secretary, and that was it.

They were at breakfast when he told them that he would ride south in the morning, leading the old bullion mule. No, he wasn't taking any men with him.... Because he didn't need any, that was why.... Robbers? What about robbers? Robbers had to take their chances same as anybody else. Come fooling around him, they probably deserved it. Shanghai Pierce had ridden all over Texas with a mule of money, time and again. So had Papa. Ben judged he could handle it.

He was leaving Cassius with twelve men, including the cook, and Andy. Four or five men, and either Cash or Andy, were going to be at the house all the time. The place would never be unguarded, regardless of the moon.

He shouted from the door for somebody to catch the mule up.

Mama exclaimed, "But I thought you said tomorrow!"

"Oh, sure; only thing, if I happen to be twelve, fifteen miles in the right direction comes sundown, hardly any sense in riding it two ways. Pretty near amounts to a day. Though it's hardly likely; I expect to be home, all right, if you want to set a plate—"

"Now, Ben, you can come home for dinner just this one last night," Matthilda pleaded. "Please, now, won't you?"

"I'll sure try," he promised. He was always shy, and embarrassed when it came time for any big build-up of goodbys. They knew he had maybe seized upon this way to get out of saying any at all. But Rachel could only take a chance on it, and bake him a birthday cake ahead of its time, in hopes he would come home, this last night he could.

When the cake was frosted, she made for Ben the creation she had invented. Summer had turned hot early this year, and as they neared the end of June the swampy sedge pockets along the Dancing Bird were green-scummed and still. This was the kind of summer that made a good firefly year. Some years they saw hardly any, but this time they were all along the creek, all through the trees, by the middle of June. And the ground cherries—the other thing she needed—were ready early, too. These were tiny plants that hid under the deep grass; they bore papery little lanterns the size of a strawberry, each with two small yellow berries inside. Experimenting, Rachel found she could get the twin berries out of the little lanterns and put a firefly in each, instead.

So she made a firefly tree—and if there had ever been one in the world before, she hadn't heard of it. She cut a dried-out smoke bush, a skeleton of silvery twigs, about two and a half feet tall, and tied the ground-cherry lanterns all over it, dozens of them— though they looked like hundreds before she was through. After that she had to wait for dusk, when the fireflies came out. Half the time she worried for fear Ben wouldn't come home, and the rest of the

time for fear he would come early, before she was
ready. If he came too soon she would have to wake
him up to show his cake to him; he always went
sound to sleep, as soon as he had eaten.

As soon as the first fireflies rose into the twilight
she began lighting the firefly tree. On and off went
the little lanterns, more and more of them lighting
as she got fireflies into them, until by full dark the
whole firefly tree was alive, working all the time. It
showed up well; for, though they were about at the
end of the current Kiowa Moon, they lighted no
candles, preferring to leave the shutters open for air.
Rachel stuck the contraption in the middle of the
birthday cake, and waited for Ben to come and see.

She sat up for a long time, in the dark beside the
firefly tree; until finally she put her head on her
arms and went to sleep.

It was close to midnight when Ben got home. The
ringing of his spurs waked her. She raised her head
as he came clumping in, and heard his fingers slap
his holster before he knew who was there, in the
dark.

"I made you a cake," she said stupidly. "It's
right here."

"Seems like some kind of a tumbleweed, or something, has grown up out of it," he said, fumbling in
the dark. "My God, am I as late as that?"

She started to say, "It's supposed to—" Then she
realized that the firefly tree was dark.

"There's a lightning bug climbing on it," Ben
said. One little lantern had gleamed weakly, once,
and then quit. She shook the tree, but nothing happened; the fireflies wouldn't light any more. Maybe
they were dead.

29

She tried to tell him how the firefly tree had been meant to work, and had worked, before she went to sleep. She wanted to make him see how pretty it had been, with the little lanterns lighting up all over it, on and off, on and off. But in a minute she knew it didn't sound like anything, just told in words. And she began to cry.

He took her in his arms, tangled his fingers in her hair, and let her cry against his chest. He said, "I believe that was the very nicest thing I ever knew anybody to do."

She realized then that she was actually close in his arms, there in the dim dark, and she forgot about the firefly tree; but she still pretended to cry a little, for a while more, so that he would keep on holding her. She thought, *He knows I'm not his sister. Shall I tell him now? Shall I tell him I know it, too?*

"Well, anyway," he finally said. "we can eat the cake."

They took it out on the stoop, in the faint light of the waning moon. He sat with his back against the house, and when Rachel had cut the cake she sat close by him, leaning against his shoulder, while they ate. Before they were through, they ate it all.

They talked about how dry it was. Ben had been up at the source of the Dancing Bird, and it was no more than a seep; though in the spring it was a little waterfall nearly two feet high, and they called it The Falls. Rachel admitted to Ben that whenever she was at the head of the creek she always looked for the bird Papa had seen there that had given the stream its name. Ben laughed a little, but as much at himself as her. He said, "I always do, too."

"Papa was chasing Pawnees," she said, knowing this was wrong. She had found she could always get him to tell her the old stories she liked by pretending she didn't have the facts right.

Old Zack had been chasing a Comanche raiding party, in the early days of the War; it was that everlasting raiding and chasing that had kept snatching him back every time he set out to enlist. This time the chase had led them a long way through the dry, until finally their loose horses had lit out, thirst-blind and undrivable. And Zack himself had left the trail to recover them. They had smelled the live water, running freshly in the heat, a dozen miles away.

Downstream, the little creek disappeared in the sands; only four miles of it ran all year round. Zack had followed upcurrent to where the water came out from under a limestone ledge. And there on the flat rock just above the water was dancing the strangest bird, some kind of a crane. Zack knew sand-hill cranes, and whooping cranes, and every

kind of shidepoke, whether it lived in Texas or just
passed through; but this was none of them. It was
bigger than a whooper, nearly five feet tall; blue
and white, with yellow legs and a red beak. Nobody
had ever heard of any such a thing. But there it was,
reflected in the water as it bobbed and wheeled and
pirouetted with half-spread wings, the way sand-
hill cranes like to do, though only around their
mates.

Papa sat neck-deep in the cool water under the
ledge and watched the dance, and the bird seemed
not to mind him. And as he sat there the notion
came to him, he used to say, that this was no natural bird, but a spirit bird, sent to him for a sign. The
Indians would have called it that. Papa told that
part as if he didn't mean for you to believe it—and
yet as if he did more than half believe it, himself.

Or maybe he didn't, Ben thought now, as a possibility occurred to him that had never come to his
mind before. *Might well be that Papa made all that up,
to kind of sugarcoat this last, farthest move, into the very
shadow of the Kiowas. . . . So maybe there never was a bird
that danced. Just only a fairy story. . . .*

"I sure miss Papa," he told Rachel. "He's four
years gone; and yet, this year, I miss him more than
I ever did before. We needed him, Sis. We needed
him bad."

In some ways he sounded weary, and about a
hundred years older than he was. But there was
something else in the way he spoke that reminded
her of a little boy. *Now?* she wondered. *Should I tell
him now? "Sis." He knows I'm not that to him. He pre-
tends it to please Mama. Because he thinks I believe it. Is
this the time to tell him?*

She was afraid. She could not remember ever having been so much afraid in her life. Ben was naturally good-natured, when not harassed, or overworked too much. Maybe he hadn't minded being so nice to her as he had always been, so long as the pretense that they were brother and sister held up. But maybe he wouldn't like to think of her in any other way; maybe he wouldn't have any use for her at all. There never seemed to be a right or natural time to tell him. Nothing they talked about ever led into it any way. She couldn't seem to find a way to tell him without it sounded far-fetched, and crude, and kind of out of a clear sky. Like a rock plunked into the pancake batter, all unexpected out of no place.

She asked him where Witch River was, where Papa had died, and why nobody outside the family ever seemed to have heard of it. It was a reached-for question, to keep him out here on the stoop a little longer. Any time, now, he might yawn and go to bed.

He explained—and this was new to her—that Witch River wasn't the right name of anything. It only ran in the spring, or during hard rains. Just one of the innumerable runoff channels that gullied the prairies everwhere. Few drivers logged it, because they crossed it when it was dry. Those who had trouble with it, during the spring melt, called it the Death Crossing, or Deadman's Creek, or the Ghost Fork, since Old Zack died there. Only the Zacharys called it Witch River, after a stock joke Papa had used, just before he started his herd into the angry water.

Old hands were always sending some greenie up

to ask the boss what river they had come to.

"Witch River," Old Zack would say.

"Why, this one, right here."

"That's right," Zack would answer, sending the boy back bewildered. If the jokers in the swing could get the boy to say he guessed it must be the Wright, they were satisfied. From there on the kid couldn't head his horse into any stream, without somebody asking him if he was sure it was the right river.

To Ben it seemed fitting that the river in which his father died should be named after this country joke. He believed Old Zack would have chosen to go to his death with any kind of makeshift, rather than with no joke at all.

Now Ben told her about the day his father had died. The family knew, of course, that Papa had been drowned, while crossing cattle, but Rachel had never known Ben to feel like talking about it in any detail before.

Zack had reached Witch River late in the day, but he had ordered a crossing anyway, though it would run on into the dusk, and maybe the dark. They put the herd through in bunches of about five hundred, going into the water where the banks were low. The current was running pretty hard, but they had enough river-wise hands to press hard against the leaders, lest they yield and be turned. Three bunches crossed all right. But as they put the fourth into the water the light was failing, and maybe the horses were tiring, for this time the leaders turned, and were swept downstream with the current. The wild Texican cattle would do that, sometimes, in spite of all hell and the best men in Texas.

The cows were carried downstream into a deeper, narrower channel, under the nigh bank, where the faster water got hold of them. Here the south bank was high and bluff, and even undercut; there was no way to turn back. The riders who fought against the sweep-away found themselves either too far across, or caught in the mix of the turned cattle—a mortally dangerous place to be.

Ben himself was in the broad shallows on the far side. The lead cattle, with thrashing hundreds behind them, rushed past and got below him in the first moments, swimming with the fast current. Old Zack—Papa, to Ben—was famous for his crossings. No disaster was in his record such as caught him this time, all in a moment. Ben was running his horse at a stumble through the shallows, trying to get downstream of the leaders. So he was well placed to see what Papa did then.

Straight off the bluff came Zack's rocketing horse, winging far out over the channel as it plunged to deep water. How far below was the river? To Ben the bluff looked sky high—crowding fifty feet, maybe. But this sounded like such a stretch that he always afterward called it "worse than thirty." Not a record jump, but one hell of a piece of cow-handling. Zack sounded the rebel long yell all the way down. An explosion of water went up as the horse hit just ahead of the leaders—and they turned.

As Papa came up he was trailing free from the saddle horn, on the downstream side of his horse—you can be swept under your animal, into the meat-chopping hoofs, from the upstream side. Papa's horse sunk its hindquarters, treading for bottom, and found it. Man and horse surged up onto sound footing, and all the hardest part was behind. . . .

Once Papa had said, "All accidents are freak accidents. All dangers are hidden dangers, by the very meaning of the word. Look out for the Indian sharpshooter where there's no cover to hide him. Watch out for the badger hole, far from where any badger should be. A man can ready himself for anything on earth, if he knows it's there."

So now the unforeseeable struck from under the fast water. As Zack's saddle horn came streaming up, some thing sodden whirled to the surface, and shawled itself over the nose of his horse. The horse reared and went over backward, and the current rolled over horse and man. They did not reappear.

Ben sent the herd on, and stayed to search Witch River. The stream emptied like a bucket in a day or two, and Ben found his father's horse, along with some drowned cattle, in a mess of drift. And with the horse was a drowned wolf. Now, how many drowned wolves have ever been seen? Ben had never heard tell of one in his life. Those varmints refuse to be drowned; too strong, too tough, too wary. Yet this one had come a long way to surface right there, at the nose of Zack's horse, in that one split second when Zack's life could be ended by it.

Though Ben rode downstream a long way, and later others rode, Zack's body was never found.

Zack had been around forty-five when he died, but full of drive, and a don't-give-a-damn quality, much like Cassius. So long as he lived, Ben would never forget that soaring leap with its ringing rebel yell, the spraddling horse against the sky above him, the incredibly tall sheet of water that went up

as horse and rider hit, turning the cattle. He remembered it all, as if it had been last night. He had
never been able to get used to the idea that a man
so much alive as Zack could just suddenly be out of
the world, completely and forever.

"Now the horses he rode are old," Ben said slowly, wonderingly, "and his bones are sand in the
sea."

They were silent. The fireflies that had failed
Rachel were thick and bright, stirrup-deep, all
along the Dancing Bird. Rachel reached for Ben's
hand, and held it hard between both her own.

"I miss him still," Ben said. "He was all I ever
knew to turn to, when I didn't know what to do. I
need him, so many times. . . . Rachel, Rachel honey, I never needed him any more than I do this
year."

*Now? Shall I tell him now? Maybe I could become what
he needs, instead.* But still she didn't know how to
speak.

"He would have known what to do here," Ben
said. "Papa knew how to face anything down."

"No," Rachel said. "If you'll think back, you'll
remember things he turned his back on, trying to
pretend they weren't there. You'll even remember
things he never faced, but gave ground to, and drew
away."

Now how does she know that? He was almost frightened, for a moment. *How much does she know, and understand, that we think she's never suspected?* He decided
to ignore it.

"He was a good man," Ben said, without change
of mood. "The best man ever forked a horse, I
guess. There'll never be another like him."

Her whisper was intense, rebellious. "That isn't true!"

"What?"

"You're a better man than Papa ever thought of being," she told him.

"Rachel! Me?"

"You're steadier, and you hold on harder. You stick to your knittin', where Papa was always getting switched off. Papa could no more stay with what he was doing when the guns and saddles came out than a yearling hound. You're the one people can tie to, Ben! And count on always."

"I—but—why, Rachel—" he was dumbfounded. "But, you loved Papa—I know you did. Because—"

"I worshiped him. I would never have known he wasn't the best man in the world, if I hadn't known you. But you're the best man."

He was silenced; and she didn't know whether he was touched, or only astonished, and shocked by her heresy.

Presently he leaned over, and gently kissed her hair. He said softly, "I'm right glad you think that, anyway."

Now? Is this the time?

But he stood up, and with an easy pull of one hand lifted her to her feet. He said, "Now, you take care of everybody, while I'm gone."

And it was time to get some sleep.

30

After Ben was gone, the summer ran on; and it was turning into one of the driest they had known since they had been on the Dancing Bird. The grass cured on the stem before it was halfway up, and the range, heavily overstocked the year before, was overgrazed and haunted by dust devils, wherever the livestock used. Trail men who drive late would bust, as most had busted, the last three years in a row.

This year the things that had made Rachel's childhood happy didn't seem to interest her any more.

Other years she had trapped pets, often collecting a regular zoo of them. Once she had raised an elf owl, no bigger than a sparrow when it was full-grown. Another time she had spoon-fed a nest of ravens until they flew. For several years one or another of them had come back, from time to time, to squawk for handouts around the stoop, but fewer appeared each year, until no more came home. She

had tamed any number of deer mice, and jumping
mice. These were magical little creatures, with delicate oversized ears that the sun shone through. If
one of them tried to hide in the grass, with no dark
place to crawl into, all you could see of it was those
sun-shot ears, like two glowing pink flower petals,
all alone. Once there had been a kangaroo rat that
Ben had caught for her somewhere in the dry, a
bouncy, tassel-tailed bit of fluff with no fear of people whatever.

Most exciting, and at the same time most disap-
pointing, had been a coyote pup. Cash had dug it
out for her before its eyes were open, and until it
was nearly grown it had seemed to be turning into
a dog. But it had ended by snapping at her whenever she touched it, and had finally run away. A few
times afterward she had seen it sitting on a hum-
mock to watch her from a long way off, but it had
never come home again, or answered her call.

But this year what she remembered best was how
much work pets make. Only children had much
fun, she guessed, and she wasn't a child any more.
Hadn't been for a long time. She dug up extra tasks
for herself, which in other years she had delayed as
long as she could. She boiled down antelope blood
to a stickum, and made a couple of quarts of percussion caps. She set up the big outside kettles, to
begin the annual soap boiling and candle making.

She was trying to forget another task that she
knew she must someday undertake. No one had assigned it to her; indeed, she would be prevented if
she were found out. Her restless industry was an
attempt at escape, for she dreaded this thing, and
even saw reason for physical fear. But she could not

drive it from the back of her mind. The five hands who were always loafing at home, a different combination every day, were a help in putting off the job she feared. They played poker endlessly, on a blanket laid in the dust by the creek, shifting position with the shade; some of them followed her with their eyes whenever she was in sight. These, with either Cash or Andy always around, gave her an excuse for believing she could not slip away. But her time was running out. July passed, and they were into August; she knew Ben might already be on his way home.

Then the grasshoppers came.

When the first great cloud of them appeared in the north, Rachel didn't know what they were. They had heard of northern Texas being devastated by them in '68, but they had not amounted to anything on the San Saba. At first she mistook the strange low darkness on the horizon for a dust storm, and she watched for twisters. The billions of grasshoppers rolled swiftly across the grassland, and only shreds and fibers were left where they touched. The cottonwoods along the Dancing Bird turned to skeletons, with only chewed tags and remnants of leaves left on the branches. The day they were thickest they made it impossible to walk outside. They covered you, and got down your neck, and tangled their spiny legs in your hair. You could not set foot to the ground without crushing them, or lay a hand upon anything without snatching it back from a bristly, kicking handful of them.

It was the grasshoppers that gave Rachel a chance to get away. When they had passed, the cicadas, which everybody called locusts, resumed

their metallic shrilling in the bare cottonwoods—
what on earth did they find to eat? But the cattle
were left standing in helpless bunches upon the
stripped land; and the prairie moaned night and
day with their bawling. Cash worked as though
possessed.

He sent riders in seven directions, hunting for
belts and pockets of grass the grasshoppers might
have missed. When these were found, the cows had
to be moved to them, with Jake Rountree on hand
to see that the Rawlins cattle got an even break.

Zeb Rawlins himself was in Fort Worth, seeking
a deal with somebody to put together a corrida,
with which he wanted Jude to drive a herd of
stockers to Wichita with the first cool weather. Jude
was the drawback, there; Zeb was not having an
easy time finding the men he had to have. But if
word went down to him that he was coming out on
the short end at home, he might be able to flood the
Dancing Bird with gun-toting riders, and take over
the whole range.

Cash still came in at night, or sent Andy, with
three or four of their crack shots, but only a couple
of hands were left home to sleep away the days.
They had almost, but perhaps not quite, come into
the first days of their next Kiowa Moon.

"One day's work more," Cash kept saying, "and
we'll have done what we could." But at night there
would again be just one day's work more, still
ahead.

No excuse was left. Rachel could get away now,
and must, if she was ever going to. Early one morning, when the locusts were already grinding away in
the heat of sun-up, Rachel saddled a fast pony, and
got away unnoticed.

She pointed downstream, and to the east, toward the Rawlinses.

She had told herself she was going there to try to make peace with Hagar. The men were feisty enough, but there was a bare chance that they would draw back from a war if Hagar could be made friendly again. Her chance of getting through to Hagar was obviously not much, but if there was any chance at all she could not forgive herself, ever, if she did not take it.

Or so she had told herself, and told herself again as she rode. Something else in the back of her mind was still unrecognizable in shadows; she would not look at it, or let it out into the light. So well had she suppressed it that she could not have named what it was, even if she had dared to try.

Half a dozen horses shuffled themselves in he Rawlins saddle corral, restless in the morning sun. They watched her approach, and whinnied at her pony, so that she was announced from a long way off. Nothing else stirred around the Rawlins place; the cabin was closed up, tight-shuttered against the morning heat, and the chimney was smokeless. Except for the corralled horses, the place might have been deserted for a long time.

Rachel did not tie. When she had dismounted she led her pony to the door, keeping hold of him, for she was frightened now, more so with every step that she advanced. At the door she raised her knuckles to rap, but still hesitated, all but unable to face the ordeal she had laid out for herself. What, after all, could she possibly say?

She never knocked. The door was suddenly snatched open in front of her, and Hagar was standing there, glaring at her with a total hostility. The

sunlight was pitiless upon the deep lines and rough-
nesses of her face, and it was a death's-head face.

31

Rachel tried to speak, and could not. She was
seeing devil-lights come up behind Hagar's eyes,
the same dreadful glow she had seen upon that awful night in this same house when they had heard
the story of Hagar's captivity. She wanted to turn,
vault onto her horse, and get away, but not a muscle would move.

"You," Hagar said. The word was voiceless, a
rasping of breath in her throat. She had not seemed
to breathe at all, at first, but now she was breathing
hard, almost gasping for air. "You," she repeated.
"You dare to come here?"

"I—only—" Rachel could not remember a word
that she had ever thought of to say.

"You come here," Hagar said. "To this house.
You come and stand afore me." She had regained
her voice, though it shook, and her words seemed to
choke her. "What blasphemy can there be, you
would draw back from?"

Looking into the terrible eyes, Rachel was certain Hagar was insane. Yet she still stood there.

"Squaw!" Hagar accused her. "Ki'way squaw! Yet you stand here afore me!" Her voice still shook but rose strongly now. "Red nigger as ever was, yet you dare face up to me? For now we know all. Your own brother put knife to my little girl at No Hope— her dear pretty hair has been seen on his shield! Yes, and he stopped by your place, as he rode to that butchery, didn't he? Boasted to you of what he would do—and from you rode straight to the massacre! And his knife—your own brother's knife —it was at work when they cut apart her darling body—past all decent laying out of it—leaving no part with another—"

Overrun by Hagar's storm of words, Rachel was in bewilderment. Hagar had seemed to accuse Ben, or Andy—perhaps Cash, even, forgetting in her madness that Cash had been far away. But Hagar's raving still poured on.

"Oh, I know you now! Dear God in heaven, how I know you! For I know the work of red-nigger squaws, when they be nigh a massacre, and get a chance at the bodies. Had you been longside your brother, you would have bloodied your hands like his own. But not again! All Texas knows the truth now, save those too blind to see. You will be struck from the face of this earth. You, and all your kin, and all who give you help or feed you—you'll be hunted and driven—"

She lost her breath in a hard fit of coughing. Yet through it she managed to force out, "Yet now— you stand afore—me—" Spittle foamed and dribbled at the corners of Hagar's mouth, and it was flecked with blood. She turned blindly from the door, went to her knees as her crippled feet betrayed her, and clawed herself up again. "Rifle," she croaked, as if someone were standing there to hand it to her. "M' rifle—gi' me m' rifle—"

The spell broke, and Rachel could leave there. Perhaps she could have moved before, had not some unaccountable inner compulsion held her standing rigid to hear Hagar out. She had a scared moment in which her pony reared and spun away from her, spooked by her billowing skirt as she whirled. The leather burned through her fingers, and she all but lost him. She made cast after cast of the split-rein, while the pony ran backward from her, and she stumbled over her skirt, unable to quiet him. But she got the rein over his neck at last, and a foot in the stirrup; she was no better than lying across the saddle, but with him, as he lit out.

No bullet came. In the Rawlins cabin, Georgia had finally got to her mother, from wherever she had been, and caught Hagar as she stumbled toward the door. Hagar had got down a heavy rifle musket, and was fumbling to seat its coiled Maynard primer.

"Ma! You can't!" Georgia threw arms around her.

Hagar fought her daughter with an unnatural strength. Georgia's lip split as an elbow struck her mouth, and a rib cracked as the musket butt drove into her body. Yet she held on; and in a matter of moments Hagar's cough came back, and the strength went out of her. She lost her grip on the musket, and went to her knees. Georgia picked her up, and carried her to her bed.

32

When Rachel could gain her seat, her knee over the
horn, she bent low on the pony's neck, letting him
bolt; and only then looked back. Hagar had not reappeared in the open door. But still she urged the
pony flat out and belly to the ground, winging over
gullies, sailing high over brush they could more
quickly have swerved to pass, wanting only more
space behind her.

By the time she pulled up, the pony was shaking
as badly as she was, and all the wind was beaten
out of both of them by the headlong run. It took her
a while to recover herself sufficiently to take a look
at what had happened. None of it made much sense
at first. The wildness of Hagar's accusations had
the effect of disconnecting all she said from reality,
blurring what basic meaning had been in it. Rachel
had the impression that Hagar had accused her of
taking part in the No Hope massacre.

Going back over it, taking apart what Hagar had

said, and looking at each piece of it alone, she found that the meanings became more clear. Hagar had not said Rachel was at No Hope; her reference had been to what could be expected of squaws, if they were present at a slaying. And the accusation of her brother—Hagar had not meant any of the Zacharys. Nor had she meant Seth, who was a savage, but not a red savage. The mad woman had been repeating some part of Abe Kelsey's babblings. She had called Rachel a Kiowa Squaw, whose brother had ridden with Seth.

Strangely, she felt no real surprise. She could not remember that the possibility had ever come to the surface of her mind; certainly she had never conciously considered it. Yet some part of awareness must have been there, someplace. She found herself calm in the face of this answer; it was almost as though she had felt relief, that the long mystery and foreboding were over. *I think, now, that I already knew it. I think I must have known it for a long time.*

She unsaddled methodically and put away her saddle and bridle. With a corncob she cuffed up the wet back of her pony, so that it would dry without chilling. She walked into the house unexcited and unhurried; yet Matthilda knew what had happened in the first moment that she saw her.

This time Matthilda did not panic. She had known for quite a while that her struggle to stand off the inevitable was a hopeless one. She said, "You've been to the Rawlinses'."

Rachel nodded. "The bones are out of the tree." It was an expression they had brought with them from the San Saba, where the Indians had formerly made tree burials; sometimes riders still came upon skeletons in tattered wrappings, high above the ground among the branches.

Neither Cash nor Andy was home that day. More than either Ben or Andy, Cassius followed the crash-on, bust-'em-down, keep-em-hustled tactics their father had brought out of the Big Thicket; and now he was trying to complete the redistribution of the herds in an all-out rush, before the Kiowa Moon came full. The two cow-hands supposed to be garrisoning the home layout were out looking for Rachel—poor trackers, obviously, searching where she had not been.

So Rachel and Matthilda were alone, and now they said what little had to be said about these bones, newly fallen from the tree.

"I should have told you the whole thing straight off, I guess," Matthilda admitted.

"Is this all of it, this time?"

"Yes; this is all of it." She told Rachel now how Papa, or Old Zack, as everyone called him, had led a band of volunteers in pursuit of a party of Kiowa raiders, who had cleaned out a whole string of isolated settlers, apparently. This was back before the War, in '57, but the Kiowas were always bad ones, even then. The raiders had captive children with them, seven or eight, at first; Papa had sworn he would follow them as long as horses made tracks. The Indians never did seem to learn how tenaciously a man like Papa could hold on. He chased them all the way to their village, far up the Salt Fork of the Brazos, and whipped their warriors in a holding action they tried. He was less than an hour behind them, at one point, as the village got away.

That was when he found her. Traveling villages

carried all their stuff—children, old folks, everything —on drag litters, or travois, which were poles dragged behind a horse, with a buffalo-hide hammock slung between. And there between the travois tracks, sat a white baby, less than one year old—

"How do you know I was?" Rachel asked coolly.

"Why, by your teeth, of course. Seemed you had bounced out of a drag litter, all unnoticed—"

"Indians have teeth. What made you think I was a white girl?"

"It was perfectly obvious. It always has been. It was only long after, when Abe Kelsey got mad at Papa, he started that other outlandish story."

Matthilda stated it as a simple fact, because that was what it was to her, and always had been; for she had wanted it that way. "Papa carried you more than two hundred miles in his arms," she said now. "Took him two weeks to get you home. How many wild cows he roped and milked to feed you, we'll never know. But Papa didn't mind. He loved you the minute he saw you. And always after. Even more than as if—"

"If I was a captive child, why did nobody ever find out who I was?"

"Maybe we didn't try too hard—though we did do what we thought we ought to. But you were so dear, and sweet, and we wanted you so—"

"It doesn't matter any more," Rachel said.

"Of course not. I don't know what difference it would make even if that foolish story had been true. There's lots of Indian blood, in some of the very finest southern families. Sam Houston himself married a Cherokee girl. And General Pickett, who led the brave charge at Gettysburg—he was married to

an Oto woman—a north-west kind of Indian. I
don't know how people get so upset."

Having seen Hagar, Rachel knew how. But she
said again, "It doesn't matter."

Mama kissed her, and praised her for being so
sensible. "You and I aren't going to be here, anyway, come winter. We have money, now; it's time
to see to your education. We'll visit a while in New
Orleans, first. After that, maybe Charleston; maybe
Richmond . . ."

Always ready to run again, Rachel thought, *every time
the truth about me catches up.* She said, "Could you ever
really bring yourself to leave Ben, and Cash, and
Andy?"

For a fraction of a moment, then, the glint of a
tear threatened, but Matthilda forced it back. She
was ready with this answer, too. She had often controlled them by letting them see she was hurt; but
she had expressed self-pity so seldom that she could
use it now, to confuse the trail.

"We must be crazy people," she said, "to live in
a leaky mud hut, at the utter end of desolation, and
put our money down a hole. The boys find their
work here; emptiness has some strange pull, for
men on horses. But it's a dreadful thing to be a
woman, out on the prairie. A woman on the prairie
is an unwanted thing. Nothing but a burden and a
tie-down, keeping the ones she loves from doing
what they want to do. Until they can't stand it any
more, and run away. Cassius will be gone soon, and
Andy too. And poor Ben—he'll feel he must stay by
us, drawing into himself, and growing old too
soon. . . ."

Rachel saw now how drawn Matthilda looked,

how terribly tired. She made Matthilda lie down, and she sang the herd lullaby, about the pore cowboy, shot five times right through his dang chest, until Matthilda smiled and dozed. Then she slipped away.

Maybe they got too much practice in facing up to the worst, out there. Rachel never doubted for a moment that she was of Kiowa blood. Too many things bore it out besides the conviction Abe Kelsey's statement had borne for so many. She remembered how Matthilda had always kept at her to wear a sunbonnet and cotton gloves when she went outdoors in the summer heat. How all the lemons they ever got hold of had been wasted trying to make creams to keep her bleached. How she never had been allowed to wear moccasins with beads, or any kind of an Indian-looking thing . . .

The Kiowas had been stealing Spanish-Mexican women, and Texican women, for somewhere upwards of half a century, and raising stolen white children as their own. Many Kiowas had the same Spanish kind of olive skin as she had—maybe lighter than her own would be, if she were out in the weather as much. And plenty of them had wavy chestnut hair, far less Indian than her own, which was straight black. Lost Bird had auburn hair; and his eyes—

She felt her stomach try to turn over as she remembered Lost Bird's eyes. Now she took down the little mirror that hung above the wash bench, and studied her own eyes. They had always looked the color of the mud in the bottom of a tadpole puddle, to her. But this time she took the mirror to the darkest corner, and saw that her eyes were nearly

black. Then she stood sideways at a window and
watched her eyes turn green. And when finally she
faced toward the bright sky she saw her eyes go
paler than a peeled grape; doubtless they would
flash like pale steel, like the knife in Lost Bird's
eyes, out in the full sun. *Is that why he looked familiar,
when I never saw him before?* She could find no other
resemblance. But she could hear Hagar saying,
"Your brother stopped by, on his way to No Hope. . . ."

She went to the slop bucket, and was sick. But
when she had drunk a pint of cold water, and
washed her face, she knew what she had to do; at
once, tonight, before Ben got home. If only Cash
and Andy would stay out one night more . . .

Nightfall did not bring them home.

She located a sheath knife, and a belt that would
carry it, and punched holes in the belt so that she
could strap it on. It was all she was going to take
with her. She had no destination, and no plan, except to get away; to the west likely, and try for the
cap rock breaks. Her brothers were trackers, all of
them, but so was she, enough of one to know how to
break her trail.

That night as she and Matthilda ate supper
alone, she could not help thinking that she was eating in this house for the last time, and a lump hurt
in her throat, so that she could hardly swallow her
food. But Matthilda was quiet too, so that Rachel
did not have to talk; and the failing light helped her
not to give herself away. They went to bed, and
Rachel lay listening for Matthilda's breathing to
become regular, so that she could creep out of the
house.

But that was the night the travails of Matthilda's life caught up with her. Something closed in, and something bore down, and something gave way.

33

Matthilda slept lightly, nervously. The twilight seemed to hold on forever, and when at last it was gone the moon rose earlier, and shone more brightly through the skeleton cottonwoods, than they had expected of it, so soon. Four times before midnight Rachel stole out of the bedroom, and each time Matthilda came broad awake.

"Rachel—you up—"

"Drink of water. It's hot tonight."

Then Matthilda would like some water too, so that she was fully waked up again. And the patient waiting began all over again.

An hour after midnight Matthilda began to moan. Rachel thought her to be having a nightmare, and tried to get out of the room. But Matthilda's voice sounded, faint but wide awake, through the warm dark. "I don't feel very good." It was almost a whimper. "I have the awfullest pain. . . ."

The pain seemed to be right in her middle, so they decided it was indigestion. Rachel closed the shutters, and saw to it that the loopholes were all plugged, so that she could build a fire. They had drawn the coals at dusk, so she had to start anew, setting tinder to burning with a flash of powder from the snaphaunce firelighter. She set a kettle on, but lighted no candles, and fumbled by memory for the herbs she supposed she should put together, verifying them close to the fire. Finally she made a brew, believed to be good for indigestion, out of peppergrass, ginger, and some pinches of stuff such as mandrake root.

This concoction, brought scalding hot, must surely have been the worst thing she could have dished up, for it induced hard vomiting. A little later, before her breath was entirely recovered, Matthilda gave a long, groaning cry of pain, and went unconscious.

The next three hours went to make up the longest night Rachel had ever lived in her life. Matthilda regained consciousness in half an hour, but moaned continuously until daylight. She tried to lie quiet, but could not; the sounds were wrung out of her against her will. Finally she took to putting words to the moans, in an effort to get control. "Oh, mercy, mercy . . . Oh, mercy, me . . . Oh, dear, oh dear me, oh deary, deary me . . . Oh, mercy, mercy . . ." On and on forever, without end. Sometimes she asked for water, but if she swallowed a mouthful she could not keep it down.

When Cash and Andy rode in together, in the first dawn, Rachel knew she had never been so glad to see anybody before. Matthilda tried to smile at them. "Something I ate," she whispered. They felt her forehead for fever, but she was wet with sweat. A little later she seemed to doze, out of sheer exhaustion; or perhaps she lost consciousness again, for her breathing sounded strange.

"Seems like a busted blood vessel," Andy thought. "Somewhere in her chest."

"You don't know what it is any better than I do," Cash set him back. "All I know, it don't look like any natural kind of bellyache, to me. I've got to get help."

Rachel was appalled. "All the way to—where? The Rountrees'? You won't be back before tomorrow night!"

"I'll fetch Georgia Rawlins."

"They wouldn't let her come here if the world was falling down!"

"She'll come."

Matthilda rested more easily after the sun came up. Her breathing became more natural, and she slept almost peacefully through the middle of the day.

Cash brought Georgia late in the afternoon. They came in at the gallop on beat-out horses—not windbroke, but spent to the last notch that they could be without permanent damage. They would not work again in a month. Cash let Georgia down at the stoop, threw her saddle on the ground, and turned loose her horse. "Got to look around a minute!" he shouted, and rode to the corral to get a fresh pony.

"What's the matter with him?" Andy asked the outdoors, afraid to speak to Georgia.

"He's been fretty the last four miles," Georgia

told them. "Something spooked him. Didn't say what it was. Let's see your mother."

Matthilda had gone worse again, seemingly half conscious but unable to recognize Georgia, and breathing with great labor. Georgia asked when it had begun, and looked overpowered. "This is bad. She's bust a blood vessel."

"I told you," said Andy.

"Shut up and fetch my saddle bags. . . . We've got to quieten her what we can. Keep her warm. Wish we could get dry sheets around her. But I don't dast mess with her. I sure hope I'm mighty wrong. She looks a whole lot like a goner."

She pounded some dried leaves and pieces of root into a powder, and made a tea of it. They got about a half a cupful into Matthilda; it was the first liquid she had kept down so far. "Make her sleep, some, maybe. Won't do no other good, though."

Rachel tried to find out how Georgia had got away from her mother.

"Ma? Never asked her. Just lit out."

"Don't she know you're gone?"

"Bound to. Saw me ride off with Cash, I reckon."

"But what will you tell her when you go back?"

"Hell, Rachel, how do I know? Maybe I'll tell her I'm carryin' by him. Whatever seems needful."

"She'll kill you!"

"Not me. Oh, she's game to pull a trigger, all right! But me, I'm all the girl she's got left."

That was the nearest they came to talking about Rachel's bad time with Hagar. Listening, they became aware that Matthilda's breathing was already quieter. Rachel was impressed and Georgia explained that it seemed like there had been a power of sick folks around, wherever she was. But she did not look confident; perhaps she was not entirely sure she had not killed Matthilda, with her witch-woman herbs.

Now Andy roused them up, speaking in a low tone, but urgently. "Stand over by the windows. No —one to each side. Get ready to bar them up. Not yet!"

They could hear the hoofs of Cash's horse coming in, walking quietly. Standing by the windows, but out of line, they could not see Cash, but they knew he had given Andy some kind of signal.

"We got trouble," Andy told them. "But don't touch the shutters! We can't let on we know it. Lest they never let Cash get here."

He pulled a loophole plug from the door, and stood behind it, ready to swing it open. The sound of the walking hoofs came on, and on. How could hoofs so near approach for so long, yet never seem to get here? Suddenly Andy swung the door wide, and Cassius, bent low over the horn, jumped his horse across the stoop and into the room. Andy slammed and barred the door behind him. "Now fort up," he shouted.

34

"I figure there's about a dozen of 'em," Cash said as he dismounted. His horse seemed enormous, in here, making the house and everything in it look smaller than they had ever seen it before; the wooden floor boomed under the hoofs. "Knock open a loophole in the west wall. Rachel—get one open in Mama's room. Georgia, pull the slide on the north lookout—better bust out the glass."

They posted themselves as he told them, each alone, one to each side. And after that there was silence in the house. Matthilda seemed to be sleeping peacefully. Half an hour passed, and the sun went down. The shuttered interior darkened, but a clear dry light remained outside; it would not dwindle enough to harm marksmanship for the next two hours.

Cassius was trying to listen. "Georgia, for God's sake, stop that damned clock!"

They had not heard the familiar ticking at all un-

til Georgia stopped the pendulum, and the little
painted ship on its painted sea rocked no more.
When the ticking had stopped it left an emptiness
that fairly rang in their ears.

"See there!" Andy spoke from the west loophole.
"One's riding in the creek bed. I can bead right on
his head!"

"I see him," Cash said.

"You want I should—"

"Let him come on."

Up over the cutbank of the Dancing Bird, square-
ly in front of the house, came a single Indian rider.
"Lost Bird," Cash said, so that they all could hear
it.

He came as he had come before, except that he
rode bareback, and with a war bridle, a single cord
tied on the lower jaw. He was without war paint,
and his shirt was on; a four-inch silver concho
shone in his hair. And this time they could see he
carried no weapon at all. It was a strange thing for
a Kiowa to present himself like that, entirely unarmed. But that was the worst thing about Kiowas;
they were always doing something original, un-
predictable, so you could never figure what kind of
way they were fixing to come at you.

"That gray he's riding is a famous racer," Cash
said with a peculiar detachment.

Lost Bird's right hand was raised in the peace
sign. He did not lower it as he pulled up five yards
out, directly in front of the door, and made his pony
stand like a rock.

Cash said something in Kiowa, and Lost Bird
began to speak. Andy had returned to his station.
Nobody was unglued from his loop to see Rachel

creep through the shadows to one of the front shutter loopholes.

She remembered the smooth, beautifully molded face, the small, pleasant-appearing smile, the dark-reddish glow in the thick braids. But his eyes were only dark slits now. Rachel felt the peculiar revulsion that she had felt before. Lost Bird was speaking slowly in Kiowa, a phrase at a time; and he matched his words with the conventional sign language of the prairies that they all knew. So this time she knew what he said.

"We many times take your people," he said, and though the sign language does not translate well in its literal meanings, the thought came through clearly; "You come, you want them, you buy. You pay us. We let you take them back. Many times. All friendly. All good."

Cash said something through the door in Kiowa, and Lost Bird acknowledged it with a brief grin. But he went on with the speech he had doubtless carefully prepared. "Long ago," Lost Bird's signs said, "you take a child of ours. You take my sister. We look for her very long. Now we find. Now we come. We want her back now. She is ours. We pay. You pay us, now we pay you. All friendly, all good. I give ten horses for my sister. You give me. I take home."

Cash spat out an angry Kiowa phrase.

"Tell what you want more. Price is good. But I give more," Lost Bird's hands said. "I do not leave this place without my sister. I have twenty-two men. You have two men, three women—one very old. No good."

Cassius raised his carbine to the loophole, aimed

steadily, and put a bullet close past Lost Bird's ear.
The blackpowder smell was plain in the room as he
reloaded. Outside, the gray war pony quivered, but
did not move its feet. Lost Bird was smiling, and the
smile expressed more contempt than he could have
shown in any other way. He believed he knew
whom he was dealing with, and how their minds
worked, and what Cassius, particularly, would do
and would not do.

"You shoot well," his hands said. "You do not
shoot to hit. You hit me, nobody in your house will
see the sun again. You know that. Now listen. I tell
you all this again." He started over with the same
prepared speech as before. "Few times, we take
your people. . . ."

Rachel startled Cash by speaking almost in his
ear. He didn't know how she got there, standing at
his elbow. "This is no good," she said.

"You get back where I put you!" he ordered her,
through his teeth. He was abruptly, bitterly angered, for her intrusion threatened a betrayal of all
their long efforts to shield her.

"There isn't going to be any fight," she said.
"Let me by. I understood what he said, this time."

"Never mind them damned Indian lies! You're
going to—"

"He's telling the truth. I've known all about it for
a long time. I'm going to end all this trouble now!"

"You'll not go out there, because I'll stop you,"
he said; but he was less sure of himself, thrown off
by her revelation.

"Maybe you can stop me. But they'll be in here,
while you have your hands full with me. Now let me
go."

He stared at her, bewildered by the flat, dead-sounding tone in which she threatened outlandish, unbelievable things. "Is everybody crazy but me?" he demanded. "By God, I know how to settle this!"

Out in the clear twilight, Lost Bird was patiently, slowly, going through his smooth, clear signs. His gruff Kiowa phrases came steadily to them, through the door. Cash raised his carbine again, and instantly fired. Lost Bird's head jerked violently with the impact of the bullet; he was dead as he fell. The whole back of his skull seemed to be gone as he lay face down in the dirt. The gray war pony shied, found itself free, and stampeded.

Cash had fired to kill, from cover and without warning, at a range from which failure was impossible to him; while Lost Bird had sat horse before him, unarmed, fully exposed under the peace sign. Any justification would have to be found in the necessity Cash had believed governed his decision. He never thereafter spoke one word in his own defense, or gave any sign of regret.

"Oh, Cash, Cash!" Rachel cried out. "They'll never draw back now! They'll fight till we're dead!"

"You can bet on it," Cassius said.

"They'll never let up, so long as—"

He cut in harshly. "Then there's no use you going out, is there? Now get back to your loop!"

35

For a few moments stillness held outside. The zinging of the locusts in the cottonwoods by the creek
had been silenced by the gunshots; and this made
the quiet unnatural, as if the whole prairie lay
stunned.

Before the locusts could begin again, the "Wa-
wa-wa-wah!" of a war cry sounded from the creek,
immediately followed by an uncountable chorus.
The creek bed seemed to be full of Kiowas, while
yet no Indian but the dead Lost Bird could be seen.
Two rifles slammed, down there; then a ragged vol-
ley. The windowpanes burst outside the battle shutters, and fell tinkling.

"Close your slide," Cash called to Georgia, who
stood at the back of the room, at the north lookout.
"Get down on the floor!"

Andy, at the end, complained, "I can't line up on
nothing from here!"

"Stay there anyway." Cash turned away from his

door loop, and leaned against the plastered sod wall, at rest. A buffalo slug broke through a shutter, and rattled, spent, across the floor. A little after that a bullet nicked a splinter out of the side of the door loop where Cash had stood, and lodged above the fireplace.

"They'll quit this, in a minute," Cash said.

He was right. The Kiowas were firing at the house in an expression of anger; they had no plan to fit what had happened. The guns in the creek bed fell silent, and Cash looked out again.

"Two-three of 'em have gone to popping up and down," Cash said, puzzling everybody. "Guess they want to see what we'll do."

"What *will* we do?" Andy asked him.

"Nothing," Cash said, but kept his carbine ready. He watched an Indian leap straight up to expose half of his painted body, then drop from sight again. Another tried it in a different place. Then a single white-streaked warrior sprang out of the creek bed, and stood in the open upon the bank. Cash fired, and the Kiowa came down in a heap. The lip of the bank crumbled, and the body began to slide over the edge. Cash fired again, and hit, he thought, before the body disappeared from view.

That was the end of that experiment. The Kiowas could not be heard withdrawing, but they could be expected to take council now. Ten minutes passed without event.

"This might be a good chance to eat," Cash said. "They're not liable to give us too many good ones, from here on in. Not for a while." He looked for the Kiowas to try a jump at them in about the last of the dusk. He believed they'd want to make use of

poor light, on account of he'd bothered them a little
bit, he thought. They had had him all figured out,
just how he would act, only he hadn't acted that
way. Still . . . all he could say for certain was that
no Kiowa was going to leave here yet, unless to
bring more. They would never leave the body of
Lost Bird lying out there in front, where it was.

Rachel accepted that the body out there was that
of her brother, or perhaps a half brother—incredibly of her own flesh and blood. Yet she felt
nothing toward him, or toward any of the Kiowas,
other than the bitter enmity you feel for half-hu-
mans who have come to destroy everything you
love.

Georgia helped her push furniture around, and
make a tent of blankets in front of the fireplace, so
that no gleam would show outside the ports. They
heated nothing but coffee. The boys had to stay on
watch, and wanted only cold meat and bread, such
as could be eaten with one hand. When each had
coffee and a sandwich, Rachel remembered grace.
Once, long ago, when Andy was too little to be still
when Papa bowed his head, she had said a stupid
thing in trying to quiet him, for she was little, too.
Her words came back to her now.

"Wait, Andy—Papa has to read his plate."

"What?"

"I'm going to say grace." The locusts were going
again, out in the limpid twilight, but her low words
came clearly through the quiet of the room. "Dear
Heavenly Father, we thank Thee for these vittles,
the—the gifts of—" She faltered. Remembering the
long ago had made her remember Ben, too, and
what this prayer had made her think when she was

half-grown. She had almost said, *these vittles, the gifts of Ben's hard work.* . . . She recovered herself. "The gifts of Thy love," she finished steadily. "Now guide us, and guard us, and keep us from evil . . ."

Cassius' horse began to paw again, making a thunderous noise on the wooden floor, so that the rest was lost. The horse was trying to fudge around toward the smell of water, in the barrel by the door. Rachel got him a bucket, unbridled, and fed him a loaf of bread; then put the bridle back on. The animal drowsed after that, well-practiced in going unsatisfied.

After that, Rachel chewed her bread and meat methodically. It seemed dry, and sticky in the throat, all but impossible to wash down. But—*No feed, no distance,* she was remembering; she made herself get through it all. The motions of feeding people brought a hard ache into her, sometimes in her middle and sometimes in her throat; too many memories went with these people, and this room. The uneasy quiet left time to think, which was the last thing she wanted to do; and she became more miserable the longer the silence held. If she had not worked in a daze, as if hit in the head, she might never have got through it at all.

They damped out the coffee fire, and folded the blankets, so that the chimney could help keep the place aired. Cash and Andy opened more loopholes, including two near the floor, at the ends of the front wall. These were intended to surprise hostiles who crawled along the foot of the wall, under the other gun ports. Cassius talked over with them how they must fight. He and Andy would defend the battle shutters because, though he did not

say so, these were an incomplete protection. No one
must fire from the same loop twice in a row. They
must put backs to the wall to load. When they
moved about, they must duck under or step over the
lines of fire radiating inward from every port. Each
must pocket the cartridges he would need. A lot of
their ammunition was out on the range with the
wagon, but Cash judged their supply would last the
night.

When they were as ready as they were going to
be, Rachel and Georgia looked at Matthilda again.
She slept so quietly now that they had to bend low
to hear her breath. They both felt her pulse. At first
Rachel could not find it at all.

"It's so weak," she whispered. "Just a cobweb."

Georgia didn't say anything. Something about
Matthilda's pulse bothered her more than its lack of
strength. Seemed more of a quiver, than a beat. But
she was unsure what this meant.

After that there was nothing to do but wait. The
last of the twilight was falling very fast. Andy said,
"Maybe they'll wait for the moon." Nobody answered.

Suddenly Georgia moved. She was sitting against
the dug-in back wall, and now she put her ear to it.
She tried to say something, but the words only
caught and whispered in her throat. On her next try
the words came louder than she meant, so that she
startled herself, and them all. "They're comin'!"

In another moment they heard the hoof-murmur
coming into the room through the earth of the hill
into which they were dug; and soon after they could
hear the horses outside, all around them.

"Well, I'll be a son of a buck," Cassius said, nonplused.

Rachel ran toward Matthilda's room; Georgia went to the north lookout slide.

"Leave that shut!" Cash said suddenly. "Rachel —plug the loops in there, and come here! Andy— block the ports at that end! I see this now!"

They obeyed him, closing the ports by knocking home wooden plugs, fitted long ago. Outside, the hoof-rumble rose and rose—an approach so unquiet that it must certainly have been meant to be heard.

"Damn fool that I am!" Cash blamed himself. Ought to have guessed the hostiles would try to come in here the quickest way. Only the door and the two windows overlooking the Dancing Bird offered openings big enough to admit a man. Except for gunports, the bedroom where Matthilda lay had only some slits near the roof, to give air. Neither these nor the north lookout were big enough to get in through. What Cash had imagined was a crawling, swarming attack—Indians along the walls where the guns could not reach, Indians digging under, Indians all over the roof, like ants trying to get into an egg. The Kiowas could dig through the thick turf with hatchet and ironwood lance, making their own gun ports, until the place bristled with guns pointed inward. They could breach the walls and come pouring in; they could level the house to the ground, if they had to.

First defense against this kind of an attack was to pick off the Kiowas as they rushed, before they got tight to the walls. If Cassius' cowhands had been here, instead of bumbling around somewhere with a bunch of wet cows, they might have fought off the whole Kiowa nation. Even loopholes made by an enemy work two ways—until they become too

many. As it was, with only one gun to the side, their
chief hope was to hurt enough Kiowas to destroy
faith in their medicine, so that maybe they would
quit.

But Cash now saw that he had wrongly imagined
the whole thing. Mounted warriors could do nothing against walls; they could only create diversion
and confusion, while delivering a badly aimed covering fire for a dismounted attack. They would not
bother with that against so few, if they were coming
from all sides. The attack would be frontal, against
the shutters, and perhaps the door.

He now posted Georgia and Rachel belly-down
with cocked carbines at the low ports in the front
walls, near the ends. If their ports darkened, they
must fire, for Kiowas crawling along the base of the
wall must pass these ports to get to the shutters.
Beyond this, they would play no other part, until
knifemen got into the room.

They were barely in position when the war cries
broke the night wide open, very near and all at
once, an incredibly loud and inhuman yammering.
A file of mounted warriors streamed across the front
of the house, firing raggedly but continuously. Except for an occasional slug that splintered through a
shutter, little was to be feared from this kind of fire.
Andy and Cash several times raised their carbines,
but lowered without firing. The Kiowas were riding
close, too close. Some hung on the far sides of their
saddle-less ponies, but even those who sat straight
up, firing coolly, whipped past the ports too fast for
a decent shot. What Cash did not want was to bring
down a horse. A dead horse would make a redoubt
at too close a range.

The riders were circling the house now, reloading as they passed behind, and the war cries never ceased. A warrior wearing a buffalo-horn headdress pulled out of the circle and stopped his pony in the open, signaling to the racing circle with his shield. Cash and Andy fired together, and a scalp flew off the Kiowa's shield. The rider seemed to fall on the far side of his bolting pony, but he never hit the ground.

"No good," Cash said. "He took cover, that's all. He was sitting up again, going around the corner."

"Those black and yellow bands," Andy said. "In his warpaint, and on his shield—"

"That was Seth," Cash confirmed. "Wolf Saddle is the one painted up with black and red snakes. Seems like he dropped out of this last round. That one I put a crimp in, down by the creek, was Fast Otter, I think. . . . Look sharp, now, Rachel, Georgia!"

The circle of racing ponies went on unbroken, and the war cries screamed continuously all round the house. Bullets still slammed into door timbers, and the gunfire out there made the ears ring. But nothing was hitting the shutters now. Cash went to stand by one window, and Andy by the other. And now Rachel's carbine crashed.

"Get him?"

"My loop's still blocked," she fired again into whatever lay against it. Then they heard Georgia's carbine go, at her port near the other end.

"Good girl," Cash said. For moment, then, Georgia let her carbine fall. She rolled away from her gun port, sat up, and what sounded half like sobs and half like laughter came through her fingers.

Rachel cried out, "She's hurt—she's shot in the mouth!" She ran to Georgia, but attempted no aid. She threw herself upon her stomach across Georgia's legs, and got her carbine muzzle to the loop Georgia had abandoned. For a split moment she saw what she took for a leg outside the port; she fired, and believed she hit it, but it was snatched away.

Georgia pushed her aside. She was breathing hard, and her voice shook, but, "Nothing hit me," she said, and she took her porthole back.

An ax, swung by an enemy who stood in the protection of the wall, was splintering into the shutter where Cash waited. He had an answer to that. He coolly studied the angle of the axblows, then struck the wall nearby with the butt of his Colt. A shard of plaster fell, revealing an opening the size of a half dollar. It showed no light, but as he fired through it, the mud that plugged it went to dust and the ax blows ceased.

At the other window the whole frame loosened, and the shutters cracked and bowed inward, under the impact of a boulder no man should have been able to lift. A split opened down the middle, and Andy fired through the crack at a shadow beyond.

And suddenly that was all. The mounted Kiowas circled a few times more, but their fire was thinning. Then both gunfire and war cries stopped altogether, and the rear wall brought them the sound of horses going away.

Matthilda had slept through it all, and still slept; making them believe now that she might never wake.

Lost Bird's body was gone, when the three-quarter moon came up, but they could see no other dead. Scoring up, they believed that three more Kiowas had been hit, one of them hard. Andy still believed he had touched up Seth, a little bit. Cash didn't think so. They feverishly carpentered the broken shutters, finding out how hard it is to get anything done right in the total dark.

When that was done, not much was left to do but wait.

"I guess I kind of slipped a stirrup, there for a minute," Georgia said sheepishly.

"You did fine," they all assured her. And that was all that ever was said about that.

Cash was encouraged, cocky, even, because they had come through a full-out assault without any hurt. "See how easy? I misdoubt if there's a Horse Indian alive knows how to fight against walls. If they can stand getting shot, we can sure stand pulling the triggers. Just as long as they want to keep up!"

He told them a story he had picked up from a cow hunter, way over to the east of their range. There had been a big fight, up on the Staked Plains —just lately, too. No more than three—four weeks ago—seemingly about the middle of June. Twelve or fourteen buffalo hunters—Billy Gibson was their ringleader—had moved into an old deserted place up there, called Adobe Walls. And here they had been set upon by the biggest passel of Comanches, along with a fair sprinkle of Kiowas, that anybody had heard of in years. The story had it that there were sixteen hundred Indians in it. "So, let's say, there maybe was about four hundred Indians," Cassius trimmed it down. He didn't know who the

war chiefs had been, except that Quanah had been
seen there.

Quanah had struck in the dark before sunup, and
might have carried the place, too; only some old
dry-rotted roof timbers had happened to fall in, and
had got two-three of the hunters up, spoiling the
surprise.

A couple of fellows sleeping outside in a wagon
had got killed. But once the twelve inside started
firing, the savages never got any farther. The fight
went on about a day and a half, and the hunters
believed they had killed about fifty Indians. "Let's
make that about ten Indians, more likely," Cash
pruned down the story again. One buffalo hunter
had got a slug in the arm, and that was all the damage inside.

"And there you have it: Walls is what you need!
Nothing but walls. I bet that us four, in this house,
could whup a thousand of 'em with these walls right
here. If a thing can't be done ahorseback, why, they
just don't know how to do it at all. We've got those
fools helpless out there!"

None of them really believed their position was as
good as that. But they did begin to feel that maybe
they had some sort of chance.

They talked about whether Cash's cowhands
would hear the firing, far off where they were. Cash
had left them moving a herd southward from the
extreme notheast corner of their range, and the
wind was from that way, what little there was. He
didn't believe they could hear. Not at worse than
twenty miles away. Besides, wet cows are always
losing their calves, when you chouse them around
in bunches; nothing else could bawl so much. Cash

doubted if you could hear the world fall down, through all that bedlam. If ever they got the idea he needed them, they'd come, all right.

"There's about four of the hands call him 'Padre,'" Andy said, as if that clinched it.

"Padre? Who, Cash? You mean like a priest?" Georgia looked blank. "Now don't tell me he preaches to 'em!"

"It generally means they got crazy-helpless on snake-head," Andy explained, "and their boss saved 'em from jail. Or maybe something worse."

"Like what kind of worse?"

"Like being dead is worse."

"Well, they're sure missing a real meaty chance to return the favor."

Cassius made no comment on all that. He wondered out loud if the Rawlins boys were liable to come looking for their sister. Georgia thought they might. "Along about late tomorrow afternoon."

Rachel didn't speak his name, but Ben was the one she hoped would come. He could have been back by now. He ought to have been back. *Ben, Ben, aren't you ever coming home?* . . . Maybe he wasn't. Papa had proved to them, four years ago at Witch River, that the Zachary men didn't always come back.

36

For three hours the people in the Zachary soddy
waited, ready to fight again, but no more attacks
came on. Cash concluded that the enemy would
hold off, now, until the last darkness before dawn.
He tried to make the others get some rest. They
remained fully dressed, their carbines in their
hands, and either Cash or Andy prowled the ports
by turns, watching the prairie by the light of the
young moon. No one could more than doze. They
knew the Kiowas wanted them wakeful through this
part of the night, so that morning would find them
fumble-handed, but they couldn't help it. They
stayed strung-up anyway, just as the enemy wanted
them to.

A little after midnight a bullet came wowling
from the north ridge, and broke a little pane in the
blocked north lookout. Ten minutes later a rifle
whanged from the creek, chugging a ball into the
door. During the next couple of hours seven or eight

more shots were fired, at irregular intervals, and
from various directions. It was the same game, to
keep them from resting when they ought to rest.
Two hours after midnight, all action ceased, and
the night was still. Now the Kiowas would give
them every chance to go sound asleep, in time for
the next assault.

Cash had them all up at their loopholes long
before the first graying of the sky. And now the
Kiowas fooled him again. Daylight came clear and
strong. The sun came up, and the locusts began
winding up again, after sleeping out the cooling of
the dry land between midnight and morning. And
no attack came at all.

Matthilda waked, and, though she was very
weak, she seemed immeasurably improved. Georgia
made her a few spoonfuls of gruel, and it stayed
down. In their unbounded relief they let Matthilda
lead them back to the theory that she had suffered
nothing worse than a severe siege of indigestion, after all. Intent upon keeping his people up to
scratch, Cassius allowed them only a cold breakfast; but the sunlight outside, and the increasing
warmth of the summer morning, were favorable to
the illusion that the worst was over.

Cassius seemed partly puzzled, and partly suspicious; but he was beginning to show what appeared
to be a curious disappointment. Finally, turning
impatient, he threw open the outer door, and stood
exposed upon the stoop, his carbine in his hands.
Nothing happened. He led his horse out, mounted
bareback, and rode it down into the creek to let it
drink. Andy and the two girls stood ready at the
portholes while Cash did that; but still nothing
broke loose.

One thing, at least, was strange, and wrong. The uphorses were still in their corral. Inconceivable that the Kiowas should have left them unmolested, unless they were coming back. Before he came back to the house Cash turned out all the horses but two, which he fed and watered.

"Nice big dust," Cash reported, "strung out to the west. The near end of it is settling down; the head end of it looks about twelve miles away, and getting farther. Like as if they're all heading back into the cap rock breaks. Only thing . . . That dust looks just a little bit too big and plain, to me. They don't need to raise that much dust. It's more like the dust you might make dragging brush behind you, in the right places."

"And I better light out, dragging some brush behind me in the right places," Georgia said. "Your maw's all right now, far's I can see. I got to get home—before my old lady runs *me* into the cap rock breaks, neck and neck with them Indians."

Cassius had to think about that a while, and he was in a quandary. If he had been up against Comanches, he would have had a chance to figure out what they would do. Comanches often fought bitterly, and with suicidal courage. If a Comanche figured his medicine was right, you could expect him to strike one more blow at you after he was dead. But they were not imaginative, nor resourceful, by comparison to their Kiowa allies. They were as liable as not to quit a fight when they had you licked, for no better reason than that they thought they had fought enough.

But Kiowas were another matter; their tactics included every form of trickery known to war or crime. Two Kiowas in a party of Comanches could double its menace—and here they had nothing but Kiowas. Best thing to assume was, whatever they seemed to be doing, they weren't doing that. That big fat trail they were laying, out there to the west, had all the look of a full scale drawoff. So it wasn't. They would be back again in the first dusk, and tonight would see the hard attack, beside which last night's attempted surprise was only a feelout.

The safe and sure pattern of defense was perfectly plain. Cassius knew he ought to keep Georgia right here where she was, and let old Hagar fume as she might. Now that Georgia was past her first moments of battle-impact hysteria, she was every bit as valuable as a man. They ought to fetch a few buckets of fresh water from the well by the creek, then spend the rest of the day strengthening the shutters and the door. They could brace these with heavy props, using the floor planking, if need be, and pegging fast to the joists, until no ram the Kiowas could devise would take effect. And the root cellar should be ruggedly sealed off. It had an air hole to the surface, much like a whistle-pig burrow, plainly visible and easily enlarged—a tempting entrance for the first buck who set eyes on it. Now that they were all battle-tested, and had the hang of it, the four of them could probably hold out forever, with only these simple improvements. A serious and organized job of digging might be another matter, but this was so unlikely it hardly need be considered.

Some Indians were getting hurt. At least one, and maybe three, not counting Lost Bird, had been killed in action. Tonight they would hurt a few more. The Kiowas wouldn't stay with a losing deal like that for more than one more night; they weren't accomplishing a thing. Cash believed they would round up as many Dancing Bird horses as they could find by the light of the moon, and be gone before tomorrow morning. Except for about one chance in a thousand of a lucky shot finding you through a porthole, they could just about assume that a good cool, wide-awake defense would bring them through without harm.

And none of this suited Cassius the least bit. He had been at his best when they were beating off those first attacks, but he had solved that, now, and knew how he could get fixed to do it more easily next time. But he was no more comfortable waiting down a hole like a badger, patiently and forever, than the Kiowas themselves would have been. To him, as to the Horse Indians, the initiative was everything. A situation in which the enemy had all the choices as to when, how, and whether they should fight was intolerable to him. Every instinct Cash had was for attack—a clever attack if practical, or head-on if that were the only way. *Impose the terms of battle, and you will impose the terms of peace.* He didn't remember who had said that; didn't think it was Hood. But Cassius was no more likely to wait out an enemy than a horse is likely to take refuge in a tree.

So now he had a different idea, and he judged he had better keep it to himself. He had developed a certain amount of reticence, even secretiveness, through having too many of his schemes sat upon as chancy, and even ridiculous. Better not upset everybody, and get a lot of arguments on his hands. Just do it.

He began by agreeing with Georgia that she must get home. The house would be safe enough while he rode with her a good part of the way—far enough to be sure she would make it safely, no matter what. He would be back in the latter part of the afternoon, at the latest. Meanwhile, Andy and Rachel were to stay forted up. He showed them how he wanted them to traverse the ridges and the cutbanks of the creek with the telescope sight of the buffalo gun, maybe two-three times an hour, until he got back.

Matthilda had gone back to sleep. Cash went and took a last look at her, assuring himself that she was indeed out of trouble. His fingers gently touched her hair, careful not to disturb her. Then he saddled for Georgia and himself, and took out.

37

By midmorning the sun outside the portholes had a violence that took all the color out of the prairie; everything showed in shades of white, and the distances shimmered. The heat would be slow to leak in behind the soddy's thick walls, but Rachel and Andy went barefoot, to fit the weather outdoors. Rachel wore nothing but a starchless cotton dress, and Andy shucked off shirt and undershirt, keeping on only his pants. This would not generally have been thought decent, among grownups, even in the same family. Rachel found it faintly consoling that Andy still felt they were only a couple of kids from the same litter, as though neither time nor anything that had happened had changed that for him.

They blocked up all the portholes except one in the end, one in Mama's room, and the two low ones in front. These, and the cracks in the split battle shutters let in only a cool and shadowless twilight. Something was missing in here; after she had thought about it a while, Rachel decided it was flies. During the hot months the air was always full of their buzzing, because of the corrals. But since they had not been cooking the house had gone back to the cellar-like feel that never entirely bakes out of places dug into the ground. The cooled fumes of burnt black powder hung acridly in the still air, giving a strange edge to the smell of the wood smoke that had steeped everything for a long time. The flies had found their way out into the sun, and there was nothing here to bring them back.

Matthilda called, faintly, and after a false start by both of them, Andy stayed on watch, and let Rachel go. But his mother wanted him, too. They stood beside her, and both held her nearest hand. She had a frail, bloodless look, as if she had been sick for a long time. Her words came to them in hardly more than a whisper, but her mind was now clear.

"Where is Cassius?" she asked them; and when they told her—"Then the fighting is over, for now."

They had not known until then whether she had been conscious during any of the firing, or had known that they were under attack.

"Be very watchful," Matthilda cautioned them. "They right often come back."

They assured her they were well forted-up, and on watch. Cash was sure to be back, before night.

"The root cellar—be careful about the root cellar. So easy to dig into, from outside. Of course you pegged the slide? But it never was strong enough. A bullet could come right through those thin boards. . . ."

Andy said stoutly that bullets could go two ways.

"You must rest now," Rachel said; but Matthilda held on to their hands. They didn't want to pull away from her fingers, so weak in their clinging.

"I may not be with you," Matthilda said, "when they come again. Something's wrong with me—just awfully wrong—inside. If I pass away—"

Rachel cried, "It isn't going to happen!"

"I'm not afraid," Matthilda said. "It's only—I don't want to leave you." Her lip trembled, but only for a moment. She went on quietly and lucidly. "But maybe I must. Soon. If I do—you mustn't be afriad of my body. It will turn all hard, and cold— but that won't be me. Just something discarded, like an old coat. You must think of me as all bright and new, someplace not too far away. And wherever I am, I'll be loving you, always, always, with all my heart. . . . Don't go away. Not yet . . ."

She closed her eyes for a moment. Tiny beads of new perspiration on her forehead told them she was in pain, though her face was still. But when she opened her eyes her voice was steadier, and sounded more like herself, than before.

"Someday, when your time comes to pass away —I want you to remember how it was this time, when you were born. Mama was waiting for you, with all your little clothes made, and everything all ready for you, to take care of you. . . ." Her eyes were turning slowly, from one to the other of them. She did not remember, now, that Rachel was not her own child; she was thinking of Rachel as having been born to her, as she had always wished it could be. "So it will be again. Mama will be there. And I'll have everything ready for you, to take care of you, and make everything all right. So you must think of it as a glad new time. You mustn't be afraid."

Andy said softly, "I won't be afraid, Mama." Rachel could not speak.

Matthilda smiled at them, a wavering, gentle smile, without sadness; and she let their hands slip from her fingers as she closed her eyes.

They wondered whether they should heat up some of the brew Georgia had made; they were a little afraid of it, so long as Matthilda was able to rest without it.

They watched, and the sun climbed; it was straight overhead. A haze that appeared to be made of pure light crept halfway up the sky from the horizon, increasing the glare. And now they saw the horsemen in the sky.

This country produced mirages every day, in the summer heat. Mostly these were a shimmering near the earth, as of distant water riffling in a breeze. Sometimes a cowhand came riding in through a knee-deep mirage of this kind, and it would reflect him, exactly as if he were riding in shallows. Other times the mirages changed different kinds of animals, like antelopes, into huge shapeless things, unrecognizable, and strange of movement. Then you could imagine that you were looking at the spirits of those giant beasts, from another age, whose huge bones were sometimes uncovered by the freshets. The Zacharys could only speculate on what incredible animals had left those mighty bones deep in the ground; if there was a book in Texas with a picture of a woolly mammoth in it, they had never seen it. The Kiowas believed the bones to be those of the Man-Eating Owl, a living monster of enormous spirit power. Watching the vast shapes in a mirage you could almost believe they were right.

But today's mirage was different from any they had ever seen before. Andy saw it first, and stood astonished for a moment, before calling Rachel. Across the sky, miles above the land, rode a file of horsemen, tall beyond natural proportions, on horses of a fantastic length of leg. They seemed to come wavering into existence from the east, moving at a walk across the sky until ten were in view at a time; then the leaders shimmered into nothing as they passed on into the west. The riders in the middle were the most distinct; you could judge them to be Indians, for some seemed to carry shields. Neither size nor distance could be judged. Except for their long legs, the horses could have been six feet tall at the quarter mile. Or maybe they were a quarter of a mile tall, at fifty miles. About twenty ghost riders had passed when the whole thing became indistinct, and disappeared.

They had heard of things like that; yet Andy seemed shaken. Rachel would have liked to help him believe the riders in the sky had been a natural thing to see. But she didn't know what to say, for to her they had seemed a sign, of unclear meaning, but ominous portent.

A little after the mirage gave out, a loud, dreadful cry came from Matthilda's room. They rushed to her, and found her half on the floor. When they had lifted her, she lay staring-eyed unconscious, her breathing hoarse and full of struggle. Too late, now, to try Georgia's brew; they could not expect a chance would come again.

When they had pulled themselves together, they went back to traversing the ridges and the cutbank of the creek with the telescope sight of the buffalo gun, as Cash had wanted. The weapon was an ancient .69-caliber muzzle-loader, once a smoothbore, but now rifled for the expanding Minié bullet they called a Minnie ball. So altered, the old gun deserved the telescope sight they had fitted to it, for it took whatever charge anybody dared to ram down it, and its range was fantastic. Because of its great weight, Andy used the telescope to sweep the land from the higher ports, while Rachel was responsible for the loopholes just above the floor, overlooking the creek. She had put a few sticks of firewood and a blanket at each port, for a gun rest, and she traversed by hitching herself in a quarter circle behind the port, on her stomach. They hadn't been finding anything.

But now, as Rachel worked the field of the scope past the base of a cottonwood, she stopped, and went back. After a moment she adjusted the great gun carefully upon its improvised rest and looked again.

She spoke softly. "Andy."

He had been chipping with a crowbar at the mud sides of the port at the other end of the room, trying to give it a wider field of fire. His bare feet were silent on the scrubbed planking as he came to her, but the floor carried his tread, so that she knew when he was beside her without looking up.

"Don't even breathe on this," she said, and made room for him. "But quick! Look where I'm sighted."

He spraddle-armed over the gun, glancing along the side of the barrel to place the scopes tight field, before putting his right eye to the sight. Rachel saw his left eye focus and stare blankly, trying to see through the wall. "That wad of leaves is a bust-off branch," she explained, hiding her nervousness.

"It's lying on that big alamo root, where the bank cuts under. See, where the cross-hairs mark?"

She waited, then, while Andy looked for a long time through the scope. From the grasshopper-stripped cottonwoods along the creek came the zinging of the locusts—winding, winding, metallic and tireless, the voice of the dry heat.

"The cross-hairs," she jogged him.

He spoke absently, as if his mind were out by the creek, but he didn't seem to be seeing much. "She won't hit there, you realize. Ben's got her sighted in at four hundred yards; God knows why. She'll over-carry more'n a foot."

"I know all that!" She would never handle a gun with the ease of daily use, as Andy did, but she remembered things better, and now she was losing patience. "Do you see it or not?"

"See what?"

"An eye."

He tensed, but in another moment rolled clear of the gun and sat up. "Nothing there now. Sun shows through."

She looked, and it was true. Only a glimpse of bright sand showed at the cross-hairs, where before had been a lightless patch, obscured by close-framing leaves, but presently resolving into part of a dark face. She thought Andy was going to ask her if she was sure of what she had seen, and she was ready to snap at him. But he raised no question, so she backed up quite humbly, of her own accord.

"Sometimes, you look at a thing too hard, for too long, it begins to look like something else. Like, maybe a bird was sitting there . . ."

Andy did not answer. He sat slackly, his eyes vacant upon the floor. "It's changed," he said at last.

Rachel knew without asking that this referred to nothing outside. Through their silence, under the spiraling zing of the locusts, they were both hearing again their mother's struggle for breath. Something was worsening. The breathing was louder, and a flat sound had come into it, expressionless and not entirely human, like the impersonal creaking of a door. Andy raised his eyes, and gathered himself uncertainly, as if he would go to Matthilda; but Rachel moved her head faintly, and he settled back.

"It couldn't just fall there," Andy said, and again her thought followed his, this time back to the mystery by the creek. "Our trees don't have any leaves, since the grasshoppers was here. That's a pulled-up greasebush, brought from someplace. And it wasn't there early on. It's never been there before. So—I guess you know what it has to be."

She knew, all right. But she just sat looking at Andy, her eyes widening a little, and seeming to darken. Her mind was at a balk, weaving like a horse that tries to refuse an ugly jump. She did not want to accept the only explanation there could be, or to believe she had really seen what she knew she had seen.

"That's a blind." Andy said. He spoke slowly, and he sounded tired, rather than under strain. He seemed to be feeling his way, as if everything that would happen here and everything they must do were parts of a pattern worked out somewhere long ago, so that nothing was left for them but to study out what it was. "They've put it there to spy on us from, without letting on."

Rachel's face came alive as her composure broke, and her words were breathless. "Then they're out there—all around us! Oh, Andy—" She broke off, stopped by her brother's quick glance of surprise, of appraisal. Perhaps a very great compliment to her was behind his surprise that she could falter, but now she was shamed by it, and made to get hold of herself. "They're watching us," she said more evenly. "Now. They've come back."

"Beginning to, anyway. Might be they're kind of sifting back, by ones and fews."

Rachel hitched herself nearer the big gun; her movements were jerky, and her hands were shaking as she stretched them to the weapon. "I'll sight her down—fix that overshoot—" Andy would be the one to fire, when the time came, because of this gun's heavy kick. "He's bound to fill the sights again, soon or late."

"Wait." Andy had gone back to thinking, methodically, carefully, wary of hurrying into some panicky mistake. These spells of stillness were new to him, and Rachel was not quite sure what they meant. He didn't look as though he were thinking. More as if he might be going to sleep. "I question," he said finally, "if it's a real good idea. Maybe they'll bide their time, a spell, if we don't seem to know they're there. And time's what we need. Cash is the one we have to make know."

They suspected, in spite of his taciturnity, that Cash meant to fetch home his crew, and maybe even his wagon—by what miracle of hard riding they could only imagine. But eleven men would melt to nothing in a hurry, if they came high-looping into an ambush. Rachel wanted to try making a smoke. In this still air, even a thread of smoke would rise tall and straight into the sky; it would be seen from far away. They could smudge it with wet rags and grease drippings, and soak a blanket for sending the smoke up in puffs, lest it be mistaken for a cooking fire gone out of hand. What they had no way to figure, Andy objected, was how their brother would take it. "Cash sets no store by any size-up us young'ns are liable to make." He said it without bitterness. He judged Cash would as lief charge in headlong as lay back; he had been that way all his life. Anyway, by the time they got through fooling with a smudge and a blanket, the place would be smoked in fit to blunt an ax, and hotter than hell's back oven besides. Which hardly seemed right, with Mama in the shape she was in.

They finally decided that the only signal Cash could not very well misread would be a sound of fighting. They would have to fire in bursts, to make it sound real, or it would have the failing of any other kind of signal. Two shots, nearly together, then one, at the space of a reload; then wait a while to save ammunition, and run it off backwards. They had not started their clock again, lest its loud tick interfere with listening. But they had a little minute glass they had made, for boiling an egg when they had an egg; its sand was measured to run through in three minutes. Guessing at how far downstream their guns could be heard, they thought they could make do with one burst to every three turns of the glass.

For their first burst they used a Sharp's Fifty, and a cap-and-ball Walker. Then Rachel watched the sand dribble through the minute glass while Andy made the round of the lookouts, to see if the besiegers had reacted. The Kiowas should be able to see that the shots from the house were going wild, as if nobody knew anything, but you could never be sure.

They went on with this for fourteen turns of the minute glass. The sun would set in an hour more. Out on the cottonwood root by the creek the up-rooted greasebush still lay, its leaves curled now by the heat; but the telescope sight had picked up no other sign that any ememy was near. Rachel was worring about the wasted ammunition.

"It's terrible, how fast the powder burns away. We're doing an awful thing, here, if it turns out we're wrong."

"Well, we're not wrong." Andy answered her. "How can we be wrong?"

"We haven't a thing to go on, but just that one, lone, single sign."

"If you find one, lone, single bear track," Andy said stubbornly, "there has by God been a bear."

"Yes, but what if—"

"Listen!" He sprang to a shutter loop, and put his ear to it. In a moment he put his finger in his other ear.

Rachel tried to listen, then went to the bedroom door, and closed it softly. Matthilda's breathing was quieter, but now they were trying to hear something that perhaps could not be heard. After a moment Rachel knew what it was. From eastward came a faint whispering that had to be far-off riflery. Were war cries sounding with the guns? Rachel thought they were. Perhaps she had not really heard them, but only knew they must be sounding, in as big a fight as was going on, somewhere far away. The distant whisper died away, rose briefly in a distinct rattle, then ceased altogether. They did not hear it again.

"That's Cash!" Andy whispered. "He's run into a fight, way off there!"

"No, he hasn't! It's something else." She was voicing no more than a wish. If he did not get back, they need not mourn for Cassius alone, but for them all. Of course, if the firing had come from a brush between Indians and a couple of companies of cavalry happening along—

"Oh, for God's sake," was Andy's only answer when Rachel suggested that. No cavalry had ever been seen on the Dancing Bird yet.

"Seems like you're cussing a good bit," Rachel commented.

"I may stop that. Sudden-like, and all at once. Sometime tonight."

Rachel could think of only one thing she could be sure the day had accomplished for them. She did not mention it to Andy, for no dust anywhere gave hope that it was going to do any good. Yet it meant something to her: Ben surely must be one day nearer home tonight than he had been when this sun came up.

Instead she said, "Cash is all right. He'll come home. He *must* come home. So he will. . . ."

38

Cassius lay in the bottom of a dry coulee, resting, and trying to save what strength remained to him. His left leg was broken below the knee, so badly that a spike of bone was sticking out of it. He had bound it as tightly as he could with strips of his shirt, splinting it awkwardly with bits of drift, yet it was all he could do to drag it as he crawled, and he had crawled a long way. The leg had been smashed by his horse as it crumpled in front and over-ended, destroyed by a bullet-broken shoulder.

Before his horse had been shot under him, he had got an arrow in the back, which was an unfairness, for it had been shot from in front of him as he charged, trying to close with his enemies. He had been lying low on the neck, and the arrow's trajectory had carried it deep along the length of a back muscle. He had got rid of the shaft, finally, by an effort that almost knocked him out. But the sheet-iron head, a slender three-inch cone of metal, had come off the shaft, and stayed. It was still lodged in his back, somewhere down near his belt.

He believed he had killed four savages. One he had got in the first brush, when they had discovered him and circled in on him. A dandy shot, when he finally got it, but he had spent six cartridges before he made it. The second he had got from behind his fallen horse, with the last shot in his carbine. After that he had taken to the coulee, trying to outwit the warriors by an interminable crippled crawling. The wound in his back was bleeding fast, and he could find no way to stanch it. He left a blood trail every yard of the way; and he had been able to make use of it.

When the Kiowas had come into the coulee after him he managed to be some distance from where they expected him, so that they followed his blood trail along the bottom of the gully. And now he used a trick that wounded bears used. Beyond a twist in the coulee he climbed out onto the bank, and back-trailed a little. Until now he had kept the empty carbine, sometimes using it as a crutch; but it wasn't much good to him, so he dropped it in the bottom of the gully for bait. Waiting on the lip of the coulee, just over the carbine, he had killed the first savage who bent to pick it up, shooting him through the head with the Dragoon revolver. Four or five others who were trailing them got the hell out of there, and he wounded one as they got away. But he didn't count the ones that were only wounded.

The last one he got with almost the same trick, but with an extra hitch to it. The Kiowas circled, to come safely at the place where he had lain in ambush; but he wasn't there when they got to it. As soon as the coulee was clear he had rolled off the edge, half killing himself in the fall, and once more started crawling. At a turn of the gully he climbed out of it again, but this time he did not watch his back-trail. The Kiowas halted, well clear of the place his blood trail disappeared around the corner. They spotted the bit of buckbrush in which he was hiding on the lip and knew he was waiting there. They left the coulee and circled to a safe distance ahead; then back-trailed themselves, to close from behind him.

Only they were wrong about the way he was facing. Once more he had thought one step ahead of them; and he killed another Kiowa who crept upon him from the supposedly safe direction.

He had missed, though, with every shot, as he fired at those who retreated. The Dragoon was empty. He rolled himself into the coulee again, and lay there. He was weak, now, and when he tried to drag himself forward he made only a few inches.

One more . . . Just one more red nigger . . .

He concentrated everything he had in an effort of the mind, so great that much of his pain was blanked off. He was trying to project himself into the minds of the savages, into their very bodies. He began to see them, one individual, and then another, wherever each was upon the prairie; and they appeared to him in a detail far more complete than any imagining he had ever experienced before. He seemed to sense not only the intentions but the thoughts of each one; and he took heart as he knew they were not leaving.

Presently he rolled himself to the side of the gully,

tight against the mud wall of the coulee, belly down, but face tuned outward.He drew his Bowie knife from its sheath, though even this was a struggle, and gripped it underneath his body. Then he waited, counting his own heartbeats. He had to be alive, and conscious when they got there; but it was going to be a horse race.

They came in time. He knew they were there before he saw them. He waited with slitted eyes, unwinking; and at last they appeared around him. Another arrow in the back, first, then another. He lay limp, but was still breathing. Suddenly he was grabbed by the hair, and a knife sliced his scalp.

He whirled, then, got the scalper by the wrist,and snatched him downward. The Bowie knife struck upward, and went home to the guard in the belly of the Indian. With his last effort Cash twisted, carving with the knife point in a circle. Then he disappeared under a mass of as many as could reach him, hacking and stabbing.

39

When a quarter of an hour had passed without
further sound of riflery, Rachel opened the bedroom door, lest Matthilda regain consciousness
and call too faintly to be heard. She seemed asleep,
her eyes closed, her breathing again so quiet that
she seemed hardly to breathe at all. The heartbreaking cycle they had gone through so many
times had come full circle once more, but without
room for hope, this time, that it was not already
starting over.

A small breeze was beginning to move out of the
northwest as the sun lowered, and, though it didn't
amount to much, what there was of it was working
against them. That mild and pleasant little stir of
air would have been welcome, and enjoyed, on any
other summer evening they had ever known. Tonight they blamed it for keeping any further news
from coming to them across the prairie miles. Raw-
nerved, they felt that every act of nature was wickedly opposing them.

In the absence of any further indications, they judged they had better make ready to last out the night without help, regardless of what they might believe, or hope. Each was trying to seem unworried, and each was thinking how scared the other looked. They set about bracing each other by turning their minds to the practical things they could do. Their ammunition had better be tallied, about the first thing, they guessed.

The repeaters, to begin with. The faster of their two magazine carbines was the Spencer, which loaded with a seven-ball tube. Its magazine, with three extra tubes, accounted for twenty-eight rounds, and the Henry was carrying six. But when they had emptied every pocket, and scraped out the corners of the ammunition chest, they found only nineteen loose cartridges more. In all, the repeaters had fifty-three rounds, which might sound like a plenty, if you didn't know how fast those things poured away lead. Every single round would have to be held back for the desperation moments of close action; and even then, the rim-fires must be hoarded with all care, or the magazine carbines would be out of action in the first three minutes.

Nothing to do about it. They could cast bullets, and make caps, but they didn't know how to refill the detonation rings of the rim-fires. The close-shooting Sharp & Hankins would have been deadly in sniping action; it might have hurt the enemy more than any other weapon they had. But it was a slow-loading single-shot, and used the same rim-fires as the repeaters, so it had to be put away.

For slow fire, they were left with only two cap-and-ball pieces. They found only seven rounds for the breech-loading Sharp's Fifty. Its linen cartridges were slow and finicky to make, but maybe they would have to try, if the Zachary marksmanship they were so proud of was to do them any good at all. The .69 buffalo gun was muzzle-loaded with loose powder; but search brought to light only one more of the huge slugs it fired, besides the one with which it was charged.

But their two cap-and-ball revolvers worried Andy the most. The big Walker Colt was loaded in its six chambers—they carried its hammer on a capless nipple—but had a reserve of only four more .44 balls. They had used it in firing for noise, and hadn't found any way to get a good bang from it, blank, without wasting lead. And Andy's treasured near-Whitney had the six loads in its cylinders, and that was all. They rummaged past hope without finding one .36 ball more. The revolvers were their final recourse if the Kiowas swarmed in, and Andy meant the Whitney for Rachel, because it was lighter, and bucked less, than the heavy Walker.

"We've got to make some—quick! Build up a fire—" He rummaged frantically for the lead strips they melted down to fill the bullet molds.

There were no lead strips.

"The saddle shed—there's lashings of 'em down there in a—"

He grabbed for the door bar; but Rachel had got there, and threw her weight on it. "Andy—no, no, no—don't you dare leave me here!"

"It's our only chance to—"

"There's nothing down there! The door's stove in! Lead would be the first thing they took!"

He knew it was true. The saddle-shed door, nothing but rawhide on a frame, was hanging antigodlin by one strap, visible from the house.

Andy scratched up one idea more. He pulled a battered two-foot chest out from behind all the other plunder under his bunk. From this old toy box, as Andy pawed everything out of it, came such a history of Andy's childhood that Rachel could not bear to look. She glimpsed the remains of a rag doll; Matthilda had seen no harm in giving a baby boy something to love as he went to sleep. Andy had decided dolls were unmanly before he was five years old, and Rachel had not known, until this moment, that he had never been able to bring himself to throw this one away.

In the very bottom of the chest, where they had sifted by their weight, lay tumbled some dozens of lead soldiers. There had been whole regiments of them once, brightly painted and tall as your finger —Andy's share of the loot Papa had brought home one time, after selling a big herd.

"Here—here!" He shoved a clutch of them into Rachel's hands, and clawed for more. "Get the fire going! Where's the melt-ladle at?"

She packed all of their lightwood splinters into a solid heap, threw on gunpowder, and set it burning with the snaphaunce. She had already blown the flame white with the bellows when Andy stacked the rest of his soldiers on the hearth.

"Get some bigger wood onto—no, I'll do it! Gimme that!" He took the bellows from her. "Get the thirty-six mold out! It's the one makes eight at a whack. . . ."

Only traces of paint remained on the little soldiers, but a picture flashed into Rachel's mind of

how bright they had been, and how pretty, long
ago. She kicked one under the table, and crawled
after it. Before she came out the other side she had
managed to wipe her nose, without blowing it, on
the inside of her skirt. If the little cracks were beginning to spread, she didn't want Andy to know it.
Not yet. Not while it could still be helped. As she
brought the long-jawed bullet mold to the hearth,
the first drums started.

A rattling noise began it, like the sound of two ax
helves pounding on a log. Then a pair of medicine
drums took it up, and finally, a flat loud clamor,
made by beating on sheets of hardened rawhide. All
of these noisemakers were struck in a unison as ac-
curate as if a single giant drumstick were hitting
them all at once with every stroke. The sound built
and built, now and then ending with a final wallop
like a cannon shot, to start over softly, and build
again. The whole thing had an odd ventriloquism,
so that sometimes the drumming seemed to be coming from down the creek, then from behind a ridge,
then from somewhere on the prairie beyond the
Dancing Bird.

Andy glanced up at Rachel, but they didn't say
anything about the drums. He skimmed the molten
lead in his ladle. "Better take a look at Mama."

The red rays of sunset were striking through the
high air-slits in the bedroom, filling the narrow
space with a strange ruddy light. Matthilda's face
quivered, and her eyes opened, as Rachel stood
looking down at her. For a moment she stared unseeing; then she knew Rachel, and her face twisted
weakly as she burst into tears.

"Darling girl," she said, as if the words were

wrung out of her, "darling, precious girl. . . . I'm so sorry. I'm so sorry."

They never knew just what it was Matthilda so regretted as she died. Maybe the last thought in her mind, as the light left it, was the simplest kind of an apology for being unable to care for them, or even herself, anymore.

The snoring gasps called the death rattle began at once. Rachel tried to call Andy, but before she could get control of her voice he was at her side. He looked at Rachel, questioning, with the wide-eyed look that sometimes made him seem a little boy. She nodded, dry-eyed. The rattle stopped, and Andy moved closer; his competent hands gently pressed Matthilda's ribs, and the effort to breathe began again. But the second time it stopped, Rachel took Andy's hand, and wouldn't let him start it any more.

Almost ten seconds after breath ended, Matthilda's eyes opened, and turned right and left, as if searching the upper corners of her room. Rachel had heard of a final flare-up of consciousness in the last moment before death, and she wanted to cry out some word of good-by, but she was unable. Later she blamed herself, for she believed a smile would have come to Matthilda's lips as she died, if Rachel had been able to speak.

Rachel drew the sheet over Matthilda's face. Andy still stood looking down at the lifeless form, his face twisting and his breath coming hard, as he tried not to cry.

"The ladle," Rachel reminded him. "I'll do what's left to be done, here."

He nodded, and went back to his work. He was

sniffling as he went, and wiping his nose on his bare
arm; but his hands were still sure as he squatted
upon the hearth.

The sun went down, and the ruddiness went out
of the last daylight, but the drums kept on, building
again and again from a softly pulsing beginning to
a thunderous climax. Sometimes the off-key,
"Hiyah, hiyah," of medicine songs could be heard.
Rachel brought water and clean clothes to the
bedroom, and closed the door.

Alone, she put a bandage over the eyes, so that
they would rest closed, and another to hold shut the
jaw. As she bathed the body she marveled a little, as
she sometimes had before, at how smooth and white
Matthilda's shoulders were, in contrast to her
work-stringy forearms and gnarled hands. *They'll
never touch you,* she promised silently. *They'll never take
away your pretty hair.*

The body seemed an impersonal thing, as Matthilda had wanted it to seem. Something lay here,
but too much else was gone. Like Matthilda's
dream of how she wanted them to live, someday,
after the one great cattle year that had only just
now come. She had held in mind a pleasant town—
a country sort of town, as you saw it when she described it, yet with shiny touches of elegance about
it, too. The houses, all painted white with green
shutters, stood along mudless streets, where car-
riages wheeled handsomely in the shade of old
trees. Each house lived in a picket-fenced garden,
with sweet williams and cornflowers, and holly-
hocks for a tall backing, and candytuft along the
walks; and, of course, plenty of pansies. On quiet
Sunday mornings the church bells tolled slowly, a

peaceful sound, sweetly solemn. And in this town the time of the year seemed always to be early summer.

Rachel tried to think of Matthilda as having gone to such a place, but she could not. She had no feeling that Matthilda was anywhere at all.

She brushed the white hair, which still seemed to have more cool light in it than there was in the room, and dressed the body in Matthilda's best clothes. The materials were pitifully cheap and worn, but well sewed, by Matthilda's own hands. She stripped the bed, freshening it with one of their two best sheets, and covering Matthilda with the other one.

It happened to her the minute I was born. She could be alive and well, and taking care of her boys. She could have enjoyed them a long time. Except for me.

Unlike the others, she had a clear conviction as to what had caused this death. She believed that Matthilda had quite literally died of a broken heart. Yet . . . she had been sure of this for too long to feel it greatly, now that the inevitable was past. What she felt was a great weight of tiredness, held up by a single thin wire of resolution containing all her strength.

40

An hour had passed, but the slow twilight was still clear, and the drums were going as before, as she came out of the bedroom and closed the door.

"Well, anyhow," Andy said, "these here will be the first toy soldiers ever did really fight, I guess. I stretched 'em into twenty more thirty-six caliber. For your Whitney."

"That was rattle-headed." Her tone was inert, and sounded cold, even to herself. "What will you do when the Walker's empty?"

"I always got my knife," he said—and immediately saw that he didn't. "Hey—you seen my skin-out knife?"

She went back into the bedroom and got Andy's narrow-bladed sheath knife, and his belt, from under her mattress.

"I figure you better wear this," he said. "I'll punch more holes in the belt, so's you can— Oh. Somebody already. . . ." He buckled the belt around her, and used the knife to cut off the long tag of strap left over. For himself he got the Bowie they used for a carver, and stuck it in his waistband, punching the blade through the cloth.

They laid out their weapons, and the few loads. Once it was dark, anything that became mislaid would be lost forever. Rachel put six rim-fires in the pocket of her dress, for refilling the Henry's magazine, and fetched the loading kit for the Whitney revolver. Each cylinder had to be charged with loose powder, then a ball and patch rammed home with the lever under the barrel, and a cap must be stuck on each nipple. She laid the things needed beside the powder horn on a corner of the table, where her hands could find them in the dark. Andy got the ax, and stood it by the door.

Now the drums built up to one more climax, and did not start again. They left a silence that rang in the ears. Andy said wonderingly, "Why, it's just as if Mama has gone out there, and stopped them some way."

Rachel said, "Stopped? They're starting now, more like."

Again the back wall brought them the sound of hoofs trampling about, somewhere nearby. But the horse movement formed no pattern, other than an unreadable shuffling about, and in a little while was quiet.

"Oh, say—by the way—" Andy had his eye glued to a loop-hole, and he kept it there. He was trying to sound about four times more casual than he knew how to do. "Remember to save your last shot. You will, won't you? Count careful—just awful careful—every time you let off the six-gun. Because you'll need one more, if they ever get in. You know?"

She didn't answer him. She threw a bucket of water on the fire, and stepped away from the answering explosion of steam.

"Rachel? Did you hear?"

"I heard you, Andy." No use arguing. But she had no intention of wasting even one lead soldier on herself, no matter what.

"The main thing is—" He broke off, and jumped for the buffalo gun. He had to replace its lost-off cap, and his hands shook as he tried to be quick about it.

Rachel got to a door loop. The twilight had lessened, but it was still clear. She saw at once what had roused him up. Two Kiowas sat their horses on the far slope of the Dancing Bird, above the holding corrals. Even at two hundred yards, and in failing light, she could not mistake the black and red snakes painted all over Wolf Saddle's body, or the broad black and yellow bands that identified Seth. Immediately Andy's .69 let go with its heavy blast.

A buffalo horn vanished from the side of Seth's headdress; he was nine-tenths knocked off his horse, and almost went under its belly, but pulled himself up. She saw him pull off the remains of the war bonnet, and slam it down, before she turned away.

Andy was pouring a second full measure of gunpowder down the buffalo gun. "Oh, *damn!* That was Seth! Seth!"

He had missed a chance to take half the hell-fire out of the hostiles, and maybe lift the siege altogether, with a single shot. She judged he would have to be straightened out, if they were to be here long. "Had to shoot at his head, didn't you? And yanked on the trigger, too—fit to bust it off! Why do you—"

"She kicked high on me," Andy stuttered, almost in tears. "Honest, I centered square on his belly-button! What-all powder did Ben have in this thing —a gallon? I should have drug down with my whole weight—" He banged home the rammer, and fitted a cap.

"Put that thing down! That's her last charge, you've got in her now!"

"That's Seth sitting out there—will you hear me? And Wolf Saddle with him—"

"Well, they're not sitting out there any more." Low-toned, unhurried, she went on to take him apart; then put him back together again. "What was all that scrabbling around? You looked something like a man trying to wash a cat. You know better than that. Now get your dang head up, by God! Because we've wasted the last shot we're going to. There's not a man in Texas shoots any better than you do. Or handles anything else any better, either. So take your time. There's a power of Kiowas out there, now. But come morning, they're going to be mighty few. And you'll be sitting with pancakes and honey to your fry-meat. Because that's what I'm going to fix."

He lowered the hammer of the big .69 to half-cock, set the weapon aside, and stood rubbing his shoulder. When he finally managed the shadow of a grin, she knew he was all right.

And now the Kiowas came, without gunfire, without war cries, without any sound heard within at all, until fifty-pound boulders crashed against both shutters at once, splitting the timbers, and loosening the deep-anchored frames. Others followed, and the same again, over and over, shattering the heavy wood. . . .

41

After the fourth attack, not much was left of the battle shutters. Andy had split up the table to brace what busted pieces the first and second assaults had left hanging; and after the third they had tied up the splits and splinters into sort of a net with strings of rawhide they had saved to make a reata. But now only some long splinters remained, stuck picketwise along the sills.

For a while they had very easily defended the opened window holes from the opposite wall. The moon was up, and Seth was running out of warriors interested in silhouetting themselves for close-range guns within. Three had been hit there, but the only Kiowa surely killed was one who was shot in the throat, and fell inside. He bled in streams, and though they heaved him out as soon as they could, he left such a great, slippery puddle that Rachel had to fetch ashes by the bucket, to restore the footing.

In the fourth assault the Kiowas had used more gunfire, and used it better, than in any previous attempt. They had found out that those inside were covering the windows from positions at the back wall. Their riflemen fanned out, using the creek bed as an entrenchment; and a heavy blanketing fire poured in. If Andy and Rachel had not gone forward at the first shot, they might very easily have been killed in the next three seconds. They stayed against the front wall after that, reduced to taking in enfilade whoever might choose to climb in.

As the fire lifted, one quick rush was made, in files from both ends of the house. War hatchets struck the splinters away, and a leg came over the east sill. Andy all but severed it with a swing of the ax; and then stepped out from the wall to fire three times into a muddle of shadows at the other embrasure. The Kiowas broke off.

Now there was a letup, during which they had time to deal with a buck who was fooling around with an idea of his own. This one had lodged himself outside an end port with a single-shot. He couldn't see anything inside, apparently; maybe didn't want to put his face to the loop. He kept poking his rifle into the room to fire blind, at random angles. Except for the near corners, no part of the room was safe from him. Andy squirmed and dodged to the end wall, and stood waiting with raised ax.

Moonlight slanted through a shutterless window to shine cleanly on the bright-metal muzzle as it next appeared. Andy's ax struck hard, and perhaps buckled the weapon's barrel, for they knew by the odd sound of its explosion that the breech blew up.

The barrel was driven deeper into the room, and stayed there, pointing at the floor.

"Never, never in all my life," Rachel said, "did I hear of 'em hanging on like this. Not even for revenge—they're satisfied to take any old scalp, anywhere, for that. Oh, Andy, what's happening here?"

Andy wouldn't admit he saw anything special about it. "Just one night? It's common."

"When they're hurt like we've hurt 'em?"

"We don't hit 'em as square as we hope," Andy thought now. "I'm only sure we killed about one. Maybe two. I don't know."

"I could have stopped this, once," Rachel said, and Andy had never heard a like bitterness in her tone. "I know what I'm called. I'm a red nigger. Cash should have let me go."

"That's nothing but Abe Kelsey's damn lie! You're Rachel Zachary, and don't you forget it!"

I am Rachel Zachary. I said that once. Long ago. The day the world fell down. . . . "Seth believes it. Lost Bird even—"

"They'd never believe Kelsey. Not in a thousand years! He only drummed on it, till he put it in their heads."

"All right." If there was any difference, she didn't see it.

"Most likely one of 'em had a medicine dream. That's how they get to believe any old damn thing they want to, that ain't so. Like, some of 'em think they're bullet-proof. A critter that can believe that can believe anything. And that's what happened. One of 'em wanted to own you, so he had a medicine dream. Or said he did."

"They don't even know what I look like," she rejected it.

"Don't they? They've watched you dozens of times. From the creek bed. From the ridge. From the brush."

"You'd have found their tracks!"

"Yes," Andy said oddly. "Time and again. Only Ben told us to shut up. One of them wants you for his squaw—or one of his squaws. We should have allowed for that. My guess is Wolf Saddle. I'm willing to bet . . ."

"Sure," she said, and now the bitter edge could have whispered just as softly if it were slicing through a bull hide shield. "I'd make a good squaw. A dingin' squaw. Once they fattened me up."

Suddenly he turned angry. With her? Maybe with the world. "Don't you play ignorant with me! Because I don't give a hoot in hell where at you were born, or who to, or who by. I'm your brother. Raised that way, and I aim to stay that. Right up to the last breath I draw—and one long spit beyond!"

He got up, his bare feet silent, and went to set his ear against the back wall.

"And another thing," he said, through the moon-tempered dark. "You're not an Indian—not a red-nigger kind, nor a Civilized Nation kind, nor any other kind. So quit fooling around with the notion you might be, you hear?"

But I am. If I'd been a boy, and raised among 'em, I'd be Seth—no, Lost Bird. I'm a girl—so I'd be one of Wolf Saddle's squaws. And I may be, yet—until the first time I lay holt of a knife— Suddenly a hard twist of disgust sickened her, for she realized that a knife in someone's belly was exactly what an Indian would think of, as easily as he breathed. She remembered what Hagar had said about the knife work of squaws, if they were on hand for a massacre . . . their bloodied hands . . .

Andy made his round of the lookouts and came back to her. He spoke softly, from close by. "I didn't go to sound so mean, and cross. It isn't you I'm mad at, Rachel. Ever."

The gentleness of his tone betrayed her, and she let herself slump, where she sat at the foot of the wall. He sat down close beside her. Awkwardly, but without self-consciousness, he took her in his arms, her head in the hollow of his shoulder, his cheek against her hair. He said, "You're the best sister anybody ever had. You're more than that. You're all the family I've got left, for all I know." They had no reason to think anything had happened to Ben; but apparently, in his exhaustion, Andy was willing to concede that Ben was lost to them too. But— "We'll fight 'em to a standstill," he said doggedly. "Forever, if they want. Just you and me. So long as you stand by me, I'll fight 'em till hell freezes. And then pelt 'em with ice."

He made her cry, at last. She wept grudgingly, without sound, holding onto him tightly; and presently she knew that he was crying a little, too. *No way out*, she was thinking. *No way out, ever. No matter what happens, now. . . .*

Or maybe there was. For now the Kiowas came again, in the weirdest way yet.

42

This time they didn't need the telltale back wall to
hear the horses come. They came fast, and from not
far out, in a thundering storm; and the war cries
clamored as never before. A few guns fired wild
through the empty windows, without object, other
than added noise. The two stood with their backs
against the forward wall, watching for any part of a
Kiowa to show inside; but no dismounted warriors
came.

Instead, a heavy bump shook the very walls, and
the door strained inward; clods and plaster fell,
loosened by the yielding anchorage of the frame. A
Kiowa rider was backing his horse against the door.
It would go, in a couple of seconds, driven inward
by a thousand pounds of bone and straining muscle. Andy got there, cocking the Walker, and for an
instant Rachel was certain Andy would be pinned
as the door crashed in. The bulging planks sprung
a sudden three inches, spoiling his first shot, but the

Walker slammed again, and the door snapped straight. The Kiowa horseman was on the stoop, and would stay there until picked up; and his horse was splashing through the Dancing Bird.

The attack on the door made plain the whole secret of their precarious defense. They could keep only two guns going—but there were only two ways in. Seth must know that now; he had tried to make another way. But this kind of an attempt on the massive door was almost certain death, with the door loopholes placed as they were. All this racket and display had to have some other object than the backing in of one horse as a ram, for although the Kiowas had given up on the door, their yelling riders still circled the house.

A new hoof-rumble began on the roof itself; boards cracked, in spite of the depth of sod on top, and showers of dirt fell. All this was bewildering, but without visible sense. Rachel did not know what snatched her attention to the back wall. Surely she could have heard nothing more; and when she tried to peer into the shadows the small indirect light of the moon was not enough to tell her what she saw. She went to the root-cellar slide, and bent low.

A split had appeared in the boards of the slide. As she watched, the blade of a hatchet struck through, and was wrenched back. She pulled the .36 revolver Andy had made her wear, and fired wildly three times through the slide as the hatchet struck again. The hatchet blade stayed where it was, stuck halfway through, into the room. Andy was trying to shout something to her, but she couldn't tell what it was. She got down on the floor,

which might have been what he wanted her to do.
She dared not leave the slide, yet to stay by it left
Andy with the defense of both windows in front,
and a weakened door that would probably go down,
now, before any kind of a ram.

A touch of panic came into her. After four com-
pound mistakes, the Kiowas were at last finding
more ways in than the two of them could defend.
She saw Andy fire through a wall port, and she
started to him with some unclear notion of shuttling
between the front and back walls.

She didn't get there. Halfway across the room she
was struck and borne down by a great mass of dirt,
sod, and broken boards from the roof as it gave way.
Her face hit the floor hard, and she lay stunned
and smothering, unaware of where she was or what
had happened to her, until Andy pulled her free.
She sat against the wall where he put her, strangled
by the dust; and blood was running down her front
from her nose and cut mouth. But as her head
cleared she saw what had happened. A horse had
broken through the roof with one hind foot, and was
trapped there, its leg stuck down through the roof
beyond the stifle. The hoof dangled loosely from a
broken cannon, yet tried to kick.

One more way in? It might be, if the enemy could
pull the horse clear. Or the struggles of the horse
might do it; dirt was still falling, and the hole in the
roof enlarging. Andy was watching the front again
as Rachel got up shakily. The holster of the
Whitney dragged at her belt unnaturally, and she
found it filled with dirt. She drew, emptied the
holster, and tried to clean the weapon of its grit.

The rocketing horsemen thinned; a horse

plunged downward past a window as its rider jumped it off the front of the roof; and once more the Kiowas broke off. The back wall brought diminishing hoof mutterings for a little while, then was quiet. The defenders were left confused. The two tries at the door and through the root cellar had been good ones, and had threatened to finish them, yet seemed but feebly carried out, without tenacity.

Actually, the pull-away had not been ordered. The warriors had drawn off of their own accord, because their horses were blowing. Such failures in following through were always putting a stumble into the tactics of the undisciplined Horse Tribes. Some part of the thing that all the uproar had been meant to cover was still going on.

Andy took the buffalo gun, and for some moments studied the position of the struggling horse, which was still working deeper into the room through the roof. He had to bend backward, awkwardly braced, to fire upward, but the double charge of the .69 took effect through boards, through turf, and through horseflesh. The great thrashing up there stopped as the bullet found the heart. Andy turned away.

He was starting to say, "Do you think, if I'd mock an owl—"

One more wild random shot came in, not even well placed, but ricocheted from the side of the west embrasure. Andy squealed from a suddenly tight-shut throat, and went down.

43

He pivoted as he fell, and came down partly on his side and partly on his face, arms and legs jack-knifing in an awkward heap. As Rachel turned him over he was in the stunned moment between the first shock of pain and its return in full force.

"I'm all right—I'm all right—" he said, without seeming to know how to help himself. "You—your mouth's bleeding. . . ."

For an instant she could not see where he had been hurt, but a rush of blood was already puddling into the patch of moonlight two feet away. It was the inside of his upper arm, just below the shoulder, and the back muscle of his arm; the tumbling bullet had torn a jagged channel, so deep that his arm seemed half severed. An artery was cut, and the bone broken—perhaps shattered—so that when she straightened the arm it had a joint where none should be.

She tore off the hem of her skirt and made a tourniquet. It had to go almost at the armpit, the wound was so high up. Nothing was in reach for a turn-stick except the barrel of the Whitney revolver, so she used that. She twisted the heavy cord of cloth tighter, and tighter, and still the blood ran in a pulsing stream.

Pain was returning, making muscles jerk all over his body. "Don't—don't—" he kept saying through his teeth, while still the pistol must be turned, and turned, and the tourniquet disappeared into his flesh. When the rush of blood dwindled to a trickle, she tied the Whitney where it was, and fetched the pillow from her bed. Ripped open, this yielded masses of raw cotton in lumpy wads, as it had come from the bale. He choked back a scream, then went unconscious, as she turned him on his face to get at the wound.

It took bandage after bandage, for in spite of great handfuls of cotton the blood kept coming through. After the bandaging she had to make splints, and by the time that was done he was able to help her get him to his feet. She half carried him, taking his whole weight when he lurched, and got him onto his bunk. He was breathing hard and irregularly, in gasps and gulps, but he cried out no more. "Walker—th' Walker Colt— Bring me—"

She put the gun into his hand, and after that he wanted water. That was all, though. He was past noticing that the Whitney revolver was in his tourniquet, so that she could no longer use a final shot as he had wished. She got the Henry carbine, and started to refill its magazine, but found it fully loaded. She didn't remember when she had done that. She sat on the floor beside Andy's bunk, and what she was feeling most was such a weight of weariness that she could hardly lift her hands. Except for those few short dozes, twenty-four hours ago, they had not slept in more than thirty-six hours. Her head ached, her balance was poor, and a steady ringing filled her ears. And yet, there was still that single thin thread of resolution to hold her up. It was stretched taut, and near the cracking point, but it had not broken yet.

She could hear the Kiowas singing again, someplace a good ways off, not so loudly this time. They were using a single drum, muffled by wetting its stretched hide. She couldn't tell how many voices there were. She tried to estimate the time by the position of the squares of moonlight on the floor. Midnight was hardly past; the dawn had a long, long way to come.

A soft, dragging sound was coming from someplace, as though the Kiowas might be creeping close again, along the outside of the walls. Somehow it didn't sound quite like that. It sounded as if it were here, near her, in this room; yet she could see nothing move. After she had listened a while she put her ear to the planking. The sound was coming from under the floor.

This seemed out of all reason, yet the dragging sound went on, stopping for minutes at a time, but always beginning again. There was a space under the joists at this end of the room, of uneven depth, but with room for one man to crawl around on his stomach. You could squeeze into it from the root cellar; Rachel and Andy had explored it long ago. Papa had brought out a bunch of friends to help him build their soddy, before the family came out.

They had used a pan of water for a level when they built the floor, but while they were digging they didn't need to be so particular, and for a level they had used a whisky bottle. Trouble with that, there was whisky in it only at first, and after the bottle was empty they had kept on using it for a level anyway. By the time they were down to grade at this end they were working with more enthusiasm than eye for straight. "There's a power of digging in a case of whisky," Papa had said.

So that was where something was dragging itself around, either stealthily, or else feebly and with great difficulty. Now she remembered the shots she had fired through the root-cellar slide, when an enemy was trying to chop his way in. Maybe one of the shots had creased one, or skulled him, so that he had come to in the dark, not knowing where he was. Or she might have put a bullet in his head. Men shot in the head did not always die at once. She had even heard of a man who had been shot straight through the temples, in the War, yet had lived, and had recovered.

Maybe the savage dragging himself around under the floor was blind—or even without any mind at all—just a body that lived, and crawled, not knowing what it did. . . . The intermittent sound of the thing creeping under there went on for a long time, and the distant singing went on, and the moonlight on the floor would not move at all.

The big carved secretary lifted two inches and dropped again, with a bump that shook the whole floor. She had to think for a while before she knew what had happened, and she had forgotten how to think. One end of the heavy walnut piece was stand-

ing on the Glory Hole, and the trap door had tried
to open. Whoever was under the floor was not
mindless; he had found the Glory Hole, and
guessed that a trap door must be above it. Not
feeble, or weakened, either—he must have the
strength of a grizzly. Under the floor was no
wounded man, crawling around blind, but a stalk-
ing hunter, carrying out a plan. Maybe he had
meant to locate them by ear, and fire upward
through the floor. Inching toward her, he must have
come upon the Glory Hole because she was beyond
it.

As quietly as she could, Rachel hitched herself
back into the corner by Andy's bunk, where the
deepest shadows were. She couldn't see the sights of
the Henry, but she would not need them, for she
could fire along the floor. She cocked the carbine
and held it in her lap, ready to fire it from there.
The carved secretary began to quiver.

Slowly, slowly, a fraction of an inch at a time, the
trap door of the Glory Hole began to rise.

44

Ben had ridden late and started early. His tired horse had gone low-headed, and its running walk had slowed; though the bullion mule, more lightly laden now, jogged steadily on his quarter. The sun was going down as he came in sight of home approaching from the south, across the Dancing Bird.

From a long way out, as he crossed a far rise, he saw that the chimney showed no least haze of smoke beyond the bare trees; and suddenly he knew that something was very wrong. He stopped a moment; then threw away the mule's lead, pulled his carbine from its boot, and went on at as hard a run as his horse had left. Behind the last ridge he stepped down, dropping the reins, and ran forward to the crest on foot. And there he stood for many minutes, looking at the soddy from across the Dancing Bird, at two hundred and fifty yards.

The door of the soddy still stood, but the windows were black empty holes, shutterless, with only

a few splinters of framing where the glass had been.
A misshapen dead horse, bloating in the summer
heat, lay on the roof, its position queerly distorted,
as if it were partly buried in the roof itself. The red
horizontal light of the sunset struck across the
house front, bringing out sharply some hundreds of
pock holes, where bullets had blasted cone-shaped
craters, big as a man's hand, out of the dry mud.
The door of the saddle shed was torn out. That was
about all there was to see. But the empty corrals left
this place more still than it had ever been, since first
anyone came here; not even a bird sailed or
whistled, anywhere along this sector of the Dancing
Bird. No place Ben had ever seen, not even No
Hope, had ever looked more dead.

His carbine slid from his fingers into the dust; if
he had been aware of it he would not have cared, or
supposed he needed it any more. He walked to the
creek, neither quickly nor slowly, but only plodding
heavily, one foot and then the other. Not even his
sick dread of what he must face within those walls
could matter to him now. He reached the creek bed,
dropped into it, and waded the mucky shallows to
climb the cutbank. Some broad bloodstains, clotted
but blackening, marked the slope; but he walked
across them unheeding, moving steadily uphill to
the house. He was within ten yards when a strange,
unnatural sound from within the dark soddy made
him falter. What he heard, he knew as he came
nearer, was someone moaning and muttering some
sort of gibberish, in a voice he did not know. It
sounded as much like Kiowa as anything else. He
drew his long-barreled Colt, and stepped over a
window sill, into the soddy; and there he stopped.

He was standing in a shambles. Great blood pools, some still clotting and sticky-looking, most dried and darkening, spread under both windows, over a great area in the middle of the room, and even showed where a flow had run out of the fireplace, across the hearth, and onto the floor. The carved secretary was lying on its face, the only whole piece of furniture in the room. Broken glass, and a great litter of shattered wood was everywhere, from splintered shutters and furniture put to the ax in efforts at repair; the table was a pile of drift. Three walls, but especially the back wall, were covered with the same bullet craters that pocked the front wall outside. A leg of the dead horse hung down in the middle of the room from a great sag in the broken roof. The clock was bullet-smashed, the water barrel was split and overturned. No greater havoc could have been expected if a regiment had fought here for a week.

The voice Ben had not recognized was Andy's, where he lay half out of his bunk in a fever delirium; and he was begging for water. He moved feebly and aimlessly in a kind of writhing, and his eyes saw nothing.

Rachel stood in the shadows at the far end of the room, a carbine in her hands; and she looked so like a spook Ben hardly recognized her. Her eyes stared at him like dead eyes, out of black hollows. One side of her mouth was puffed enormously; her nose was skinned, and perhaps broken. Blood smeared from her mouth and nose was crusted all over one side of her face, and what remained of her dress was stiff with great dark stains.

He failed to speak, on his first effort. On the second try he said, "It's over, Rachel. Now everything's going to be all right."

She stood the carbine on its butt, out in the middle of the floor, as if she were leaning it against an invisible wall. It balanced a moment, then rattled on the planks as she turned away. She stumbled to the bedroom door, and got it open. She almost reached the bed, but struck its edge as she fell; and lay face downward on the floor.

He picked her up, and started to put her on her bed; but he saw the sheeted corpse in the other bed, so carried her away. At the other end of the soddy he found his own bunk smoothly made, untouched in all that chaos. He stripped off the ruins of Rachel's dress, and put her poor dirty little body between the clean sheets, before he went to Andy.

45

Nine of the range crew came in soon after daylight. They had lost the cook, whom the Kiowas had caught in his overturned wagon. And they thought they had had a pretty bad time, until they saw what had happened here. The two men who had gone missing when they went to hunt for Rachel had not been seen again. And nobody knew where Cash was.

They moved both Andy and Rachel to improvised beds in the saddle shed, and strapped Andy down to dress the wreckage of his arm. Ben himself bathed Rachel, and made her as comfortable as he could. Sometimes, for a few moments, she came half awake; she knew Ben then, but said very little. She knew that Matthilda was dead, and that they had forted up, and Andy had been hurt. For the present she didn't seem to remember much more, and Ben was glad for that. He poured soup into her when he could, and she slept.

Between stages of delirium, Andy was able to tell Ben what had happened here, but only up to a point. He remembered Rachel's firing through the root cellar slide, but he didn't know what had overturned the walnut secretary, or what had happened in the fireplace—or maybe the chimney; or what had busted the water barrel. He thought that after he was wounded he had fired at something, from where he lay—maybe several times. And he knew a gun had continued to let off near him, from as far back as he could remember. He had the impression that he had lain there many days.

Late in the morning, shortly after they buried Matthilda, a rider from the Rawlinses brought word that Cash had been found, and he was dead. But he didn't seem to know anything more about it, and rode away without dismounting. They learned nothing else, until Georgia Rawlins rode in at noon.

She said somberly, "I'm glad to see *you* here, Ben." Her face looked bloodless under her tan, and very drawn; somehow harder, around the mouth and eyes. She made Ben walk out to the creek with her, where they could talk. "I sent a man. Did he get here? We found Cash."

He nodded.

She went on in a lifeless monotone, and told him of the night she had spent here, describing that first night's fight as a "brush." After Cash rode her home or pretty near, he seemingly had lined out to fetch his crew in. But after the Kiowas cut him off, she believed, he must have tried to fight his way home. The signs appeared to show that he had fought a long way from where he was hit, and his horse killed, to where he had ended. Georgia herself had gone out to identify him for certain. She had sewed him into a wagon sheet; and they had buried him on the hillside above the place where he fell.

"Ben, can it be, that was only day before yesterday, he was alive!" Her face crinkled up, and the tears came. "I loved him, Ben. I was going to marry him, soon as we could tell you. It was always him, I guess, in spite of all different I knew I should do. It can't ever be no other man."

She leaned against him, much as she would have leaned against a gentle horse; and her tears wet his shirt. Her words came muffled. "You're the better man. You're a better man than Cash ever could have been. But somehow, nothing like that seemed to matter. . . ."

She stood back, and dried her tears. "You want me to look at Andy's arm?"

They walked back toward the saddle shed. Ben had sent a rider to bring a surgeon from Fort Richardson, but he might have to go all the way to Fort Worth. Might be days. If he didn't get here in time, Ben would have to take off the arm himself, or they'd lose Andy, next. "Will you help me, Georgia?"

"I'll help you all I can. Always."

46

The swarm of hands cleaning up the house found
two corpses still hidden in it. Wolf Saddle was dead
in the root cellar; and Seth, shot through one eye,
was in the Glory Hole. That the two war leaders
had died trying to come to close quarters was no
coincidence. They were the ones with no way to let
go. Doubtless they would have chosen this, rather
than a return to the Kiowas in defeat and dishonor.

Only a few Kiowas, such as Kicking Bird and
Hunting Horse, were able to see that the tribe itself
had little farther to go. Others of the Wild Tribes
would presently lose out as the buffalo vanished;
but the Kiowas would be whipped and driven, and
broken as power, even before that. The Kiowa raids
into Texas and Mexico had never been in defense of
their lands. The Kiowa homeland had been north of
the Red, in what had become the Territory itself,
since long before the Texans came. The Kiowas
raided for glory, loot, and sport.

And now the military was in charge, and the cavalry moving up. A handful of hard-riding warriors, kept few by their very way of life, could no longer use the Territory as a sanctuary from which to launch their forays. Satank was dead, and his son, Sitting Bear; young White Wolf, and Lives-in-the-Saddle, favorite son of Lone Wolf, died in a defeated raid. Within six months Yellow Wolf, Rising Bird, Wild Dog, Singing Tree, Striking Horse, Red Otter, and Lame Wolf would be dead. Of those who survived, Lone Wolf, Satanta, Big Tree, Sky Walker, Woman's Heart, War Eagle, White Horse, and Bear Paw, and fifty more—all those who had been the hard cutting edge of the Kiowas—would be on their way to imprisonment and exile. And the great Kicking Bird would die, poisoned by the warlike of his own tribe, because he had preached the ways of peace.

The vast areas the Horse Indians required, in order to live by the hunt, could not much longer be held against a race that fed a thousand people upon land the Wild Tribes needed to feed one. The buffalo, the one great essential to nomadic life on the prairie, was already going, and would soon be gone. The Kiowas as a people would survive, and someday increase. But the Kiowas as the great war tribe of the southwest prairies would be gone before the buffalo.

With more hands at work than there was room for, the soddy turned new again overnight. The roof was mended, the floors scrubbed and sandstoned; new battle shutters were built. A new smooth-over of plaster dried overnight, and was whitewashed the next day. The place looked kind of bare, but they moved Andy and Rachel into the lower bunks of the main room. And still Rachel slept.

Now other people began to come; they were going to keep on coming for days. People they had known long ago, and people they had never seen, would travel from as far away as the Palo Pinto, as the story spread, all of them eager to help in any way that could be found. Not one of them all could remember having called the Zacharys Indian-lovers, or ever questioning for one moment the origins of the girl Old Zack had found upon the prairie, seventeen years ago. Only Zeb Rawlins, when at last he came, would recall his errors, every one; and own to them as forthrightly as he had stood against them.

For while Andy would become a hero, Rachel was going to be idolized. She could have anything in Texas; she could have Texas. Though Ben didn't believe she would want it, any more.

But up through the third day after the fight, the cowhands were able to keep people out of the house. Andy was resting easier, and Rachel asleep; and Ben sat on a box near the hearth, keeping an eye on them. He didn't want to see anybody else.

A cowhand named Roddy came and hung around near the stoop, balancing on one leg and then the other, and bashfully trying to see in; he didn't want to disturb anybody by knocking. Ben went out to him.

"Indians lanced a caow last night," Roddy said. "Just out of pyore meanness. Never took no part of her. Then they taken the lance, and stuck it straight up in her ribs, plain to be seen. Right close here, too. It's getting so they not only jump you, and steal

you blind, and murder the hell out of you. Next
they got to come back and taunt you."

"What color was it?" he asked Roddy.

"Oh, I'd call it a kind of a yalla caow."

"No, damn it, the lance!"

"Oh, I'd call it black, mainly, with a lot of
rawhide wrop—"

"Good God almighty! Where is it now?"

"Well, last I saw, the boys was horsing
around—"

Ben recovered the thing, finally, and took it into
the house. It was a short lance, no more than eleven
feet long—a good three feet shorter than the typical
fourteen-foot Kiowa lances. The shorter the lance,
the braver the Indian, everybody said. Its needle-
tapered ironwood, from a perfect shoot of the incredibly hard Osage orange, was stained black and
polished to ebony, except for two feet at the tip,
which turned out to be painted red, after the clotted
beef blood was cleaned off. It was Striking Horse's
lance, all right. His medicine feathers had been re-
moved, but seven spaced ringlets of rawhide showed
where they had hung.

The hand hold, placed slightly toward the butt
from the balance, was wound with whang, aged
iron hard, and worn to a black shine of its own by
half a century of use. But six inches of similar winding at the butt did not belong there. Grease and
charcoal had been rubbed into the rawhide string to
make it less conspicuous, yet it was new. Ben began
to suspect what he had here, when he saw that.

He picked at the winding with his knife. It was
glued with boiled-down antelopes' blood, but only
at the ends. He unwound the whang, and found it

had secured a parchment-like tube of doeskin,
which he was able to slide off the butt of the lance.
A strange, creepy excitement of imminent discovery
stirred his scalp; for he knew, now, and for sure,
what this was. Turning the tube in his hands, he
read the message picture on the outside, skillfully
drafted in delicate, even lines.

An Indian, conventionally represented as having
feathers sticking straight up out of his head, was
handing something to a white man identified by a
stovepipe hat. A wavy line from the Indian's head
led to a small drawing of a horse striking with its
forefeet, and a similar line led from the high hat to
something like a gourd. "Striking Horse gives Stone
Hand a present." Couldn't have been any plainer.

He stood up for a look at Andy and Rachel, in the
lower bunks at the end of the room. Andy was restless in a fever doze. Two or three times a minute his
head rolled and he often murmured, unintelligent-
ly. But Rachel was sleeping quietly. Ben let his eyes
rest on her for half a minute, before he pried the
tube partly open with his thumbnail.

The doeskin had been scraped very thin, but
nothing had been done to keep it soft. He supposed
the drawings had been made while it was still
green, for now it had hardened in the shape of the
ironwood butt, and wanted to stay that way. He
had a glimpse of something that might have been
the forequarters of a horse, and the speckled face by
which the Kiowas indicated 1857, the year of the
spotted death, when Old Zack had found a lost
baby on the prairie.

So here was one more incomprehensible paradox
of Kiowa integrity. Cash had made his brash visit to

Striking Horse at a time when the Dancing Bird was being closely and almost continuously scouted, as the sign had plainly shown. A raid in strength must already have been under debate. When Cash asked the old warlock what child, captive or Kiowa, had been lost by Kiowas in the year of the spotted death, he had as good as told Striking Horse outright where that child was now. Ben did not doubt that Striking Horse had used that intelligence, without hesitation and at once, to unleash Seth's murderous assault. Never said he wouldn't.

But at the same time, Striking Horse had promised Cash to send him the answer he wanted, if he could find it out. And now he had sent it—even wrapped on his own lance, in token of validity—because he had said he would. Only an Indian would see no contradiction in sending destruction and the fulfillment of a promise almost hand in hand. The warlock's answer would be the truth, for if he had not learned it he would have sent nothing at all. This thing in Ben's hand held the secret of Rachel's birth.

Shakily he pried at the brittle parchment; then stopped abruptly. Some kind of warning had sounded inside his head, unclear in meaning, yet definite as the dry buzz of a sidewinder. He sat down on a box by the hearth, the tube dangling from his fingers, and his eyes brooding upon the ash-banked coals; and he was wondering why he felt suddenly ashamed. He was missing Cassius in a way he had not expected, for though he grieved for his brother he had not expected to need him so soon. What Ben realized now was that he had no one left to talk to, any more.

Andy had been clear-headed for a while today, but it wasn't the same thing. Andy had felt it important to make Ben know that it was Rachel, and not himself, who had got them through the siege. He thought he would have gone to pieces very early in that night of terror and endless desperation, if she had let him.

"She sure fought for her life," Ben said.

"No," Andy said. "No. She wasn't fighting for her life." Almost the last he remembered was Rachel blaming herself, in the belief that she could have prevented the whole thing, had she not moved too late. In those last hours she admitted to Andy that she had been trying to slip away, when Matthilda was taken down, without other plan than to lose herself past finding; and so take out of their lives the disgrace and the danger she had brought them. "It was me she was fighting for. Not herself. She didn't care about her own life, one way or the other."

Ben believed it. And he saw now why he had drawn back from prying out the secret of the doeskin scroll. Nobody, not even Andy, knew Rachel as he knew her, or ever could. If she could not look to him for understanding, she could not hope to find it on this earth. *Yet I was fixing to ask one mean-minded question more,* he thought, *that I don't even give a hoot about, one way or the other. She'd quit me, she ought to quit me, if she knew it even entered my mind.*

He leaned down and shoved the parchment into the heart of the banked coals. A little shaving of flame had come alive at one end of it before he turned away. He went and stood beside Rachel, looking down at her somberly as she slept; and he had never felt more humble in his life. *God help me to make it up to you. For without you I don't know how to go on.*

When he turned back to the hearth only a crinkled black twist remained of the parchment scroll. He touched it with the toe of his boot, and it went to dust.

ALAN LE MAY was born in Indianapolis in 1899 of parents who had both grown up on the plains frontier and from whom he learned firsthand of the hardships and the romance of the pioneering life about which he later wrote. He began an unusually varied career by playing football at Stetson University in Florida. During World War I he served as a lieutenant of infantry, afterwards continuing his studies at the University of Chicago. After graduation, he worked as a geologist in the jungles of Colombia, lived for a year in the Vieux Carré of New Orleans, and spent the following winter skiing in Massachusetts. Then, he went West to work on ranches in Texas, New Mexico, and Arizona. Between 1927 and 1937 he wrote a series of adventure tales that quickly won critical acclaim both here and in England. For the next sixteen years, he divided his time between writing screen plays (among these *Along Came Jones, San Antonio, Cheyenne,* and *The Sundowners*) and short stories for magazines, and working his own cattle ranch in California. This life was interrupted by a stint in Korea as a war correspondent for the United Nations. His first novel, *The Searchers,* was published in 1954 and was later produced as a motion picture. This highly successful work was followed by *The Unforgiven* in 1957 and *By Dim and Flaring Lamps* in 1962. Mr. Le May died in 1964.

No one knows the American West better.

JACK BALLAS

☐ *THE HARD LAND*

0-425-15519-6/$4.99

☐ *BANDIDO CABALLERO*

0-425-15956-6/$5.99

☐ *GRANGER'S CLAIM*

0-425-16453-5/$5.99

The Old West in all its raw glory.

PETER BRANDVOLD

❑ ONCE A MARSHALL   0-425-16622-8/$5.99

The best of life seemed to be in the past for ex-lawman Ben Stillman. Then the past came looking for him...

Up on the Hi-Line, ranchers are being rustled out of their livelihoods...and their lives. The son of an old friend suspects that these rustlers have murdered his father, and the law is too crooked to get any straight answers. But can the worn-out old marshall live up to the legendary lawman the boy has grown to admire?

❑ BLOOD MOUNTAIN   0-425-16976-6/$5.99

Stranded in the rugged northern Rockies, a wagon train of settlers is viciously savaged by a group of merciless outlaws rampaging through the mountains. But when the villains cross the wrong man, nothing on earth will stop him from paying every one of them back—in blood.

"Make room on your shelf of favorites:
Peter Brandvold will be staking out a claim
there." —Frank Roderus